THE FIRS

LYNN UNDERWOOD

HighTide
Publications, Inc.

Deltaville, VA

High Tide Publications, Inc.
Deltaville, Virginia 23043
www.HighTidePublications.com
Printed in the United States of America
First Edition

Edited by Cindy L. Freeman

Book design and production by FirebelliedFrog.com

ISBN: 978-1-945990-35-9

The teachers of the law and the Pharisees brought in a woman caught in adultery. They made her stand before the group and said to Jesus, "Teacher, this woman was caught in the act of adultery. In the Law Moses commanded us to stone such women. Now what do you say?" They were using this question as a trap, in order to have a basis for accusing him. But Jesus bent down and started to write on the ground with his finger. When they kept on questioning him, he straightened up and said to them, "Let any one of you who is without sin be the first to throw a stone at her."

John 8:3-9

What readers like you are saying about this book:

For all of us who are on a journey of enlightenment (we all are), The First Stone provides one stepping stone on the path you've chosen.

Generations are haunted by decisions and guilt, but a tangled web connects them in their humanity and for some, absolution.

A story about the weight of vengeance and the need for redemption, The First Stone admirably intersects the lives of very diverse and unlikely characters. When the complexity of the war in Vietnam collides with immigrants from Mexico struggling to find their place, the tension carries the reader through the struggles of finding one's moral compass.

A deeply moving, sunny novel, full of humanity

With his Southwest heritage, Lynn Underwood writes like Tony Hillerman with a civil engineering degree.

If you enjoyed *The First Stone*, please consider leaving a review on Amazon.com. Amazon accepts reviews from readers even if they did not purchase the book on Amazon. Sign in under your Amazon account, enter **The First Stone Lynn Underwood** in the search block to find his book. You can add a review when the Amazon page with *The First Stone* appears on your screen. Thank you so much for supporting our authors.

DEDICATION

To my older brother, Larry, who has been a spiritual guide throughout my life.

and

To my older brother, James, who helped teach me right from wrong early in my life.

PROLOGUE

Mexico, 1919

His tunic looked more beige than black after a minor dust devil had whipped through the small town of La Calera. He was the first and only priest the community had known. Mexico's government, recently rocked by revolution and social change, had become hostile to the church, but the padre wasn't troubled by these circumstances or the secular concerns that preoccupied the average Mexican citizen. Nothing rattled this priest who never seemed to age, despite his graying hair. He always had a soft smile and a kind word for all.

Padre Juan was on his way back to the church to meet Antonio and Carmelita Gonzales for a baptism. Carrying water from the nearby creek, he approached the sanctuary in preparation for the baptism of a baby girl.

While he knew his heritage was rich, he also knew he needed to keep it a tightly nested secret. He never spoke of his history or mentioned where he had lived before, often referring to the past as life that is finished.

Today's special celebration was for Concepcion Gonzales. The daughter of Antonio and Carmelita Gonzales would come to be known as Conchita. Their daughter's *padrinos* (godparents) accompanied the proud parents.

Padre Juan performed the sacrament of baptism, freeing Concepcion from original sin in the tradition of the Catholic Church. Upon concluding the rite, he smiled at the parents and said quietly, "Your child is free of sin. Help her grow into the life God has chosen for her."

Mexico, 1927

Working at the orphanage suited him because he loved children. He remembered his father's words about them, "The Kingdom of Heaven belongs to them." He murmured the words as he gazed upon the innocent babies lying in cribs.

"Padre come quickly. Alfonso was bitten by a snake." Sister Maria Elena, standing at the entrance to the orphanage, summoned the priest with a frantic waving motion.

Padre Juan was diminutive in stature but large in presence. He exuded strength and confidence with the gentle smile crowning a slightly weathered face, his forehead remarkably unmarked by lines. After turning to face Sister Maria Elena, he asked, "What kind of snake?"

"No mas un serpienta de cascabel." She told him it was a rattlesnake.

"Trae me un cochillo y medicina en el bolso de cuero." Maria responded by grabbing the leather bag which contained a very old knife and some medicine. Padre Juan flew out the door toward Alfonso, who sat near a fence post and was now writhing in pain.

"Relajarse, Alfonso. Todo esta bien." He told the child to relax and that all would be okay. Alfonso, though scared, trusted this man who had been his father-figure since he was born seven years before.

"Relax, my child. The more you relax, the less the poison will hurt you." Abiding in his trust of this man, Alfonso reclined on the rocky ground while Padre Juan told him the next step would be painful.

With Salvador, the name he gave his Syrian scalpel, Padre Juan made an incision resembling a cross on the snake bite. Then with only a small trace of blood trickling out of the wound, he proceeded to suck the wound, spitting as he did. After a few minutes, he could see that blood was flowing more freely. Satisfied that the venom was reduced enough to prevent death, he applied fabric compresses soaked in whiskey to clean and seal the incision he had made.

"Alfonso, you're going to be just fine." Looking up at the priest, the child's face registered a weak smile. "Maria, help me bring Alfonso into the orphanage. We'll let him rest in the quiet for a bit."

Just then, Alfonso's older brother came running into the orphanage after hearing that his brother was dead. Jorge Morales was beside himself with anxiety as he searched for the body of his younger brother. Padre Juan caught him amidst his fury and told him that Alfonso was okay.

"Padre, I left Alfonso to hunt rabbits with my sling shot you made. He always tries to come with me. I told him to stay at the fence post and I would be back. He did." Now bawling, he continued. "I caused this, Padre. I caused my little brother to almost die. I caused..." As Padre Juan placed his hand on the teenager's back, both grief and solace converged, each struggling to dominate the older brother's emotions. It would be up to the priest to reconcile them.

When Jorge dropped to his knees next to the cot, Padre Juan joined him, kneeling to look him in the eye, and said, "Jorge, you are a good brother. You love Alfonso. You are blessed for that love. What happens in life is not always your responsibility. Things happen for a reason. You can never know."

Jorge, still in tears, looked at his younger brother lying on the cot in the small anteroom just inside the orphanage's entrance. The priest felt he needed to say more to comfort the young man who now stroked his brother's brow gently.

"Your love gave your brother his early life, remember?" Padre Juan saw a glimmer of recognition. He paused to allow Jorge to recall the incident.

"You alerted us to his choking when he was just a baby. You saved his life, remember?"

Now Jorge turned to face the padre, giving him his full attention.

"You have always been a good brother, watching out for Alfonso. You were doing that today when you told him not to follow you into the desert. You were protecting him until he was old enough to know better."

The steady stream of tears traveling down Jorge's brown cheeks confirmed that Jorge blamed himself for his brother's near-fatal encounter.

"Jorge, do you feel responsible for the snakebite? Do you think it was your fault?"

"Si," he answered in the affirmative. "Soy culpable."

"As I have told you, you are not responsible for this." Padre Juan tried consolation, but he could tell Jorge wasn't convinced. As a last resort, he gave Jorge the forgiveness he so desperately needed.

"Jorge, God has asked me to grant you forgiveness. He knows you have a good heart. He asked me to grant you a pardon with one condition that you must carry with you."

"Si, Padre. Cualquier cosa. Anything."

Now Jorge looked at him with fewer tears, but his face registered apprehension.

"Jorge, Dios te perdona." Telling him that God forgives him, he added the condition.

"You will find someone in desperate need one day. It will be a struggle, but you must grant this person help." Seeing the quizzical look in Jorge's eyes, the priest added, "You will know when the time comes. Nothing more need be said. You will know."

With that, the priest dipped two fingers in the font for holy water and made a cross on Jorge's forehead, saying, "May the merciful Lord have pity on thee and forgive thee thy faults. As a priest, and through the authority of God, I absolve thee of thy sins. You are forgiven. Go and sin no more."

Now Jorge cried tears of joy as he and Padre Juan stood by the makeshift cot where his younger brother was recovering.

***

Eight years later, when Jorge moved to Ciudad Juarez, Padre Juan had finished teaching the now fifteen-year-old Alfonso how to use the sling shot he made for him. He bent back the brim of his sombrero and looked at the midday sun then hoisted his travel pack around his shoulders and with his shepherd's crook, he walked away from the orphanage and Anahuac, Chihuahua north toward Los Estados Unidos.

–1–

MEXICO, 1936

"How can you charge me that much to cross a border?" Conchita asked the Coyotaje, the man standing beside the truck at the end of a dirt street in Juarez, Mexico. The day was cold and gray which was uncommon but symbolic to Conchita. It was March but the overcast skies seemed to match what life had presented her over the past year.

The bright and shining years of her youth gave way to her passion for freedom and making her own way. She could see that her craving for independence and her trust in a young man—a handsome young man— had led to this.

"Rayaldo, callate … silencio mi hijo!" She commanded her infant to shut up then added the gentle instruction, "Be quiet, my son," realizing she should not scold her three-month-old for complaining about their lack of comfort. She knew that if she could, she would be crying too.

Coyotaje was a slang term referring to a person who recruited then transported a Mexican national into the United States to a pre-arranged job destination. The Coyotaje offered her a job and passage into a nation with a better economy and a brighter future. This informal profession developed then flourished when in 1917 and again in 1924 the U.S. Immigration Act required literacy tests, medical exams, head fees and visa fees. Passage via a Coyotaje was cheaper and faster with the same result.

"I charge what my costs are, my child. And besides that, I've got you a job there already," he said unapologetically in Spanish. She didn't know that she had a dependable job as part of the agreement. She was now grateful to this man and a little more willing to part with her savings. She never thought getting a job would be so easy.

Conchita's mother gave her a few hundred pesos she had collected from neighbors in La Calera. She guarded the last of that gift, realizing she needed to feed her child and herself.

"Here," she said. "This is all I can spare. I must keep thirty pesos for my child," she pleaded. In a moment of weakness, Jorge Morales, self-proclaimed coyotaje for six years now, looked at her and relented when he thought about his little brother at that age and the charge the priest at their orphanage had given him.

"Muchacha, por usted solo, y esta vez. No dicerle a nadie." He told her he would do it for her this time only and that she should not tell anyone.

He opened the passenger door to the cab for her. "Aqui a delante," he said, inviting her to sit with him up front.

"Si, señor. Muchas gracias." With Rayaldo in her arms, she climbed into the cab, sharing the bench seat with him. The men who were paying a higher price for the trip would sit in the back of the truck where they must hold onto the sideboards to keep the bumpy ride from bucking them off.

Morales had arranged to deliver the men and Conchita to an estate southwest of Mesilla, New Mexico, the original Spanish settlement from which Las Cruces grew. The owners of the large farm had asked for seven laborers and one maid. He was only slightly concerned that his clients would balk at the infant in tow, recalling that Americans loved babies ... of whatever color.

How long the work would last for the men wasn't his concern. They would be okay. But he wasn't sure about this young muchacha with an infant. He hoped she could keep a job for a while and avoid deportation. He sensed a glimmer of innocence yet determination in this young woman, clearly still in her teens.

***

The drive across the border was on a back road just west of Juarez and central El Paso that Morales knew well. It was more of a trail, never guarded and near Puerto de Anapra into New Mexico. They could avoid the constantly guarded bridges across the Rio Grande River and be closer to the farm near Mesilla. Morales had blazed the trail a year before and used it to ferry dozens of Mexicans into Los Estados Unidos. It was almost a private road known only to him.

The men in the back knew what to expect, all being residents of Juarez, but he could tell this kind of journey was new and foreign to Conchita. Morales supposed she'd been on bumpy roads before but this one, rough as a washboard, felt like riding a bucking bull. She tried to pacify Rayaldo from the violent rocking of the truck. It wasn't working. The child finally grew weary of crying, it seemed, and now was only moaning.

Fortunately, the trip was not a long one. Within an hour they were at the farm estate. "It is a pecan orchard," explained Jorge as they drove up. "They grow pecans, harvest them, then process them by shelling and packaging them into containers for shipping to stores in the east and north."

He could tell she did not know what a pecan was. She didn't understand it was a nut, until he gave her one shelled after he picked up a few from one of several barrels under a lean-to roof attached to a tin storage barn near where they stopped.

"It is sweet," she proclaimed in Spanish. Still savoring the pecan, she noticed the owner who stepped out of the barn and greeted Jorge. "Hi, George." He waved then stretched out his hand to greet his friend. Although he could speak fluent Spanish, George Marcak knew he and Jorge had the same name and relished the opportunity to remind him. Jorge returned the favor. "Señor Jorge. Como esta?"

After they exchanged pleasantries, the men turned to see the new migrants who were still shaking off the bumpy ride and regaining their composure. "I see you delivered as arranged," Marcak observed. "What have we here, Jorge? Two for the price of one?" George turned to see Conchita cuddling Rayaldo.

"George, this is Conchita, your maid and her son, Rayaldo." Coming closer, he said in a voice meant only for George, "I reasoned that the child would keep her focus on her job here ... you know, considering the last maid I brought." It sounded like an apology. The last maid he delivered only a month before had already left, absconding with some pay advanced by Marcak.

"Not bad thinking, George. Not bad at all." With a smile, Marcak eased Jorge's anxiety and Conchita seemed to relax as he shook hands with his new maid.

"Glad to meet you. Come in, Conchita." Marcak motioned the two toward the farmhouse.

"Luis, show mother and child to their quarters." Marcak said. Luis Garcia grabbed Conchita's small bag of personal belongings so that she could more easily carry Rayaldo. With Conchita following, Garcia, a seven-year veteran working for Marcak and the self-proclaimed estate attendant took her to the maid's quarters in the rear of the farm estate and explained the rules of the house in Spanish, the only language Conchita knew.

"Always stay in your quarters unless you are working or outside. Don't go into the house without being invited," he started. "Don't eat the pecans. They're the farm product. Don't speak in Spanish if you are with the missus. She doesn't speak Spanish. Always keep your room neat and clean. Always start work on time and stay busy. Don't sit on the furniture in the big house … and don't drink or smoke," he added with his index finger pointing at her.

***

Conchita's new home was clean but small. Almost an outbuilding, it was connected to the main house through a breezeway with a trellis outside the entry, which held a climbing vine. This breezeway defined a path from her quarters to the kitchen in the main house.

The maid's lodging had a living area and a bedroom with a cot. There was a tiny bathroom with a shower consisting of a floor drain and a garden hose running through a hole in the block wall. Completing the space was a room that could be confused for a kitchen except that no cooking equipment was evident. Conchita asked about it, but Luis only shrugged his shoulders and left.

A woman stepped into her apartment with Mr. Marcak. Conchita knew instinctively this must be her boss. She was older than Conchita's mother and seemed to be accustomed to hard work. However, she had a limp, and Conchita spied a clue. There was a metal brace on the bottom of her right foot. It looked like a stirrup. That foot shuffled when she walked, lifting only slightly to allow her to advance forward. Now Conchita understood why she was hired.

"Good morning, Missus Marcak." It was her first attempt at speaking English to a non-Spanish speaker.

"Well, hello there. And who do we have here … a little helper?" Conchita understood only bits and pieces of Mrs. Marcak's response.

With grins and nods, Conchita got through the first interaction successfully. Now Mrs. Marcak was holding three-month-old Rayaldo and taking him on a tour of her home, with Conchita and Mr. Marcak following.

"These are the rooms you will need to clean," she pointed out to Conchita.

"Not this one." She pointed at a bedroom off the hallway, shaking her head. "This is George Junior's room and *he* must keep it clean by himself." Later, she learned that George Junior was fourteen and still in junior high school although he stood taller than Conchita and almost as tall as his father.

***

Conchita had arrived on Saturday and had only Sunday to rest from her trip.

Monday, the first workday started her training from Mrs. Marcak, who began with simple dusting and sweeping.

Tuesday, she learned how to operate the new Hoover. Conchita had never seen a vacuum cleaner before. She jumped, startled when Mrs. Marcak turned it on but caught on quickly and finished the entire wall-to-wall carpet in the living room in no time. It was a new sensation.

Wednesday, she learned about washing and hanging out laundry to dry on the four-wire clothesline in the backyard. Mrs. Marcak had some trouble getting out and then back in the house with her right leg at the mercy of the three-legged walking cane she kept at the back door. She kept it there for occasions where she must walk outside on the rough surface of concrete, earthen grade and Bermuda grass lawn. Then, of course, Conchita had to learn how to fold and put away freshly laundered clothes into the linen closet. She still needed instruction in pressing with the electric iron. That exercise happened the next day. Mrs. Marcak ironed a cotton cleaning rag, which she scorched intentionally to make the point about pressing lightly.

Cooking was last on the schedule. Conchita followed Mrs. Marcak's directions on how to prepare breakfast, the only meal she was expected to cook.

***

Undergoing this training helped Conchita with her English. The booklet Mr. Marcak gave her helped, too. It was a book of conversational English for Spanish speakers, provided by the local Farm Bureau, a loose-knit organization dedicated to helping farmers and promoting their interests.

Over a few weeks, Conchita adjusted to life in Los Estados Unidos and the Marcak farm which was more of a hacienda than a farm. It was large and bustling with activity, almost like its own small community. The farm boasted barns, workshops, a garage for the missus' car and several pickup trucks. It had another large barn where farm equipment of all kinds was stored out of the weather. She had no idea what they all were used for and she never asked.

-2-

VIETNAM, 1969

Zachary Martin turned nineteen in the rolling hills of South Vietnam among sixty-five of his brothers in Kilo Company, Third Battalion, Fifth Marines. Even at nineteen, his face carried lines of experience. He'd been in the country for almost eight months and learned the routine well.

Zach grew up in the sunshine, working the fields of his father's farm in southern New Mexico. The farm was almost as far from the Mexican border as from Deming, the town where he graduated from high school.

A close friend and partner for the last year, Billy Braun had been helping him dig a foxhole for the last hour. They would both use it tonight. Billy was from Canada, having joined the Marine Corps to gain U.S. citizenship. He did this knowing that his commitment included an obligation to put his life on the line for his new country.

Neither young man was a warmonger in the sense ascribed by college student protesters. Zachary had used a rifle for deer hunting in the mountains of southern New Mexico. But he got better at shooting during the two weeks of rifle range training in boot camp. Not only was his aim better, he was now willing to point his weapon at another human and squeeze the trigger if that human was a threat to him, his family, his nation or democracy in general. In 1969 that threat came from the armies of North Vietnam and the Viet Cong.

Zachary was over six feet tall with proportionate features that reflected a young life filled with hard work and plenty of protein. He could bench press over two hundred pounds and catch a steer with a rope thrown from a horse galloping at twenty miles per hour. His face seemed chiseled from a mountainside with rugged lines and angles that matched his former life, that of a farmer and rancher. He was accustomed to wearing M.L. Leddy boots, slim jeans, and a well-worn cowboy hat.

Now he wore jungle boots, camo fatigues and a bush hat. The difference in attire didn't alter his natural commanding presence. He was in charge wherever he went, despite his age.

"Watch where you're digging," yelled Private Ray Gonzales Kouris, a member of First Platoon and generally known as a fuck-up by most of Kilo Company. He was speaking to the air, his jab roughly aimed at Martin and Braun although he was reluctant to disparage them directly. Ray (known as Greek by his fellow soldiers) carried ammunition for the company's M-60. That was just about the lowest job one could have in a rifle company, a sign that you were less than trustworthy with important things. The tasks like squad leader, walking point, radio communications, forward observation, medevac, and the like were for more competent Marines. Those jobs had to be earned. By people like Zach and Billy.

Kilo Company was exactly like other rifle companies. It had four platoons of riflemen with four squads each and a Command Platoon (CP) that included a small group of specialists offering embedded support like forward observer teams for mortars, artillery, a forward air control, sometimes a sniper team, and always a Navy corpsman or two for emergencies.

Zach and Billy were part of this CP. Corporal Zachary Martin (Marty) and his partner, Lance Corporal Billy Braun, were a team. Together they plotted fire missions for 81mm mortars and called them in to their rear unit headquarters.

Zach was the team leader who carried a map with unit grid lines identified with a three-digit number in each of two directions in the traditional Cartesian coordinate system. So, a six-digit number could identify a target for fire missions, narrowing the target to an area of a hundred square meters. That was close enough for an 81mm mortar. Billy carried the radio and would call these numbers into the rear area where the mortar team awaited their orders.

"Shut up, Greek," replied Billy. "Watch your own ass and get the fuck out of CP's area. You're supposed to be on perimeter watch, not up here."

"Yeah, I'm supposed to guard your white asses tonight," Greek threw back at Braun. While most racism had been driven out of Marine Corps recruits during boot camp, it was clear that Greek wasn't like most. In fact, he always seemed to go out of his way to find something he didn't like about anyone who was white. The irony was that Greek didn't have a specific heritage. He seemed to be a mixture of different ethnic backgrounds, Mexican, some Anglo and Greek ancestry that led to his nickname, Greek.

"The day we need your sorry ass to keep us safe is the day Ho Chi Minh holds a parade in my hometown to celebrate their victory in this sorry-ass war," echoed Martin. His imposing frame subdued the diminutive Greek.

"All right, I'll tell Gunny and leave you two to Charlie. See if I care. I'll go back to see if Jenkins finished digging our foxhole." As he walked away, Greek casually threw his entrenching-tool over his shoulder with the middle finger of his right hand stuck up discernibly in the air.

Martin shook his head, ignoring the middle finger pointed at him and Braun from behind Greek's head, as Greek sauntered back to his squad.

-3-

NEW MEXICO, 1936

The whole Marcak family was good to Conchita and Rayaldo. They helped her furnish her maid's room and even contributed some appliances not needed in the main kitchen. Mr. Marcak had a makeshift baby crib assembled by the carpenters in the shop. The two immigrants were given free room-and-board and Conchita was paid two dollars per day for working six days a week. She never felt mistreated. Mrs. Marcak dearly loved Rayaldo and often pampered him while Conchita worked. Soon, Conchita began to feel as if she were part of the family. She returned the favor, making huevos rancheros for Mr. Marcak on Saturday mornings that included her own made-from-scratch recipe. He said they were the best he'd ever eaten. Mr. Marcak brought milk from the barnyard for Conchita to use when she stopped nursing Rayaldo. The Marcaks grew as attached to Rayaldo as grandparents would be. Family life suited Conchita. For a while she missed some of the adventures that she might have had with Rayaldo's father. But that feeling vanished quickly even in favor of diapers, nighttime feedings, and baby baths.

Helping others was both rewarding and fulfilling, she found. Her life after Rayaldo arrived had changed her. She knew it. She was less focused on her personal wants and needs than she had been growing up. She now appreciated the relative idyllic life she had once taken for granted, growing up without a care. She appreciated the Marcak family for their benevolence. She felt blessed by Rayaldo, her gift from God.

Conchita turned eighteen years old without a word to her hosts, and soon Rayaldo was walking.

Now resting in the recliner in her little home next to the Marcak household, she thought back, as if in a daydream, about her past and the terrible mistake she made that delivered her to her new-found home and adoptive family.

-4-

Mexico, 1934

At the blackboard, Conchita struggled to answer the question posed to her by the teacher in the rustic, almost run-down school room. Her full, black hair accented her youthful beauty which along with her personality was her delightful charm. Her weakness was in 'paying attention', something she had trouble maintaining. Her other weakness was boys.

"Concepcion, responde la pregunta, por favor." The teacher firmly asked her to answer the question. It was polite but she was tired of this child's indolence.

"Maestro, yo no se," she said in such an impish and coquettish manner as to cause the class to break out in laughter. While she viewed it as positive attention from her peers, the teacher saw it as shame by the other students.

"Concepcion, you must try harder next time. Take your seat."

The next student clearly had studied the lesson and wrote the answer in white chalk on the blackboard with hardly a thought. Conchita was less impressed by his scholarly talent and more impressed by his physical features. He was tall for his twelve years and had a composure that made him look like a man. She gave Ysidro a yearning look as he stood in the teacher's adoration.

Walking home after school, Conchita's older sister scolded her for not paying attention in school. "Conchita, you must learn to concentrate and learn. Not everything is about you." Conchita looked up in amazement as if she were stunned at the assertion.

"Hermana mia, es la cosa. Soy yo mismo." She replied to her sister that she was herself and that's all that mattered. Her sister was clearly frustrated with this head-strong child.

✱✱✱

Over the course of her younger school life, Conchita was always popular, gaining attention from her peers both boys and girls. She never tried very hard to excel in schoolwork nor housework at home. She did just enough to get by in both areas. Unlike her sister, she preferred to be left alone to daydream about a future as a wife and mother. Though there was a limited selection, she changed boyfriends quite often.

When she was fifteen, Conchita 'fell in love' with a young man who refused to pay attention to her. No matter what she tried to get noticed, he disregarded her advances. It came to a head one day when he started holding hands with her sister. Not only did this act distance her from her sister, she swore never to be upstaged again.

After this incident, attractive Conchita made sure she was the center of attention anywhere she went, although there were few places for Mexican youth to gather for any reason. Initially, the little village of La Calera in Central Chihuahua, Mexico had started out as a collection of rancheros with the addition of an *iglesia Catolico* (Catholic church) and a public school arriving in 1919. Other rancheros and farms followed, along with an almacen general, a general store that doubled as a post office. The community boasted almost a hundred citizens when Conchita turned fifteen.

Of course, Catolico Mass on Sunday was a must. The Gonzalez family would travel by buckboard pulled by their two horses, Dario and Pancho. There was a public school where Conchita managed academically despite her social proclivities.

Once a month during the summer, fall and spring there was rodeo. The rodeo was the entertainment scene for young and old alike.

Conchita loved to watch the boys she knew perform in the rodeo. She was sure they did it for her. After every event, a young *vaquero* (cowboy) would stand up and tip his *sombrero* … to her—not the crowd, as her sister kept correcting her.

Calf roping, bull riding, and all the other rodeo events sprang from Mexico as a cross between cattle wrangling, necessary to daily life and bull fighting, a popular sport. Demonstrating these skills became the foundation for rural Mexican youth's socializing and entertainment in the early 1900s. This rodeo in La Calera was a two-day event. Today was the first day.

"Mira, el vaquero esta saludar a mi." Conchita exclaimed to her sister and girlfriends gathered around her that the cowboy just waved at her. They were sitting amid the crowd in the central section of the grandstand. The young vaquero was taking off his sombrero and bowing to the crowd. He had just tied up a calf after roping it from the saddle of his horse that was in full gallop.

When the vaquero tossed the swinging rope toward the calf's head, the horse had been trained to halt abruptly, stopping the calf's forward motion and allowing the vaquero to leave the saddle and run toward the calf. With the horse trained to keep the rope taut, the vaquero would bulldog the calf to the ground and tie up three legs with a short piece of rope—all within a matter of seconds. The vaquero's teeth usually held the short rope while he was riding. The reason for tying three legs instead of four was because four legs tied together allowed the calf more muscle to attempt a release. The knot holding three of the calf's legs could be released with one pull of the short rope. While the event was called calf roping, it was clearly much more than that to Conchita. The current star of this Saturday's rodeo was an older, but still teenage vaquero from Nuevos Casas Grande, a larger town neighboring La Calera. Santiago Alamosa was nineteen years old and already working full-time for a large hacienda. "Look at him," remarked Conchita to her friends. "He is tall and strong and has a great smile."

"Who is he?" asked a friend.

"I will tell you who he is," announced Conchita still staring, starry eyed at the young vaquero. "He is my future husband." She turned her face to see her sister and friends' reactions. All were now looking at her in disbelief, too stunned to even put together a clear thought much less any dismissive response.

***

"Como esta, señor?" she asked through a wooden fence, gazing still mesmerized by his biceps.

"Estoy bien y usted, chica?" he replied. This had two effects on Conchita. First it was endearing to have him address her informally and second it enraged her to know he thought of her as a young girl, a child.

Does he think I'm too young for him? I will convince him that I am a woman. I am already sixteen years old. She spoke, trying to sound confident. "Te vi en la rodeo (I saw you at the rodeo). Vi tomar tu sombrero por mi (You took your hat off to me)."

Would he get the idea or think she was just a child flirting with him? He stood and looked at her again slowly, up and down. From his kneeling position and through the wooden fence he had failed to notice the figure of the young woman he had just called a child.

"Lo siento señorita. No podria ver (I am sorry miss. I couldn't see you). Pero sabia ques estaban alli (but I knew you were there)." He added a wink.

He introduced himself. "Santiago Alamosa, señorita. Y tu?" she replied, giving her name, and the two chatted across a rodeo fence like the teenagers they were.

A dusty vaquero walked up to hand Santiago a Manila envelope. Conchita watched as he opened it, revealing many pesos. "Para ti," said the vaquero as he handed Santiago his prize money.

"Seguro. Gracias a Dios." Santiago looked up to the heavens and kissed the envelope. He had won the calf-roping event and collected his prize money. With no other events he was registered for, he knew what he should do now.

"Señorita, tu quieres un Coca Cola?"

"Of course," she replied. Santiago threw himself over the six-foot-tall rodeo fence getting a foothold on the lower rail. This gave Conchita another chance to see the bare shoulder and arm muscles bulging from his short-sleeve shirt.

"Cuantos años tienes?" he asked.

Asking my age is a very serious question, she thought. What should I say? The truth? That I'm only sixteen? She wanted to be older anyway. But she didn't want to lie either.

"I'm old enough." It was the best answer she could give under the circumstances. She hoped it satisfied the criteria for both his curiosity and her honesty.

"Bueno." The two sauntered toward the nearby tienda for two bottles of Coke chilling in an ice bucket. Then, her sister called her name.

"Conchita, we have to go home now." Conchita faced her sister with a scowl then turned to smile brightly at Santiago. She stole a kiss when he wasn't looking, turned away rapidly and joined her older sister.

***

Although Sunday meant attending church, the Mass ended promptly at noon, allowing all worshipers to watch the second day of the rodeo. Conchita sat on the edge of her seat on the bleachers when Santiago was up in the calf-roping event. The calf squirted out of the chute followed by Santiago's horse. The cowboy was already swinging his rope, tossing it almost immediately out of the chute. He swung himself off the saddle effortlessly as the horse came to an abrupt stop. His left foot was still in the stirrup as his right foot dug into the earth. Pulling his left foot out of the stirrup with ease, he ran for the calf that was being held taut by the backing up action of his horse. He bulldogged the calf, catching him by the head and flank. His right knee in the calf's mid-section held it prone. Santiago had the three loops around three legs of the calf in a loose knot and stood with his upward and outstretched arms, signaling the end for the timekeeper.

"Twelve seconds," the announcer said speaking through a megaphone, declaring Santiago the winner of this event by over five seconds.

It wasn't even close, Conchita thought. Then she saw it. He had spotted her in the crowd and did a full bow directly to her with his sombrero covering his heart. As if that weren't enough, when he raised upright, he blew her a kiss. She had to go see him and congratulate him. She needed more than a kiss. When she finally reached him, it was clear that he felt the same way.

They spent Sunday afternoon with Cokes at the same store and walking around La Calera's main street. Everyone saw the young couple. "Conchita, que quieres (What do you want)?" It was a simple question, but Santiago made it complicated when he asked, "Que quieres en su vida (What do you want in your life)?" She was at a standstill now, looking intently at Santiago. The question went to her core, but she answered without thinking.

"I want to be with the man of my dreams and have a good life together." His smile led her to believe he shared her deepest desire. Was it possible he wanted more out of life than to ride in the rodeo every day?

***

Later that evening, Santiago and Conchita shared intimacies on the hay storage loft of a stable in La Calera. The two had sneaked in from the back door unnoticed. Santiago tied his mustang pony to the hitching post out front and removed the saddle. After an hour of passionate lovemaking, he returned to his horse.

He could avoid the thirteen-peso charge to rest his horse, but he would sneak some alfalfa hay and grain for later that night. Horse water was available near the hitching post. He and Conchita could spend Sunday night in the loft without interruptions.

It was her first time, and despite the bloodstained mess, she was positively radiant. It was everything she'd hoped it would be … and more. The two talked as lovers would all night. Santiago talked about his hacienda in Nuevos Casas Grande. Well, not exactly his. It was where he worked. Conchita listened dreamily, asking more questions. She romanticized about being by Santiago's side all her life, making his meals, washing his clothes, and making love to him.

When the barn was lightly illuminated by the morning sun, Conchita asked Santiago what she had been wondering all night. "Santiago, what will you do now?" The question was laced with a desire to be included in the answer.

"I'll probably go home to Casas Grande. Do you want to come with me?"

***

Suddenly tense, Santiago realized he had given in to the unspoken longing of the girl now transformed into a youthful woman.

She is beautiful, he thought, as he gazed at her naked body resting on the saddle blanket he had spread on the loose hay.

"Oh, Chago, do you mean it? Would you really take me with you?" Already she was using his nickname. He liked the way it sounded. "I don't even want to go home after last night. It was beautiful—being with you, I mean."

Well, now you've done it, he chided himself, trying to hide his regret at extending the invitation. She was a simple girl from the barrios of a rural village in Chihuahua. She might even be the daughter of a mere ranch hand like he was. He realized they knew hardly anything about each other. For him, it had been just sex. But she was beautiful. Perhaps he could grow to love her.

How could she live with him? Would the *patron* (boss) allow him to bring a woman—a girl really–into the bunkhouse?

"Do you really want to come with me? My life is not easy. I don't make *mucho dinero*. I enter rodeos because I need the money. I'm good at it and normally win. But I'm never home." He hoped the idea of ranch life would frighten her away.

"That's okay," she countered. "I'll go with you wherever you go. I'll be by your side."

"But I'm just a ranch hand living in a small room of a bunkhouse with other men." He was sure his confession would stun her, maybe discourage her, but it didn't.

"Oh Chago, I'd be with you anywhere. I slept with you here last night, didn't I?" She was sitting up now, naked, her tender breasts more visible thanks to the morning sun that shone through cracks in the barn's siding.

From the look on her face, Santiago could not tell if this pose was instinctual or an effort to tempt him with desire. It surely was working though. He could feel his *verga* stiffen. "Chica, lo cierto." Telling her that she was right was all he could muster in response, as his groin took control of his thought processes. He held her in his arms and felt her body melt into his. The saddle blanket would get another workout on this beautiful Monday morning.

-5-

MEXICO, 1934

Days turned into weeks, not because the time passed quickly but rather each day felt like a week at the ranch bunkhouse. In addition to the close quarters with men, Conchita was now expected to provide cleaning services for the ranch owner's home in exchange for her room-and-board. She didn't mind the cleaning. It gave her something to do during the twelve-hour days when Santiago was riding in the Chihuahua desert or the mountain ranges that were part of the hacienda.

"Jovencita sus pechugas son grandes." The senior maid, Consuela, told Conchita that her breasts were big, larger than before. At first Conchita smiled, thinking it was a compliment, but the maid's glare was both patronizing and sympathetic causing Conchita to comprehend the truth she had tried to ignore. Now the fatigue and early morning vomiting made sense.

"I'm pregnant," she whispered looking downward. Her mind raced. How would this affect her new life with Santiago? Would he accept her condition? As she and Consuela resumed their cleaning, Conchita realized neither her mother nor her sister had ever discussed pregnancy and childbirth with her.

She had no idea what to expect.

She had become friends with the older maid, who had little children of her own. Consuela, only ten years older, lived on the ranch too, but in a small detached house with her husband, who was more than a lead ranch hand but less than a foreman. Dark skinned, Lorenzo, at thirty years old was called upon to run teams of vaqueros. He was well respected by both those running the ranch and the vaqueros like Santiago. Consuela's children bore the dark skin of their father, a Mulato.

Lorenzo is a good man, thought Conchita. Consuela is a lucky woman. Conchita daydreamed that she and Santiago would move into a small house like Consuela and Lorenzo. Now, with a baby coming, that would become a more urgent need.

After Conchita broke the news to Santiago, he acted like the world was caving in on him. She began to sense that he felt burdened by this added degree of responsibility.

"Conchita, quit crying, would you?" Santiago said in a demanding way. "You know I have to leave. I have to go to work." He hadn't kissed her as he normally did before he swung himself into the saddle. She was emotional. That was for sure. Consuela had warned her about her emotions changing during this time. But she couldn't help it. She felt empty … without hope … as if she were dying a slow, painful death.

She hesitated then inhaled the tears flowing from her eyes and nose. Trying to regain control, she looked up at her lover. For some reason, she felt a need to urge him to be careful. "Tienes cuidado, Chago. Tienes cuidado." She meant to ask him to return to her soon but withheld that request to keep from appearing as abandoned as she felt.

"Hasta luego," he said without looking at her and rode away. She stayed, staring … hoping he would turn around or at least wave as he had done every day since she moved here several months ago. He didn't.

It was only then that it registered in Conchita's mind. A bedroll, a rifle and saddlebags were secured to his saddle. That wasn't typical. He had no need of a bedroll "except to … sleep … at night." And a rifle. His father's rifle. Why?

When Santiago's horse carried him in a different direction than usual, Conchita fell to the ground, erupting in desperate wailing. "He is leaving me! *Dios mio*, he's leaving me!"

At last, managing to stand, she ran to the main house to see Consuela. "Conchita, what's wrong? Is the baby okay?" Conchita couldn't be consoled, though Consuela tried.

"Infanto esta bien," she choked. "Es Santiago. El se fue, Consuela. Se fue!"

Consuela embraced the young woman who now looked more like the child she was ... except for her expanding belly. The two stood there, Conchita sobbing and Consuela trying to comfort her.

"Como esta? Que tal?" Lorenzo asked his wife, surprising the women with his entrance.

Consuela answered for Conchita, "Es Santiago, Lorenzo. El hombre se fue su esposa." Although the two were not married, Consuela explained to her husband that Santiago had left his wife.

"Que cabjron. Chinga su madre. Es no hombre. Es un muchacho." Lorenzo expressed his feelings for the fleeing deserter with a few expletives that refuted Santiago's manhood. With the hacienda owner away, Lorenzo could not leave the ranch and hunt down this *puto* (male whore). Besides, he could never force the coward to become a man and honor his commitment to the mother of his child.

Lorenzo's angry words did not help to console the woman Santiago had left behind. Seeing that, he left her in his wife's care. But before walking out, he whispered a prayer for Conchita and her child.

-6-

VIETNAM, 1969

Zachary Martin gazed at a scene in the distance, perhaps a few miles away. It was a small cluster of thatched huts next to a meandering river. Passing the village earlier, they had only noticed women, children, and old men. That could have meant that the younger men were working in the rice paddies. But sometimes it was a clue that the village might be under Viet Cong control. It was enough to attract the attention of Corporal Zachary Martin.

He noticed a trail of silhouettes. The shadows looked like adults walking in from a distant tree line toward the settlement. Using field glasses borrowed from the scout sniper team, he saw young kids running around the village scantily dressed, as kids would be at that age. He saw a woman attempting to gather them like a mother hen collecting her wayward chicks.

Then his gaze returned to the men walking in what looked like formation. There seemed to be a dozen men carrying farm tools over their shoulders. He wanted to believe they were farmers like he had been.

He thought about farm life at the end of the day in New Mexico. He imagined what life was like for farm workers around the globe and from where he grew up. It helped him to remember his youth, what was left of it.

Another reminder of home stepped into Martin's view.

Clevis May was the son of a rancher from the same hometown as Martin, nestled in New Mexico's Florida Mountains. They were separated by a few years and miles but relied on each other for comfort. "Whatcha lookin' at Marty?" PFC May asked.

"Farmers, I guess. Sort of reminded me of home," Martin replied.

"I think they're NVA or at least VC," May replied. He had noticed them too. "Look at the way they carry themselves. They're disciplined, in a column, and they don't have that peon shuffle."

Martin looked back at the last one slipping from view into one of the many tree lines across the meadow. It was then that the villagers seemed to welcome the men. For a moment at least, he doubted they were the enemy. "The village greeted these guys," he said.

"Watch your ass tonight!" Martin directed.

"Fuckin' aye. I'm on LP." May sauntered off toward his squad. "You keep down too, little brother. I don't want to write your mother about your sorry ass stopping one of Charlie's rounds," he said, carrying his radio on his back and his M16 John Wayne style, slung under his right shoulder.

"For a big ass." Martin replied in the colloquial expression conveying his agreement.

They had arrived an hour ago across the Song Vu Gai River separating this area from An Hoa, the outpost named after the nearby village about four klicks (kilometers) away. The landscape was mostly rolling plains and small hills with significant vegetation. It was in the Phu Nahm region, an area named the Arizona Territory, after the name of an operation two years before. It was also a region frequently inhabited by the Viet Cong and the North Vietnamese Army.

In the mid-1960s the U.S. military found itself committed to guerrilla warfare, a type of combat it didn't know well. The enemy's hit-and-run tactic was meant to demoralize the U.S. military, and it worked. When the enemy retreated into civilian population centers, the military had a hard time distinguishing the difference. Collateral damage resulted. Public pressure caused the U.S. military to enact a policy of not chambering a round in a weapon unless fired upon under rules of engagement … unless you were in a free-fire zone. Fortunately, the Arizona was a free-fire zone.

Kilo Company was on a search-and-destroy mission. It was part of several regiments that formed a ring around the airbase at Da Nang twenty-five miles to its northeast. This ring was informally known as the Rocket Belt. With a circle around the Da Nang area, its radius equaled the range of Chinese

122mm rockets. The North Vietnamese army humped these rockets down along the Ho Chi Minh Trail into Laos then entered South Vietnam at the western edge of the Arizona Territory and included the Phu Nahms.

Kilo Company was charged with defending against such infiltration. Today, Kilo Company had arrived for a thirty-day tour of the Arizona, relieving Mike Company who would rotate back into the An Hoa and take up a defensive position guarding the base camp against Viet Cong or NVA assault.

***

At the perimeter of the company encampment, Greek was getting ready for the night. He and another member of Kilo Company were to be together on perimeter watch. They would alternate sleeping and serving as perimeter watch throughout the night to ensure the enemy would not breach their lines without warning. That detail was usually left for soldiers of junior rank. PFC Jenkins had been digging when he finally stopped to rest.

"What are you looking at, Greek?" The village was alive with activity that was hard to characterize. But he could see that the women and children were in a line facing the center of their village. He could distinguish the shorter human shapes interspersed among them and identified them as children.

Greek stood three meters away from Jenkins using the squad's binoculars to stare at a tree line. "Here. Take a look," he answered handing the pair of field glasses to Jenkins. What both had seen was curious but had no immediate consequence to the company. Jenkins observed the same image that Greek had seen, women and children being lined up … but it could have been anything.

Jenkins handed the binoculars back and kept digging what would become a meter-deep foxhole. Greek continued looking.

Then Greek said, "Holy shit, Jenkins! One of the women just fell to the ground like she was dead." Jenkins grabbed the glasses and saw the empty space in the line of women where one had been standing. He saw a shorter shape … a child probably … bending over the mound on the ground. Then he spotted a figure wearing black pajamas raise his hands with some object and swing down on the shorter shape. The line of women shifted. He handed the glasses to Jenkins who confirmed his opinion.

"Something's going on over there, Greek. We should tell Farnsworth."
"No fuckin' way. He'll make a big deal out of it. We'll have to do a night move or something." Greek grabbed the glasses and looked again.

"Keep it quiet, dude."

A line of five or six black-pajamaed figures with what looked like rifles prodded the women and children out of the camp. What looked like two lifeless bodies remained in a heap as the villagers marched out carrying baskets balanced on their shoulders. Greek lost sight of them after a minute or so. He shared this information with Jenkins who looked again and caught a glimpse of the figures being marched out of their village.

Jenkins was still digging a foxhole when Lance Corporal (LCPL) Farnsworth approached the two men. Farnsworth was a fire team leader and had been reassigned to LP duty that night. "Jenkins, I need you with me on LP tonight. You're relieved from perimeter watch. Get your gear and come to my hooch in thirty minutes. Greek, you'll have another partner with you on perimeter."

Greek sat at the foxhole and kept watching the village. There was no sign of life. It looked deserted ... except for the two bodies on the ground. PFC Jenkins' replacement came, and Greek greeted him by handing the e-tool to him. "Hey boot... I dug this much. You can dig the rest."

The greatest jeopardy for a combat soldier was darkness. Tonight, as every night in the bush, the men of Kilo Company would work to survive the dangers of darkness that they had experienced first-hand over the last year. Zach and Billy had learned that lesson, as evidenced by the depth of their foxhole. They were true believers in the savagery of the enemy, whom they discovered was motivated and cunning.

It was December 10, and night came fast. Company Commander, Captain Drake, called an evening meeting of his command platoon (CP). Included in the meeting were the executive officer (XO), his radio operators, the four platoon leaders, and the forward observers for mortars, artillery and forward air control (FAC). The meeting was a strategy session for getting safely through the night. The XO pointed out defensive positions on a map to the entire senior staff. He discussed combat response scenarios and identified listening posts (LPs).

These LP units were four-man teams sent out beyond the perimeter to listen for enemy activity. The listening posts were a sort of tripwire for an incoming assault on the company. They kept their position secret by informing only perimeter defensive riflemen when they moved into position after dark and never mentioning them on radio communications.

The mortar, artillery, and forward air control observers were part of this briefing to ensure that any of their harassment and interdiction (H&I) fire would not hit the LPs.

Zach was walking back to his dugout with Billy when the absolute darkness of the moonless night struck him. "Just dark enough for Charlie to hit us," he said.

Soon fire team Alpha from the third squad of the second platoon moved into a sector about a klick from Kilo Company's perimeter. A little more than halfway to the site, they had quietly crossed a small stream and started to climb a steep embankment. It was during that climb that the four men were caught in an ambush.

They stumbled into a group planning to stage an assault on Kilo Company that very night. LC Farnsworth had led the team for the last hour and was walking point when the crack of an AK47 rifle from the top and sides of the embankment halted the fire team's progress. The first volley of fire from the NVA riflemen severed the team's ability to contact the company. The radio operator, PFC May, a close friend of Martin, died instantly with armor-piercing rounds traveling through the upper portion of his half-open flak jacket into his chest and then through the PRC 25 radio on his back. The radio was their lifeline to rescue.

LC Farnsworth answered the ambush by emptying a thirty-round magazine of 5.56 mm rounds from his AR15 assault rifle that had been switched to full-auto when he took point. He was sure he took out the primary rifleman in the ambush since he received no response for several seconds. Then, an eruption of small-arms fire from their flank further crippled the listening post, followed by another crushing blow to the fire team.

A Chi-Com (Chinese Communist) grenade landed close to their position. A second team member was now seriously injured. Jenkins was hit, bringing the fire team down to two men. Farnsworth was responsible for all their lives. He knew the company had probably heard the small-arms fire and was trying to raise him on the company push (slang for unit frequency). He also knew they would be trying to send a reaction team their way soon. But their response could not come soon enough. His team's survival depended upon what happened in the next sixty seconds.

-7-

MEXICO, 1935

Sixteen-year-old Conchita rode in the rear seat of a covered carriage pulled by two horses. Lorenzo was driving with Consuela, as always, by his side. Conchita was now six months pregnant and showing. The three were headed to La Calera, Conchita's home. She couldn't exactly call it home, but it was where she grew up. She had no home.

What would her parents think? Would they accept her back after she ran away? She considered her choices.

"No tiene miedo. Tus madre y padre siempre tu parientes," Consuela said, trying to console Conchita. She was telling her to have no fear … that her mother and father would always be her parents. New tears flowed from the mother-to-be.

They arrived in La Calera mid-day Sunday, just as Mass was being observed. The timing allowed them to move without being seen through the little settlement toward the ranchero where Conchita grew up.

Lorenzo stopped the team and unhitched the wagon. He put the horses into the corral allowing them to drink from the water trough. He brushed them as he always did after a long journey and fed them. During this time,

Conchita and Consuela sat in the swing on the front porch waiting for what Conchita had been dreading more than death itself. In fact, as she thought about the inevitable rejection, she decided death might be better than confronting her parents.

Mass ended on time at 1:00 pm and the Gonzalez family returned home directly afterward. They saw the unhitched carriage first, then the extra horses in the corral. When they focused on the front porch where two women rested on the swing, Carmelita shrieked her recognition. But, when Conchita stood and her mother saw her condition, her elation changed. Conchita had the answer to her unasked question.

***

Three months passed slowly for the Gonzales family. Conchita's parents had taken her in reluctantly, but their disapproval and disappointment in their daughter caused a strain in the relationship.

Her mother engaged a midwife who visited Conchita regularly and did her best to reassure the young mother-to-be about the nature of childbirth.

Conchita experienced several false alarms, summoning the midwife who lived over a kilometer from the ranchero. Each time the woman would stay for a while then leave with reassurance that she could be summoned at any time. The family even missed Christmas Mass because of another false alarm.

Conchita deduced the lack of tolerance from her father was because of the disruption in their lives. Her mother began to provide support, but her father had had enough of this wayward child. Conchita knew that her father sat in judgment. Her sister, now properly married and living in a home of her own, stood in contrast to her own life of iniquity. Her father had already told her she would have to leave soon after giving birth.

The day after Christmas was the special day. Her water broke on December 26, and Mrs. Gonzales called the midwife shortly after dinner, saying, "Ella rompia se fuente." The midwife came and assisted Conchita with a normal delivery shortly after 9:00 pm in the little ranchero. Mother and child were fine.

The new grandparents had mixed feelings even between themselves. They had to endure public humiliation and innuendo from the new priest for their poor parenting. Antonio wanted nothing to do with his ungrateful child. While Carmelita was sympathetic to her husband, she still loved her daughter and now her first grandson.

Still, the patriarch's wishes prevailed. Antonio said Conchita must depart when she was strong enough. She could either take her son or leave him to be raised by her parents, but she must find a new life away from her home and the family she had shamed.

Conchita resolved that she could never leave her child with whom she had fallen in love instantly.

-8-

NEW MEXICO, 1937

Conchita fell asleep in the recliner with Rayaldo in his crib. The next morning, she asked her La Patrona about churches in the area. Mrs. Marcak told her about a Catholic church in town that many Mexicans attended. She was sure Conchita would be welcomed there. She had heard there was a new priest who just arrived from Santa Fe.

The young mother approached the front entrance to St. Anne's Iglesia Catolico. Opening the door and crossing the threshold, she dipped the middle three fingers of her right hand into the holy water and genuflected. It was no surprise to find the church empty on a Saturday morning. She approached the altar slowly and knelt to pray.

"Buenos dias, my child. Bienvenidos," a voice announced from the entry behind her. He introduced himself as Padre Juan and invited her to join him in the rectory. After crossing herself again, she followed him around the side of the altar.

"Tell me about yourself, my child," he began when they were seated in his office. "From where do you come? Where is your family?"

"Padre, mi nombre es Conchita Gonzalez. Soy del Chihuahua. I want to join and attend your church. I have a young child, and I want him to grow up as a Catholic."

With a nod, Padre Juan urged her to continue. "You see ... we have had a very bad circumstance. I lost my Santiago and now Rayaldo has no father."

"I see."

"We moved here in March to earn a living. We are fine now, and I want to show my thanks to God for all he has done for us."

The priest nodded again with an air of understanding. Conchita wondered if he understood more about her circumstances than she had revealed. But his smile and his words contained no judgment.

"My child, I am new here just like you. I don't know many people yet either. But I assure you that our Father welcomes you and will embrace your child as his own. I welcome you and accept your profession of faith."

She needed a church home and others around her offering emotional support. Maybe she would even make a friend or two.

***

Padre Juan's welcoming speech was one he had employed before, but each time he spoke the words he meant them with all his heart.

As he surveyed the young woman before him, he noticed she was doing the same. He could tell it would take time for her to trust him. He wondered what experiences in her young life had caused her to be wary of others.

Juan noticed Conchita's natural beauty, and there was a delicateness about her. The freshly developed callouses on her hands indicated she was new to hard work. She had tied her dark black hair back in a pious manner and covered it with a veil. Her clothes, which fit poorly, were obviously hand-me-downs, but they were clean. The dust on her shoes implied she had walked a considerable distance. He wondered if she would accept an offer of a ride home.

"My child, where do you live now?" he asked, hoping to find an opportunity to extend the offer without frightening her.

"I live on the Marcak Farm where I keep house for Mrs. Marcak. It's about—"

He interrupted her.

"I know the Marcak Farm," he said, looking upward as if he was trying to recollect something about the family. Then he nodded and looked at her. "Now, I remember. It is south on Old Mesilla Road about five miles, right?"

"Yes, about. Do you know the Marcaks? They suggested I join your church."

He did not answer her question. "Would you welcome a ride home when we're finished here?"

"Thank you for the offer, but Mrs. Marcak is watching Rayaldo," she answered. "She just loves him. She gave me the day off so that I could visit here. I wanted a chance to walk as well."

"Very well. I will see you next Sunday, and I look forward to meeting your son."

***

It is time, Conchita thought. Mrs. Marcak had suggested it yesterday, and Conchita considered it overnight. Yes, it was time for her to become a citizen. The United States was her home now. She was now a member of the church. She had held a good job for almost a year, and her son was adapting well to his new life. The Marcak family had been a dream-come-true after the nightmare she endured during her last year in her native Mexico.

Mr. Marcak said he and his wife would attest that Rayaldo had been born at their farm so she, as his mother, could claim citizenship. The ruse seemed innocent enough, and Conchita thought that Mr. Marcak must know best.

After Conchita signed the notarized documents, the Marcaks, who served as her sponsors, added their signatures. Holding Rayaldo throughout the ceremony, the Marcaks looked overjoyed as they witnessed her oath of allegiance to the United States Constitution. Conchita felt pride in her ability to do so in English.

Tears of joy streamed down Conchita's face when the Marcak couple hugged her after the ceremony. As one of three to become citizens that day in Las Cruces, Conchita knew it was an event she would never forget.

***

At last Conchita felt settled and content. She was now a US citizen and attended Mass every Sunday on her day off. That led to Rayaldo's baptism shortly after joining the church.

Because of the Marcak's generosity, she wanted for nothing. Even after making contributions to the church, she was able to save most of her two-dollar-a-day wage.

After five years of employment, with an increase in pay, Conchita had accumulated enough money that she asked Mrs. Marcak what she should do with her savings.

At Mrs. Marcak's recommendation, Conchita opened a savings account at the Farmers and Merchants Bank in Las Cruces. FMB had just opened and was overseen by a board of directors that included George Marcak. Although not a paltry amount, the $500 was not quite enough to fund her dream of being independent. She would need to save a few more years for that.

-9-

VIETNAM, 1969

Listening posts were not typically heavily armored. They just acted as a tripwire. Each of four men carried an M-16, with an ammo belt and four fragmentation grenades. The radio operator carried two white phosphorous (WP) illumination flares. With one KIA (Killed in Action) and one WIA (Wounded in Action), his team lacked enough firepower to defend against the crushing enemy contact. Farnsworth grabbed the flares from the KIA radioman and pulled the injured team member, PFC Jenkins, up the embankment onto level ground behind a large outcrop of rock. Since Jenkins had been carrying an M-79 grenade launcher, the remaining member, Lance Corporal Peters, grabbed it and followed up the short hill right into the enemy ambush staging area.

Farnsworth reloaded his M-16 with a new magazine and fired full-auto as he ran into the dark tree line ahead of Peters. The NVA ambush team hiding in the trees never expected a charge directly into their position. Confused, they retreated. Although he had learned the technique at Advanced Infantry Training School at Camp Pendleton, Farnsworth never expected to use it. It was facetiously nicknamed the John Wayne maneuver, but it worked. They were safe, at least for the next few minutes.

***

In the company field camp, Martin grabbed the PRC 25 from Braun. He had already chambered a round in his M-16 and added magazines to his bandolier of ammo. He put on his flak jacket and ran toward the CP, where the company commander was using the radio to assemble a reaction team to rescue whatever was left of the LP.

Martin interrupted Captain Drake, who was on the radio. "Skipper, I'm ready to go out on the reaction team." Typically, members of the CP did not go into these situations. That was mostly grunt work. Riflemen with the 0311 MOS were the ones who did this sort of thing. But Martin knew the reaction team needed a medevac. They also needed a trained radioman to conduct the extraction of the injured.

He surmised that the squad had lost their radio operator since communication from them had ended.

Seconds passed. Drake was speechless. He didn't want to lose a member of the CP. On the other hand, any reaction team would need the skills of this forward observer for fire direction control and probably a helicopter evacuation.

Martin had successfully mastered forward air control and medevac helicopters. He was also the best damn FO for mortars Drake had ever seen. He was able to memorize the grid coordinates in this area of operation (AO) and could call a mission in the pitch-black of a moonless South Vietnamese night and hit the target. He seemed capable of visualizing the map and knowing where he was at any given place in the field.

"Martin, you can't go," insisted Drake. Captain Drake was twenty-three years old and the youngest company commander in the Marine Corps. He achieved that position because of his cool and calm decisiveness and talent for leading combat Marines as a platoon leader and then XO.

"Skipper, I have to. There's no one else who can go out there and run a medevac." Drake knew he was right and finally relented.

"All right, Corporal Martin, Second Squad is staging to go out there now. Stay within their perimeter. Can you run FAC?" he asked.

"Of course, sir."

"Then, keep. your. ass. alive! That's an order, corporal." Drake's right forefinger on Martin's chest punctuated each word.

Cpl. Travis White, the company FAC from Sunnyvale, California, had grown to be Martin's good friend, and they respected each other's skill. They even taught each other their respective roles. It would come to be known as cross-training in a few years. This was something else Captain Drake started when he came aboard. But Zach and Travis had another bond deeper than most. They trusted each other. Travis had even asked his sister to write Martin and become a pen pal. That trust was rare for combat Marines with sixteen-year-old sisters.

"Listen, turn the radio to the company push and we'll run the extraction through the one frequency. That'll make your life easier. And for God's sake, keep your fuckin' ass down," said White while walking with Martin toward Second Squad. "I'll tell air support and medevac to use that same com channel," he added, making it clear that Martin would not be alone. White slapped Martin twice on the helmet for luck and he was off.

Zachary Martin ran full speed in the darkness, toward where the reaction team was staging. Thankfully, he had memorized the coordinates of the LP at the evening briefing.

The reaction team waited impatiently for him at the perimeter of the company's defensive line. He joined them on the run and fell in the middle. Within the perimeter of Second Squad, he felt like a quarterback being protected by linebackers. In the distance, he still heard small-arms fire, and then a pop-up flare lit the sky.

Martin ran at top speed in the middle of the entire Second Squad, toward the flare that drifted downward under a twelve-inch parachute about half a click away (500 meters). Halfway there now, he kept running.

He heard men yelling from the ambush site. He was closer. The reaction team member on point was yelling, giving away their position to both the injured LP and the enemy, but it couldn't be helped. The reaction team might just as easily have taken friendly fire from the LP. Second Squad arrived at the site and dispersed quickly around the injured LP.

Martin had now run almost a thousand meters while mentally preparing an LZ (Landing Zone) brief for evacuation of the wounded while simultaneously preparing his mortar battery in An Hoa for strategic fire on suspected enemy ambush sites. Slowing to a trot, he pressed the button on the handset. "Whiskey Base, Whiskey 5 Alpha, Fire Mission." The "Alpha" denoted that it was Martin, the actual FO, making the call, not just the radio operator. The 81mm mortar team heard the ominous request and was already busy stripping away surplus charges from the tail fins off the 81mm rounds in the mortar pit.

"Whiskey 5 Alpha, Whiskey Base, go ahead."

Martin was still running when he delivered the coordinates. "Base, 5

Alpha, Fire Mission, Two, Seven Five … Five, Niner, Two, Fire for effect," he yelled into the headset.

That gave the mortar crew authority to send live rounds to a suspected target without the customary white phosphorus spotter round to mark the location. The mortar base's NCO had a lot of faith in this FO's ability. Zachary Martin's aim was legendary. God help the target. The rounds would fly.

Martin heard the mortars flying overhead from the base camp a few clicks away. They were impacting right on target. He picked up White's voice on the handset wedged between his ear and helmet.

"Marty … White here … Medevac is inbound … ETA four minutes to rotation. Prepare LZ brief. You'll need to finish up mortars before the bird arrives."

An LZ brief would prepare the CH46 chopper pilot and its Cobra escort with necessary information about the landing zone. It included the grid coordinates for medevac extraction, number and location of friendlies (them), number and nature of casualties, location and strength of hostile fire and if the landing zone was hot.

Normally, helicopters avoided a medevac landing site that was taking fire for obvious reasons. Because of that, the chopper required two things: confirmation of no hostile fire and a landing zone brief. Martin needed to give succinct details for the LZ to prepare the chopper crew for a hot extraction. Of course, Martin had the LZ brief in his head. The NVA ambush team had retreated with the imminent arrival of Second Squad and the mortar barrage. Even so, the enemy was still firing small arms in more of a chaotic response while running away. Members of Second Squad crossed the same stream and climbed the same embankment as the LP. Doc Evans, (the Navy corpsman assigned to Second Squad) failed to find a pulse. PFC May was now officially KIA.

PFC Clevis May died that night from a gunshot wound to the chest. Martin saw his eyes staring from within his helmet as he lay still on the embankment. A single hole had torn through his half-open flak jacket. "What a lucky shot," Martin said then corrected himself. "What an unlucky shot."

-10-

New Mexico, 1941

Conchita could tell the Marcak family was distressed. It was December. The news was about the invasion of Pearl Harbor, a place she had never heard of. Was that even part of the United States? she wondered.

She had learned to speak and read English well enough. She read the story in the Las Cruces Daily News that lay on the divan where Mrs. Marcak would rest her leg and read books. She saw pictures on the front page of billowing smoke above a large Navy vessel with a familiar name.

She knew Arizona was a nearby state. They named the ship after a state, she realized. The news was that the Japanese sank the Arizona and that Congress and President Roosevelt declared war on Japan.

The Marcak's concern was two-fold. First, they had their business to consider. How would war affect the pecan market? But they had a personal interest as well. Their nineteen-year-old son had to register the year before for the Selective Training and Service Act of 1940.

George Junior was to be drafted into the Army and trained at Ft. Bliss near El Paso.

Conchita looked thoughtfully at her own son and wondered how war would affect him and his future. She said a private Hail Mary.

Next week Rayaldo would start first grade at Gadsden Elementary School. She wondered how he would react to other boys and girls, not having met many people in their current circumstances.

***

Two years later, third grade had become an especially hard year for Rayaldo. The white kids picked on him more ... for his heritage and his appearance. They made fun of his clothes and shoes Conchita learned from the teacher's note he carried home that afternoon. She saw the hurt in his eyes as he told her what the other children said.

Conchita had enough money. She would use some this weekend to buy him new clothes and some shoes that did not have holes in the soles.

The problem was that with a war on, certain things were rationed, including shoes and boots. It was the rubber on the soles that was in short supply and only so many were manufactured. With the rationing, you could only buy three pairs of shoes per year.

Since Conchita and Rayaldo were citizens, she did have a war ration booklet. She hardly ever used the stamps but instead chose to give most of them to her employer, Mrs. Marcak. After all, she had plenty of food that the Marcaks provided from the farm at no cost. She never gave a thought to shoes for herself.

"Miho, please don't cry. We'll get some blue jeans and a new pair of boots tomorrow, okay?" She tried to reassure her child, adding, "And maybe even a straw hat." She didn't mention shirts since Mrs. Marcak enjoyed making shirts and had already made three for Rayaldo out of flour sacks, using patterns from McCall's. The woman enjoyed sewing on her Bernina zigzag sewing machine. She had even made Conchita two dresses that she wore to Mass regularly.

***

After ten years working for the Marcaks and living in the attached maid's quarters it seemed time to move. Conchita would always be there for them, but Rayaldo was getting older, and he needed his own space instead of the tiny room furnished with hand-me-downs and only a divider separating their beds. It was a difficult decision.

The Marcak's had been like parents to Conchita. Since George Junior had been killed in the Pacific theater of WWII, Conchita's relationship with the Marcaks was even closer. She was as devastated by the news as they were.

When she attended the funeral, she felt the grieving family's pain at losing their only son. She couldn't imagine losing Rayaldo.

Conchita looked in her savings book. Four thousand five hundred forty-seven dollars. She had saved enough to buy a small house, but she wouldn't do that. She had no other source of income except for the Marcak family for whom she fully intended to keep working. But a conversation after Mass the previous week still resonated in her head. A new friend, Teresa, gave her the idea.

"Conchita, you can still work for the Marcaks for maybe two to three days a week and offer your services to others the rest of the week. You could double your income. I do that," Teresa told her.

It was something she had never considered, but she had met a lot of Helen Marcak's friends. And the extra income would allow her to buy clothes for her growing son more often. Yes, it was time to have a conversation with her benefactors.

The new arrangement Conchita struck with Mrs. Marcak was too good to be true. Conchita would work only three days a week but be paid for a full week if she agreed to clean on Saturdays. Conchita could take care of the Marcak home adequately and still expand to provide service to others.

The others included people referred by Mrs. Marcak. Now Conchita had all the work she wanted and more than she needed. With the economy humming along after the war, soon she had doubled her income and was now living independently in an apartment in Las Cruces.

As much as Conchita knew it was time for her to move on, to be self-sufficient, departing the Marcak's was bittersweet. Yes, she would continue to see them, but she and Rayaldo now had a place of their own to call home.

The memories she made with the Marcak's would last a lifetime. They had sponsored her citizenship, provided employment, and given her and her son food, shelter and clothing when they had no one else, no other place to go.

More than that, they had been her family. She knew they loved her, and they loved Rayaldo as much as a grandchild.

No one ever knew that Conchita lighted a candle in the church every Sunday for Jorge, the man who had brought her and her son to America.

-II-

NEW MEXICO, 1948

They were waiting in the hallway next to the entry door to the hearing room. Rayaldo was fidgeting. Then again, Conchita was also fidgeting. Her mind would not stay focused. Rayaldo never should have been expelled. None of this was his fault. She dreaded what was surely to come. It was not fair. In her lap, her hands twisted the notice she had received in the mail last week.

This is called a hearing, she thought. Will they hear me? Will they hear my son? She felt like the deck was stacked against them. For a year, a white boy had bullied Rayaldo at school. She brought it to the attention of the teacher and the principal. "But that was a waste," she said under her breath.

"Ms. Gonzalez, the boy you're talking about comes from a well-to-do family who have lived here for a generation. He's a good boy," replied the teacher, stressing the 'good boy' in a southern drawl. This was after Conchita had made repeated trips to reveal the bruises and scrapes on her son's face and arms. Good boy, my ass, she thought, knowing that as a Mexican and a woman she could never say that aloud.

Mexicans on work visas were deported for less. At least she and Rayaldo were citizens and would never face that fate thanks to the Marcak family.

"Gracias a Dios for esta familia," she uttered so quietly that Rayaldo didn't even raise his head in curiosity.

Conchita's wild mind kept jumping among the past, present and future. She was sure this hearing would be farcical. She railed on that word again: hearing. It was just not fair. Rayaldo was only doing what I told him to do.

That kid bullied him for a year. When no one helped, I told him to stand up for himself and fight like a man. He did what I said. The kid got a bloody nose. So what? No one gave his parents a hearing for the year of bruises, cuts and scrapes their son gave Rayaldo.

The door opened without warning and swung without stopping until it hit the end of the oak bench in the hall on which the two were sitting. The school board sentinel spoke to them, "Ms. Gonzales you may come in now." His tone had an ominous ring of finality to it, as if the final score in a game was announced as the players took the field.

As Conchita and Rayaldo entered Court Room Three in the Dona Ana County Courthouse, they noticed seven men seated on an elevated dais.

The courtroom was normally reserved for county commission meetings and other public gatherings, but the school board had worked out an arrangement with the Dona Ana Court system to use it once a month.

On this occasion, Conchita and Rayaldo were the sole subjects of the hearing. As they entered, Conchita noticed that three others were already seated. The boy who picked on Rayaldo and his well-to-do parents sat midway in the audience chairs on the left.

So, this is how it works, thought Conchita. They're white and well-known, and I'm brown and don't know anyone. How she wished for the Marcak family to be with her.

The courtroom had an American flag hanging on a platform pole on the left side of the dais and a mostly yellow New Mexico flag on the right. The state was only thirty-six years old, having established statehood in January of 1912. With a heritage of outlaws like Billy the Kid and territorial law enforcement like Pat Garrett, the state judicial system experienced lots of growth pains over those thirty-six years.

With the primary population being a mixture of Indians and Mexicans until the mid-1800s, New Mexico experienced rapid changes after becoming a United States territory in 1850. White settlers moved in from surrounding states by overland wagons pulled by oxen and riding on horseback from Texas, Oklahoma, Arkansas and Louisiana. Conchita had learned this history by helping Rayaldo with his homework.

White ranchers moved in claiming large estates, and white settlements dotted the region on land that several tribes of Indians had previously called their nation. The Mexican population was sometimes seasonal, not establishing a permanent claim after territorial acquisition. For these and many other reasons, white hegemony reigned in the late nineteenth and early twentieth centuries. Conchita suspected this history would impact the tone of her hearing.

"Ms. Gonzales. Take the seat up front here," instructed the sentinel. The seat was at a table beneath and in front of the elevated dais where the board members sat. Conchita noticed she had to strain her neck backward in order to address the board. The boy's family by contrast could look straight at the group. She felt like a crook who had been dragged before a town council for discipline.

"Rayaldo, are you okay?" Staring at the folded hands in his lap, he nodded almost imperceptibly.

Once they were settled, the sentinel spoke first. "Ms. Gonzales, we are here tonight to discuss a recommendation by the school superintendent that we permanently expel your son from the Dona Ana County School System."

He paused and looked up from his bifocals before continuing.

"In today's formal hearing, this body has the final decision. It may be appealed to the State Department of Education in Santa Fe within thirty days. He looked and sounded ominous to Conchita and she squirmed in her seat.

The sentinel continued, looking straight at Conchita. "You will be allowed to address the board at the conclusion of this hearing. Mr. Chairman, you may start the meeting."

The chair opened the meeting by banging a gavel on the hardwood rest at his station. He required everyone to stand and face the flag to recite the pledge which was led by the sentinel. Conchita noticed that one corpulent board member seemed to intentionally stress the words "under God," glaring at her as he did.

These men—white men in authority—were an accurate representation of the men in Conchita's community.

"This hearing is now convened," announced the chair. "Ms. Gonzales, we are here to listen to the facts, hear a discussion, and reach a decision on the superintendent's recommendation. I invite the members of the board to ask questions or comment as they wish. The audience must wait to be called upon to speak."

"Gentlemen?"

"Ms. Gonzalez, you are single. Is that right?" asked the burley board member who had stressed "under God."

"Yes. Ray's father died." It was all she could summon as a response.

"Without a father, your son is just a Mex'can bastard." Conchita spun her head toward Rayaldo hoping to deflect the slur cast toward him. Her son seemed oblivious. Was he so accustomed to bigotry that he scarcely noticed anymore?

Working to preserve what little was left of her patience, Conchita said, "His father died before he was born. That shouldn't make him anything other than a boy who will be a man someday like each of you.

And he is a U.S. citizen as I have been for the last twelve years."

The man shot back, "Well that's your problem right there. You need a man around to set some discipline. No offense young lady, but a man has a Christian role in raising a boy. Your son has lost that advantage. That's why we're here."

The gavel struck loudly, followed by the chairman's warning that racial slurs would not be tolerated. "Other comments, gentlemen?"

After a grueling hour of defending her son, her culture and her ability to serve effectively as a single parent, Conchita felt defeated. As the proceedings ended, she was convinced her son's fate had already been decided before they entered the courtroom.

"Gentlemen, we've had lots of discussion, and I think it's time we hear a final statement from Ms. Gonzalez. Mr. Sentinel, please allow the respondent to address the board."

"Yes sir, Mr. Chairman. Ms. Gonzales, you have heard the board's questions and concerns and other testimony as conducted. This is your opportunity to address the school board directly. You have five minutes." Through the amplified speaker on the dais, he sounded like the crackling in Conchita's radio at home whenever she changed stations.

Conchita positioned the microphone in front of her and taking a deep breath, tried to speak with authority. She knew it would be an uphill struggle to change the minds of these men who must have surely decided her son's plight before they even came to the hearing.

"Thank you. Gentlemen, I implore you to please consider my son's future. Let me explain that Rayaldo was acting as I instructed him after enduring a year of abuse. You see, that young man sitting back there with his parents …" She pointed toward the boy who now had a smug look on his face. His parents shifted forward in their seats as if they wanted to stand and argue. "… that young man bullied my son.

"I cried with him each day when he came home complaining about a bruise, a scrape or a black eye. Oh, I went to the teacher more than once and even the principal one time to show them what was happening. All I got was denial ..." She straightened up and pulled back her shoulders. She was the only person who could change her son's future. "... denial based on nothing more than the good standing of his parents. Every time I was told that the boy's actions were justified. That he was merely retaliating for some assumed action by my son."

Conchita's voice was audibly shaking now, and she tried to control it. "The intentions of Mexican-Americans living with Anglos are considered suspect and the words spoken in our native language are judged to be offensive." *Under God* rolled his eyes and even scooted his chair back as if he were ready to leave.

"Mr. Chairman and members, after my pleas with the school authorities were ignored, I finally told my son to stand up for himself and fight like a man. He did. The bully stopped, and now his parents complained. But they were treated differently. Their words were believed, and my child became the problem.

"When Rayaldo spoke in Spanish it was not because he was trying to talk about the teacher behind his back. He didn't know what an English word meant and being frustrated, the only way he knew to ask was in Spanish."

Determined to use her whole five minutes, Conchita continued. "Each one of you or your ancestors came to this town from a foreign land just as my son and I did. Some didn't speak the language when they arrived. They had to learn. I did too. I had to ask my employer to explain English words when I first started, even though I was told not to use Spanish around her. But it was the only way I knew how to communicate.

"Because of that, she now speaks Spanish and I am conversant in English. Rayaldo did the same thing, again because I told him to do so. I thought the teacher would be as understanding as my employer was." Only one of the board members was paying attention and listening intently at this point. The others, including the chair, were looking at their watches and rummaging through papers on their section of the dais.

"If you expel Rayaldo, it will show him that the white community has no use for him." She did her best to hold back the tears that wanted to flow.

"One minute left, Ms. Gonzalez," intoned the sentinel abruptly. "Rayaldo is a good boy, just as I am sure *he* is," she said, motioning with her head toward her son's abuser. "He just needs understanding and a helping hand from the teacher and the school. Please allow him the opportunity for a good education. Thank you."

"Thank you, Ms. Gonzalez. Mr. Chairman, the board may close the hearing now and deliberate on the matter," said the sentinel.

"Thank you, Mr. Sentinel," answered the chair, banging the massive gavel for the third time. "Board members, I need a motion."

"Mr. Chairman," bellowed *Under God,* "I move that the student in question be expelled and not permitted to return to the Dona Ana County School System. Further, I move that he be remanded to the authorities for placement in the Youth Correctional Institute in Springer, New Mexico for a period not to exceed one year."

The audience's collective gasp indicated that this recommendation surprised everyone in the room, especially Conchita. Had they heard anything she said? Taking her son away for a year and placing him in a youth prison school in another city was beyond her expectation for the outcome of this hearing.

A second to the motion came almost immediately.

A stunned Conchita shifted in her chair to place her arm around her son. A thousand thoughts swirled through her head in those few seconds. "What would happen to Rayaldo? How would he cope? Surely the bullies in a place like that would be far worse than the one sitting in the courtroom.

"Gentlemen, there is a motion and a second to expel the student in question and remand him to Springer Institute. Any discussion?"

Before anyone could respond, the chairman called for the vote. "Those in favor of the motion say aye." Conchita heard several ayes and her heart sank. "Those opposed to the motion say nay." One loud nay was all she heard, a single nay vote.

The chair spoke next. "I have five ayes and one nay. Mr. Sentinel, please record the decision of the board."

Conchita swallowed hard and whispered a quiet Hail Mary. She looked at her son whose dark eyes registered confusion and fear. She was helpless to reassure him.

Then it seemed her prayer was answered when the sentinel spoke. "Mr. Chair, I have noted the vote. However, according to the State of New Mexico Department of Education regulations, any decision that includes incarceration must be unanimous. So, I am afraid the decision cannot be recorded."

"So be it," announced the chair who carried the meeting forward. "Is there another motion?" The single nay voter raised his hand. For the first time Conchita recognized the man. It was Simon Kouris, a man for whom she had started cleaning recently.

"Mr. Chair, I move that Rayaldo Gonzalez, the student in question…"

Conchita noticed that he was the only one who used Rayaldo's name. "…
be suspended for a period of two weeks to see if he can learn his lesson about
fighting in school."

"As far as speaking Spanish in school, I find no rule against that in the
regulations promulgated by the local board of education and no law in New
Mexico making English the only language in this state. If it were, I would
not have been as successful as I am."

He continued, ignoring the chair's attempt to call for a second.

"I now ask my colleague, Mr. Mario Lucci, at the other end of this dais to
offer a second to my motion. Mario, you came here the same time I did. We
both learned English together back in 1912. I challenge you to recall what
it was like for you and me during our youth. Would we have had the same
dilemma if we were younger when we came here and started school, with
you speaking Italian and me speaking Greek?"

"Do I hear a second to the motion?" the chairman asked again.

Lucci responded, "Mr. Chairman, I will offer a second to the motion for
what my colleague posited but for another reason. I realize this isn't a court
of law, but I am now recalling another circumstance. You all know that I
run the candy store across from Alameda Junior High. I recall seeing the
young man in the back …" He pointed at the boy who responded with a
sneer. "… tossing stones into the store during recess. It was disruptive to my
other young customers and created a mess that he refused to clean up. That
said, I am now more intrigued by the young woman's claim about bullying.
I second the motion."

The chair again called for a vote. This time the result was four to two in
favor of Simon's motion.

"I have four ayes and two nays. Mr. Sentinel, please record the board's
final decision.

"Ms. Gonzales," the chairman announced, "Your son will be suspended
for two weeks. He may then return to school. Please coordinate with the
principal for a return date." Immediately, the chairman turned to the
sentinel. "Mr. Sentinel, do we have any further business tonight?"

"No sir. We are finished."

When the meeting adjourned, the bully and his parents left the
courtroom. Conchita did not notice them waiting outside the courtroom
door. She moved Rayaldo toward the dais and thanked both Simon Kouris
and Mr. Lucci then collected Rayaldo and turned to leave the room.

When they passed the threshold the young bully spoke, surprising
Conchita and Rayaldo. "Come tomorrow, you're dead, Mex'can." Except

for the three adults and Rayaldo, no one else heard the exchange. The boy's threat which was obviously sanctioned by his parents, sullied the optimism Conchita had dared to feel only fifteen minutes earlier.

"Comi verga cabrajon," Rayaldo retorted. Conchita couldn't believe such vulgar profanity was coming out of her child's mouth. The stunned parents were outraged. Again, no one else was within earshot. With that, Conchita reasoned that a draw was better than her son losing the confrontation. She felt it would be best to quell further escalation by removing Rayaldo. Quickly, she coaxed him from the courthouse.

As far as she was concerned, they had won their case.

-12-

VIETNAM, 1969

Clevis May was lying face up with his radio still fastened to his back. Zachary's friend was dead, killed by their enemy. He remembered the last words they had spoken, not an hour before. Then, he recalled what they had been looking at.

"A group of farmers, my ass," he said to no one. "Those were NVA, and they were headed toward that village. May was right." He was shaken into consciousness by the corpsman that brushed by him.

Doc Evans moved up the riverbank and checked Jenkins, who was now half-leaning against a large rock behind the point of ambush. He was bleeding from his mid-section. Shrapnel from the Chi-Com grenade had entered his groin. He was also bleeding from his arm from a gunshot wound. He should live if his injuries were treated in a hospital ... soon, Evans determined. He reported this to the squad leader, Cpl. Wade. The Squad leader asked Martin to request an emergency medevac.

At precisely that time, the crackling sound of a helicopter erupted in his headset. "Whiskey 5 Alpha, this is Tango Zulu Alpha. How are you guys doing down there?" Martin was stunned by the call. The "Alpha" meant that the chopper pilot himself was making the call. Usually pilots had their navigator or RIO make such calls while they concentrated on flying the chopper. This pilot was taking a personal interest. Martin responded automatically.

"Tango Zulu Alpha, 5 Alpha. We're doing fine, sir. Just need a little help with some uninvited guests. We have two medevacs, one routine and one emergency." The designation for a medevac was tertiary: routine, priority, and emergency. The emergency medevac was Jenkins. The routine medevac was PFC May, the KIA.

"Roger that. Keep your heads down and pop a yellow smoke at your twenty," crackled the voice in Martin's handset.

"Corporal Wade pop a yellow smoke now," Martin yelled. A member of the rescue squad discharged a yellow smoke grenade in Martin's direction. It would mark the zone of the friendlies for the team of Cobra gunships. Their 20mm cannon fire would strafe suspected enemy territory and limit their fire to a distance outside the boundaries of the smoke. Even in the darkness, the yellow color would be visible to the choppers.

Martin then delivered the suspected POSREP (position report) of the enemy ambush. "Tango Zulu, 5 Alpha."

"Go, 5 Alpha."

"Enemy suspected at grid two, seven, four ... five, niner, six. Over." "Roger, two, seven, four, five, niner, six. Stand by." The location of small-arms fire from the enemy had changed. They were on the move, hearing aircraft overhead.

Zach knew this for two reasons. First, he heard small-arms fire noise coming from the short elephant grass the enemy was now wading through, and second, based on eight months of combat experience, he supposed they would be headed toward the village from where they had staged this ambush.

Now Martin was standing at the peak of the small rise on the embankment and realized he made a perfect target against the brilliant illumination of the white phosphorus flares. He squatted his tall, thin frame behind the rock where Jenkins rested, using the butt end of his M16 as a crutch against the sloping grade. He looked at the injured Marine who was leaning his shoulder against the rock. He could see the fear in his face. Jenkins' blood-soaked jungle fatigues looked pale against the light of the flare.

The sudden realization that he was mortal and could die replaced the light of a warrior in his eyes. "Cheer up, Jenkins. You're going home." Martin said, trying his best to maintain his own composure. After all, the LZ was still hot and they both could be going home ... inside a bag.

"Thanks for coming, Marty," Jenkins managed to say just before the corpsman applied a chest-size compress to his lower abdomen. The pain kept him from restraining a guttural scream. Martin turned his attention to the sky to prevent his becoming distracted by Jenkins' condition.

The two Cobra gunships provided air cover for the CH46 medevac assigned to this mission. They were both stationed out of Da Nang Airbase. With a flight time of less than twenty minutes, Cpl. White had called for them as soon as he thumped Martin on top of his helmet before he left.

In less than twenty minutes, the reaction team had traveled almost 1000 meters in the pitch-black night, carrying full combat gear. Even so, Martin felt electrified, ready to engage the enemy and rescue his brethren. And here came his weapons: two fully loaded AH-1J assault helicopters in strike formation, one slightly behind and to the side of the lead. Captain Newman, the team leader for the cobras, came in low and fast. The 20mm cannon switch was in the fire position. Newman targeted the coordinates given by Martin, the Ground FO.

The rules of engagement allowed air assault to fire at-will on a target called in by ground forward observers and cleared by their command. Radio communication between the pilot and the ground FO was picked up by air command center in Da Nang. Repeating the target coordinates allowed the command centers to double-check them on their base map.

They would look for Army of the Republic of Vietnam (ARVN) units, international peacekeeping forces such as South Korean Marines, or even Marine Corps recon units on concealed missions. After searching the map for these friendlies, command center looked for South Vietnamese civilians on a different map that was typically out of date, due to the mobility of the people in a war zone. He then cleared the target for hostile action.

No village showed on the twenty-year-old map and the target was cleared by Da Nang Air Control. The Cobras came in hot. Captain Newman used an onboard communication channel to talk with Captain Remington, his sidekick in the companion Cobra.

"Tango X-Ray, Tango Zulu."

"Go, Zulu," Remington replied in the crackle voice distorted even further by the twin 1800 HP engines of the AH-1J.

Captain Newman replied, "We're coming in on target cleared by CC at two, seven, four, five, niner, six. I call tracer fire on left. Take the vill' on the right. Let's do twenty mike-mike on first inbound. Then we'll burn what's still there on return at two, seven, zero, right. We'll be flying right over the LP. If we can, let's do a victory-pass for those heroes down there."

The order came from Zachary Martin and would be answered by two M61

Vulcan 20mm Gatling-style rotary cannon ordinance. The next reference was an order for a right-hand turn of 270 degrees and return to deliver the lethal burning kerosene known colloquially as napalm. The subsequent order to Remington called for napalm to be sent via sidewinder missiles. Those would burn what was left.

The first pass was an incredible display of destruction and mayhem. Nothing within fifty meters of the target survived. The sound of the M61 rapid fire was heart thumping, capable of 6000 rounds per minute. The second pass, then a third with additional cannon fire allowed the pilots a chance for target practice and a victory pass over Martin and the LP.

By now, smaller fires lit up the dark Asian night. Grass-thatched hooches were the main source of fuel for the fire now and probably included human flesh. Martin's rage against an enemy fed his hunger for revenge. His friend, Clevis May, was gone, killed by a nameless enemy who conducted a war dressed in tattered black man-jammies. Vengeance was his. And it was massive and thorough.

Captain Newman contacted Martin via the FAC channel. "Whiskey 5 Alpha, Tango Zulu. Over." Zachary Martin, watching the air response from the ambush site, swallowed hard, recognizing for the first time what he had done. His radio voice, transmitted through the air via transistors and battery power, had given the death order for dozens of human beings over the last few minutes.

"Tango Zulu, 5 Alpha," was all he could muster, his cold hands still pushing the handset hard against his ear. His throat was dry with a lump that refused to be swallowed.

"5 Alpha …Tango Zulu, target area green. Doc inbound in zero two," Newman announced.

"Roger that, Tango Zulu. Doc inbound in zero two. LZ Green, one routine, one emergency." Martin managed to stretch beyond his weakened vocal strength and emotional capacity. He released the push-to-talk handset, throwing it on the ground and threw up. In the milieu, no one noticed.

Captains Newman and Remington assumed wide area rotation for the medevac's security. They orbited around the LZ at a radius of one kilometer, looking for telltale tracer fire from the ground. None came. The CH46 was ready to extract the wounded and deliver them to Da Nang's medical hospital, twenty minutes away. Martin advised the squad leader of the inbound helicopter.

"Corporal Wade, you've got a chopper inbound in less than two minutes for Jenkins and May. They'll land at this site right here." Martin pointed at an area twenty meters away in some grassy flat land. "Get your men to establish a perimeter around the LZ and put the doc inside with the medevacs. You can help Doc, and I'll handle the landing. They'll be here in just over sixty seconds."

"Whiskey 5 Alpha … Romeo Sierra 23. We're coming up to your nine o'clock. Tango Zulu reports LZ may be hot. Do you have perimeter secured?" It sounded like the voice of a calm surgeon asking the nurse if the patient's heart was still beating.

"Romeo Sierra 23 … 5 Alpha. Roger that, LZ is no longer taking fire. We have a secure perimeter and one heartbeat that needs outa here," answered Martin. "Pop a smoke now," he instructed Farnsworth. "5 Alpha, we have a yellow smoke at LZ. We're coming in now. Stand by." If the chopper crew had reported seeing other than yellow smoke, Martin would warn them that an enemy was attempting to lure them into an ambush.

"Roger that. Yellow smoke. We're ready for you," he responded to confirm the correct location.

The machine gunners on the CH46 would become the unsung heroes of the Vietnam war. They manned two 50-caliber machine guns mounted on either side of the front of the cargo bay of the CH46 choppers. They protected more lives by accurate use of this gun than any other MOs in the war. They were also the bravest and didn't hesitate to remind others of that fact. Martin had seen one wearing a flak jacket that proclaimed his courage. It read, "Yea, though I walk through the valley of the shadow of death, I shall fear no evil, for I am the meanest son-of-a-bitch in the valley."

The 50-caliber machine gun was slow by comparison to the M-60 machine gun, and it sounded distinctive. It may have been slow, but it was powerful in its explosive report.

Boom…boom…boom...boom...boom.... Martin could just distinguish the thumping of the chopper's blades from the 50-caliber's deep throated, explosive sound. They never shot … except at a target. But there was always concern about a sniper being left behind.

Martin and Farnsworth each had separate duties that would be affected by the presence of a sniper. The response was simultaneous and tactical. Farnsworth yelled for Second Squad's concurrence with the CH46 gunner. "Lay down a field of fire toward that tree line," he yelled at four different riflemen.

The tracers from the chopper's 50-caliber told them where to direct fire and they did. Martin called for a similar response, but via his PRC 25 radio. "Tango Zulu, 5 Alpha," he yelled into his handset.

"Go, 5 Alpha," echoed in his ear.

Timing was everything. Martin knew that. He had to make the right call and now. "Tango Zulu, 5 Alpha …Doc is on the ground and taking fire from tree line at grid 302 … 513. Fire for effect! That last directive was code language for "Kill these bastards … now."

"Roger that, 5 Alpha. Keep your heads down."

"Break … Romeo Sierra 23, Tango Zulu. Over."

"Go, Tango Zulu."

"Romeo Sierra 23, Tango Zulu, stand by in place. We're coming in hot. Tell your riflemen to lay tracer fire in the direction of Charlie. Over."

"Roger that, Romeo Sierra. Out."

-13-

New Mexico, 1949

The war was over. Ration stamps were now a thing of the past, and the construction boom that followed enabled New Mexico to grow economically. George Marcak had expanded his pecan farm by purchasing three more sections of land. His farm now covered nine square miles in the Rio Grande Valley. With water rights being discussed for the first time, he was now the largest single owner of water rights in the valley.

The right to irrigate farmland had been enacted by the U.S. Congress and the State of New Mexico legislature to preserve the dwindling reserves of water in the Ogallala underground water basin that included land in six states in the U.S. with New Mexico and Texas and northern Mexico on the southernmost zone. This act led to another post-war economic boom since there was a rush to beat the five-year deadline set for an established farm that could be granted free water rights.

The New Mexico Water Rights Act of 1949 also gave another family business in nearby Deming, New Mexico, an economic bootstrap. Oliver Martin, now thirty-eight years old, had a thriving business in heavy equipment.

He began work at eighteen years of age in the Civilian Conservation Corps (CCC) started by President Roosevelt as one solution to end the Great Depression. Martin was filled with ambition after leaving Llano County, Texas and his family in 1935 to seek independent living. He was sent to Cloudcroft, New Mexico working in the Lincoln Forest using a Caterpillar to carve roads out of the Sacramento Mountains. That's where he met his future wife, Hazel, who was just seventeen, on a school ride sponsored by the CCC. The CCC was taking high school kids to White Sands National Monument. Hazel recalled insisting that she be allowed to sit up front in the cab with the driver, Oliver Martin.

Eventually Oliver and Hazel got married. Then, after working for the CCC, Oliver joined a construction company in Arizona as a driver for large earth-moving equipment. He was known as a Cat skinner, having learned to operate a Caterpillar. With that skill and experience, he acquired a contractor's license from New Mexico and started a heavy equipment business at Deming in 1942. His first job was to assist in the development of the Deming Air Base, a training facility for pilots of Army bombers.

He then created a robust career removing mesquite bushes from the southern New Mexico desert for land buyers who wanted to start a farm and claim the water rights. These new farms increased value to land heretofore without irrigation.

Oliver Martin would help nearly a hundred would-be farmers get into the field and in doing so, he acquired some land of his own … in trade for his Caterpillar skills. His first child, Zachary, was born after they built a home on the 160-acre mesquite-laden plot of land he acquired from a neighbor. The neighbor wanted to trade half the 320 acres he had purchased in exchange for Martin's earthwork, making the other half a viable farm. Martin did what he usually did. He cleared the newly acquired land and turned it into a sustainable farm.

This type of work was demanding but there were rewards. Typically, the roots and stumps were dragged together, piled in a loose stack, and allowed to dry. He would sell them as firewood when they were dry enough. Several surrounding neighbors vied for the opportunity to purchase the mesquite firewood from Martin.

Several years later, one out-of-town customer for the firewood was Bartolome Valles from Las Cruces, who drove his 1948 Ford truck to make a purchase. He would become a regular client, looking for the firewood in the late fall of every year. Although they were distant business colleagues, their personal connection would not be realized for more than two decades.

-14-

New Mexico, 1949

Bartolome Valles had left high school and just started a construction business in Las Cruces. Work was good and Valles benefited with a substantial income while gaining valuable experience in the field. He mastered English for business reasons, having grown up in Anthony, New Mexico in a Spanish-speaking home.

After joining St. Anne's Iglesia Catolico in Las Cruces, he attended Mass regularly in part to continue the religious tradition his mother instilled, but more than that, to meet other people … including young women.

A sixteen-year-old caught Bartolome's eye. Catarina Guzman had her *quincinera* (coming out celebration) only a few months before. Mexican society allowed families to present their young women to the world and of course to young men just after their fifteenth birthdays. They would do so in a party that included dancing. They could not date yet but were now allowed to associate with boys in chaperoned settings such as church-sponsored gatherings.

Bartolome, although only a year older than Catarina, was not shy about nodding and saying hello at Mass. He spoke directly to Catarina afterward as the church youth held their own conversations while the parents spoke to each other before departing. Since Bartolome was by himself in Las Cruces, he was a subject of suspicion by the parents of young ladies such as Catarina. His parents from Anthony, a nearby town, did not attend this church, but Padre Juan assured other parents that Bartolome's parents were good Catolicos and so was Bartolome. At least he hoped the younger Valles met that measure.

Bartolome met Catarina in the garden of St. Anne's. She had sauntered away from the other girls to the flower garden on the side of the church grounds. Bartolome seized the opportunity. It was exactly what Catarina had expected … and hoped for. She had been watching him as much as he had been observing her.

"Hola. Como esta, señorita?" She turned in a demure manner and pretended to be surprised.

"Estoy bien, y tu?" she answered in familiar rather than formal Spanish. It was more to relax the young man than to extend an invitation.

He needed relaxing. He had been a bit tense thinking about this introduction. Catarina was the prettiest girl at St. Anne's. In fact, she was the prettiest girl he had ever seen.

The two walked together in the garden and engaged in small talk … just getting acquainted when Padre Juan came around the back corner of the church, surprising them into silence. They didn't get a rebuke. Padre Juan was a man of God but had been young once himself. He knew what life was like.

"Como estan muchachos? Enjoying this fine day God has given us?" His comment set them at ease. Bartolome spoke first.

"Si, Padre. Es un bonita dia." All he could come up with on the spur of the moment was to agree with Father Juan that it was a beautiful day.

Catarina added, "We were just admiring your skill as a gardener."

They all now focused on the rich colors in the shrubbery and flowers. Padre Juan liked to call this work his Garden of Gethsemane. Although it was desert, Padre Juan had managed to grow vibrant red and yellow roses, along with grape vines and varieties of blooming cactus.

Smiling at the young people and motioning toward the garden, he said, "Esos son bonita regulos del Dios … como ustedes." He told the young people that these flowers were beautiful gifts from God … just like the two of them.

-15-

NEW MEXICO, 1949

Conchita's cleaning for Simon Kouris led to an unpredicted arrangement. One day after she had finished cleaning, Simon waited to pay her including a tip but also to give her something else. He handed her the present, a box wrapped in shiny white paper with a bright red bow. She was beside herself. No one had ever given her a gift except the Marcak family and only at Christmas.

She put her pocketbook down and carefully opened the present. It was a square box with tissue paper that she pulled back to reveal a delicate white silk nightgown trimmed at the neck with a pink ribbon. It also had a pink embroidery pattern on the front. She pulled it out, exclaiming her delight.

"This is beautiful. I have never had anything like it before. Thank you, Mr. Kouris."

"Call me Simon, Conchita. And you're welcome. I am happy to see you smile. You have made me happy, not only from your work for me but by your cheerful tone and your pleasant smile, my dear." She noticed the stress on my dear.

"I'm overwhelmed, Simon. I can't thank you enough. Please know how much I appreciate this gesture. Your kindness is such a reward for working here. Thank you again."

"I am pleased when others appreciate my generosity. You are more than welcome," he replied. "Someday, you'll have to show me how it fits."

Conchita held it in front of her pretending to model it over her work dress. She gave a perky coquettish smile and rocked back and forth on her hips. She felt positively giddy. She hadn't felt like that since she was sixteen years old. She suppressed a private regret for her flirty behavior.

He grinned his approval.

"Why don't you come over … say Friday after work. We can have dinner that I will make for you, and we can enjoy a relaxing evening by the fire. We can get to know each other."

Conchita had not had a suitor since she was a teenager. She thought she had forgotten how to respond to such an invitation.

"I had no idea you could cook, Simon. I would be happy to join you for dinner. You're just full of surprises." She gave him a peck on the cheek as she turned to leave with her present and her delight.

"Oh, here. I almost forgot. There's a small bonus in there for your hard work." Simon pulled an envelope from his shirt pocket and handed it to her. She did not open it in front of him.

"Thank you, Simon. I will see you Friday night," she said as she closed the side door on her way out and walked to her car that was parked on the street outside the estate and its circle drive.

In the car, she opened the envelope. She was stunned. Simon had placed a check for ten dollars for her day's work plus a fifty-dollar bill as her tip. She had never seen a fifty-dollar bill before. She looked back at the house on Maple Street through the entrance to the circle drive.

She could see Simon watching her from his front porch. She waved at him and even blew a kiss. He waved back.

-16-

VIETNAM, 1969

Roger Sammon, Cpl. Machine Gunner, USMC was instructed through his on-board headset to lay down heavy fire in the enemy's direction. He obliged them. 50-caliber tracers, along with 5.56mm tracer ammo from Second Squad were aimed toward the treeline in question. Captain Newman and Captain Remington headed in from rotation, ready on their final approach.

Suddenly, the smell hit Martin. It was like nothing he had ever known on the farm where he grew up. This was the scent of war. The smell of gunpowder, burning grass homes, phosphorous candles, kerosene napalm, gasoline from turbine engines all mixed with the stench of human blood, flesh and fear. A smell Martin would never forget. The rhythm of the 50-caliber gun sounded like the bass in a rock concert. The crescendo would be the strafing run from the two Cobras, coming up ... right about ... now.

Both Captain Newman and Captain Remington positioned their AH-1J Cobra gunships alongside each other for the run on the suspected target, a tree line into which tracer fire was being directed. Their armament was targeted on a hostile force directing fire toward a rescue operation. That was enough to justify the assault. Their directive was clear: destroy the enemy who was intending to kill them. Enough was enough! The 20-caliber guns issued report in unison, side-by-side. The sniper fire ceased at once. Martin and Farnsworth relaxed a little while Doc Evans and Cpl. Farnsworth carried May's body onto the CH46. The chopper team had already loaded Jenkins, who was being treated by an on-board Navy corpsman. CH46 choppers did not like to stay on the ground long. They were big targets with little means of defense. In fact, their average life expectancy while on the ground was said to be twelve seconds. They had been on the ground for almost two minutes.

In fact, sometimes insertion teams had to jump a couple feet because the pilot didn't want to overstay his welcome. These guys were ready to get the fuck out of Dodge.

The blades increased their rotational speed and the pilot motioned for Martin to duck. The crackle in his handset said it all, "Whiskey 5 Alpha ... Romeo Sierra 23 ... It's been a pleasure working with a real pro. Keep your head down, son. We're out 'a here," the pilot said as he issued Martin a genuine Marine Corps salute.

With that, the rear rotor of the CH46 climbed upward in its classic take-off maneuver. It was headed back toward the Da Nang with one beating heart and a still one, both heroes from Kilo Company, Third Battalion, Fifth Marines. Their escort, the Cobra gunships, departed a few minutes later, staying until a Spooky Gunship arrived on-scene. Spooky was called in to deliver its supply of white phosphorous flares. A welcome voice came a few second later. "5 Alpha, Tango Zulu ..."

Captain Newman would forever be a friend. "Go, Tango Zulu."

"5 Alpha ... Tango Zulu, we're going to have to play sidekick for Romeo Sierra 23. We're going to pass tactical control over to a Spooky for cleanup. You guys doin' all right down there?"

"Roger that, Tango Zulu. We're all here ... thanks to you. I owe you one." The debris of war was messy, causing warriors to ignore their manners. Martin realized he was being too informal with a commissioned officer and added some formality. "Thank you, sir. And skipper, thanks for the victory pass. You helped cheer up some guys down here."

"Roger that. Look me up next time you're in Big D (Da Nang) and we'll split a keg. Tango Zulu out."

The night sky lit up with a million candlepower from the dozens of white phosphorus flares transforming the dark Asian night into artificial daylight for a square kilometer. Already, kills started being counted in the tree line and the village that was no more. Within an hour, there had been an estimate of twenty enemy kills. Kilo Company had won tonight based on the scoreboard. But a lot more had been lost, including one good friend from Martin's hometown.

Zachary Martin lost something else that night. He couldn't give it a name. But it left him with emptiness, almost as if he wished he had died instead of PFC Clevis May.

What he had lost was his control, which was dangerous for himself, his enemy, and anyone else who happened to get in the way. Instead, he was filled with rage. It was this rage that caused him to lose control. He was responsible for the deaths of over twenty humans, all in retaliation for killing his friend. Could war be personal? Wasn't war supposed to be devoid of emotion? How many of those who died tonight were warriors? How many kids? He felt sick to his stomach. He thought he was going to retch, but he closed his mouth and swallowed.

He felt responsible. The deaths of any civilians were on him.

"He's a baby killer." That's what those war protestors would say about him.

The aspersion stayed with him for most of his life. There may have been some justification for killing those under twenty-one because warriors started out younger here. But a whole village? After being in the country for eight months, his perspective on war changed in one night. It became personal and a source of lasting grief.

During the Vietnam War the U.S kept score through body counts—theirs and ours. After a firefight, it was essential to go in immediately and evaluate how many of the enemy died. The North Vietnamese Army quickly learned the procedure and compensated by removing as many bodies as possible before the U.S. could make an accurate assessment. This occasion was different. There seemed to be no one left to remove the bodies. No enemy survived.

At daylight, the evaluation team reported to HQ that twenty-three enemy and zero civilians were found KIA. So, the score that day was 23-1 U.S. Zachary should have felt relief hearing that no civilians were killed. But he dismissed it as inaccurate. He knew someone washed the report, eliminating civilians from the kill list to prevent exposing a public incident. He wondered how many of the twenty-three dead were women and children.

-17-

GREECE, 1916

Simon Kouris had built an empire in the small town of Las Cruces and was comfortable. That much was undeniable. His father would have been proud if he only knew. He reminded himself that his father from the old country, died at work when Simon was a mere lad of sixteen.

"Wet behind the ears," his father would always declare.

"Now look at what I have achieved—a fine home, a growing business, well respected by the community and ..." He stopped short of adding any reference to a family. He knew he had none, not formally anyway.

He had no brothers or sisters. He never married and had no children—well, no legitimate children anyway. That should have delighted the bachelor, almost sixty years old now. He so enjoyed the time as an unattached man. As a youth he knew plenty of young women who could have been Mrs. Kouris. Was it my impertinence? My pace? My quest for the perfect one?

He knew the real reason.

He liked the private life. He was born to live alone. His father worked six days a week away from home most of the time. Their home was just outside Piraeus, a port suburb of Athens. His father was a mason and helped erect many buildings in Athens at the turn of the century.

Construction work was plentiful as a result of Corinth Canal. Because of increased trade through the port city, new buildings were plentiful. Simon's father told him that he built the Central Market and Town Hall in Athens.

He couldn't say that he ever really loved his father. He never felt loved as a child. He grew to be much like his father in that regard.

He never knew his mother except for a crudely framed tintype picture of her as a young woman. He grew up alone except for Reah, his father's hired babysitter.

Reah would walk the short winding road in the pre-dawn hours every day to the Kouris home when the senior Kouris was ready to leave for the day's work. She would return home after dark. For this she was compensated one Drachmae every day. She accepted it eagerly considering the prevalent rural living conditions.

Simon did not attend school until he was almost seven years old. There simply was no school near his home outside rural Piraeus. The one he did attend was in a small hamlet within walking distance of his home.

The school building was primarily a bakery, its use switched to part-time school midway through the day. Teaching the school was the baker who volunteered her time. The school had about ten kids of ages varying from six to thirteen. The two subjects included reading and writing. School didn't start until noon, as the bakery was always busy in the morning.

School lasted around three hours, and Simon walked there and back home in the company of Reah. The makeshift school lasted for five years when another one was started in central Piraeus—too far for Reah and Simon to walk. After all, most kids stopped going when they turned twelve years old. He would begin to work soon, he was sure.

Greece was virtually bankrupt in 1890 and poverty was common within the outlying areas and the islands. Wars, invasions and revolutions were a regular occurrence in Simon's youth. The first he could remember was what is now known as the Young Turk Revolution in 1908. He recalled that when he was ten his father's concern was not how it would affect his home but rather how it would affect his work.

Reah served as a child-minder. But she had another obligation when Simon's father returned from work. Every so often Reah would say goodbye to Simon then attend to some other work in the tool shed with his father before returning home. His father had told him to stay in the house.

As he grew older, Simon would venture out back to the shed and hear moaning. He had been tempted to ask about this but withheld his inquiry, afraid his father would raise his voice as he always did when Simon asked uninvited questions.

He felt safe enough to ask Reah one day when he was nine years old. She politely changed the subject, so his curiosity remained unsatisfied for another year. In fact, he never understood until one day when he was eleven.

Simon had begun to have peculiar sensations down below. This happened one day when he climbed the rope hanging from a tree out front. He couldn't explain these sensations, except for being tingly. His father was no help, ignoring the question. Older children at school laughed at him about it. He had no one else to ask. So, he asked Reah. "Do you really want to know?" she asked. When he assured her that he did, she asked if he would do her a favor.

He replied, "Yes, of course, Reah."

She stood and began slowly disrobing. "Take off your clothes," she instructed.

He had never seen a female body before. Hers was twenty-seven years old. She began with her top followed slowly by her lower wrap, as if still considering it.

After seeing her completely nude, he still didn't know what to expect. Being nude for him had been associated with taking a bath. She moved him to the cot, cleared the tool bags, and sat him down next to her.

"You may not know Simon, but your body does," Reah said to him, now looking at his rigid penis that was curving slightly upward.

What followed seemed at once strange and strangely familiar. But this time, the feelings explained themselves. He now knew what his father had been doing all those years with Reah. He felt oddly guilt-ridden. He would never bring it up again.

When he turned thirteen, he started going to work with his father. His first job was to carry tools and clean them when his father finished. He watched and learned the trade from "a skilled mason hailing from generations of masons," as his father described himself.

From that early age he also learned how to wield power. He saw it in his father's personal life and overheard political conversations of his father's fellow workers. One co-worker often quoted Italian Niccolo Machiavelli. "It is better to be feared than loved if you cannot be both." Simon learned that maintaining control was essential to success. That lesson stuck with him.

Simon recalled his immigration to the United States in 1912 after his father died. The Balkan League had just declared war on the Ottoman

Empire. Assassination attempts against King George caused the nation further alarm. Concerned about conscription and seeing no future there, Simon made the decision to abandon his home of sixteen years. And now after forty years in America, the lessons he learned and the instinct he gained from his father's limited parenting was enough.

He had achieved success. Sipping a glass of red wine in front of the fireplace, he realized his life was comfortable.

-18-

New Mexico, 1956

Simon heard a soft knock at the side door. He lifted his right hand, pulled back the sleeve and glanced at his gold Paneria Luminor, a recent acquisition, a testament to his hard work and success. He wished they made watches for left-handers.

He knew who it was. He expected her to come to the side entrance to avoid idle gossip. As a housekeeper, Conchita Gonzalez was fastidious, always keeping the house immaculate. As a lover? Well, she was not bad at that either.

"Hello Conchita. Please come in. Would you care for a glass of wine, dear?"

"Simon, thank you. I would." She joined him sitting in the second leather chair by the fireplace. Their elegant wineglasses nestled together on a solid mahogany parlor table between them. She sat, tucking her right leg under her exposing a sliver of her inside left thigh. Simon noticed, wondering if she had practiced that move in her new dress.

She was wearing the Dior sack dress he had given her at her last visit. He managed to get it from the designer on a recent trip to New York. He knew

Conchita's size from peeking at the dress she had hung on his armoire while showering.

Yes, they were now sexual partners. After years of cleaning his house she also shared other aspects of his life.

"That dress looks splendid on you, my dear."

"I agree. I love it," she responded. "You shopped well, Simon. Thank you again."

"Nonsense. It pleases me when someone appreciates my effort." He knew she liked him, but that she liked his money more. It made no difference just so she was discreet about their affair.

"Hard day, Simon?"

"No, pretty good actually. I am moving along well on a large commercial project and am looking forward to getting the contract for the first high-rise building in Dona Ana County." He didn't elaborate on another success he had achieved. He wondered if her son had shared that with her.

"How is Rayaldo doing in his job?" she asked.

Rayaldo Gonzalez, he had assumed, was Conchita's bastard son of her youth. The bastard part was something he didn't ask about.

"He's doing fine, Conchita." He decided to see how much she knew. "We had some trouble on a job earlier this week. Rayaldo was right there to help. Good kid. What did you hear?"

When Rayaldo was only eighteen, Simon Kouris gave him a present and told him it was a reminder that he was now a man. He had purchased the gold ring from a jeweler and presented it to Rayaldo at a Sunday dinner in his home. Ray Junior, Conchita's second, was a child still, but attentive enough to ask if Kouris had a present for him. Simon replied that when he was old enough, he might get a similar gift.

"Thank you, sir." Rayaldo had said, admiring the gold ring. "It just fits." Simon accepted the thanks and gently stuffed the red jeweler's bag in his pocket. He could see the potential in the lad, but knew he was filled with a deep-seated rage.

That rage could be useful, Kouris had thought more than once.

He also gave Rayaldo a job. Now, two years later, at twenty, Rayaldo could handle himself well and was strong for his age. Simon also hired two other high school dropouts that hung around the boy. He knew he could use them for muscle whenever necessary. When he didn't need it, Rayaldo drove for him and ran other errands. Rayaldo and his friends' reputations were useful to Simon. Ruffians known to frequent bars with the occasional bar fight suited Kouris' need for intimidating his competition.

Conchita, who had been sipping her wine, interrupted Simon's thoughts. "I heard just enough from Rayaldo to know there was some trouble but nothing more than that. Are you okay, Simon?"

Looking up from his glass, he responded, "Well, a new guy came into town a while back trying to undercut me on jobs. He was nosing around our sites trying to lure some of my workers away. Rayaldo told me about it and we waited for 'im. Caught 'im too. We taught him a lesson. Rayaldo and his friends taught the lesson, that is. I don't think he'll be back. I heard he was moving to El Paso."

Conchita breathed a sigh of relief.

"So, what about this new building?" she inquired.

"It's a mixture of offices with stores on the ground floor."

They clinked their glasses and toasted the weekend. "It will be the largest project I have ever built, Concha." As far as he knew, she liked it when he called her his pet name. He didn't know that in Spanish, it referred disparagingly to female genitalia, and she never told him.

"It will come up for bid in a few months," he continued. "I just learned about it Wednesday."

"Well, I am sure you'll get the contract. Who else would dare to compete with you, Simon?"

"No one. Not if they want to keep their arms and legs," he said, flicking up his wrist. It was not an idle threat.

"You are dressed so elegantly. We should go out. It's time we had dinner together. Someplace nice, Concha. You know, to show the town that we're together."

"Simon, are you sure we should? What will people say? What about your business? I don't want to cause—"

"Nonsense. Shall we dine, my dear?" Standing, he held out his hand. She smiled as she accepted it, and he ushered her out the front door instead of the side door.

***

Dusty Trails was a steakhouse owned by a business acquaintance. Simon didn't build the restaurant, but he did build a new home for the restaurant's owner near the Las Cruces Country Club.

No, Simon didn't build many homes, sticking to more profitable commercial work, but he wanted the Uzueta family to owe him a favor, for later. Besides the steaks were second to none, although expensive. Tonight's meal might set him back as much as twenty dollars, but it would be worth it. There was something important to discuss.

"Greetings." The proprietor welcomed his favorite guest and seated the couple at the best table in a private room overlooking the golf course. Rather than the train tracks on the other side of the restaurant, their view encompassed the beautiful Organ Mountains.

Simon knew that Uzueta would not charge him for the meal, but he would make up for that by leaving a heavy tip. After all, they had been seated at the best table. They were isolated and away from earshot of Las Cruces' finest citizens.

Conchita opened the conversation. "Simon, I have never been here before, only driven by. This is very nice. The leather seats, the beautiful décor and the view."

"I don't come here often but it's a special occasion," he answered. She cocked her head. It was the second reference he had made to a special occasion.

Simon ordered for both, as was his custom. They would have the ribeye steak with some side dishes. Then he chose his favorite vintage red wine. Conchita smiled, obviously admiring his societal skill and prominence. Simon knew she was attracted to him, despite their age difference. Their sexual encounters were pleasurable. But he also knew she had never felt an emotional connection.

"Concha, I want to ask you something." Simon noticed the straightening of her posture. He had her attention.

"Concha, it's about Rayaldo, Ray Junior, and you." Now her face registered confusion and her gaze dropped to the napkin in her lap.

They both knew that Rayaldo never had a child. The name, Ray Jr. was another ruse. The child had been born to Conchita and Simon five years before. The respectable thing for her to do in this community was to stay out of sight while pregnant with an illegitimate child. Paid for by Simon, Conchita had traveled to El Paso and returned several months later with a new "grandson." They had agreed to tell everyone that the child was Rayaldo's and she was raising him.

Ray Jr. had just started first grade at Bell Elementary School near their home. It was the school where Mexican Americans were expected to attend, not Smith Elementary, central to the town and populated by over ninety-five percent white children.

Redemption was too late for Rayaldo, who had left school and was now merely a hired thug for Simon. His worth to Simon Kouris was no different than a vehicle that might be traded in for a newer model. While Kouris may have respected some of Rayaldo's skills, he didn't respect his character.

Ray Jr. was still young enough that Simon could sense some innocence in the child. He hoped his child would not turn out like his older half-brother.

"I know we've never talked much about him," Simon began. "I hope you will indulge me some honesty. Rayaldo's a little rough around the edges as I'm sure you agree, but he has a lot of potential to be a leader. He can attract and maintain loyalty. That's rare, and it seems to come naturally to him. On the other hand, he has a penchant for drink and roughhousing. I don't know how to help that part of him. He could be a success, but he needs to grow up, don't you agree?"

Simon saw her shifting in her seat. With a deep breath, Conchita raised her head. "Yes. I know we haven't talked about my first son in much depth, but as a single mother for twenty years, I never knew how to fill that gap of his missing father. I tried. We went fishing at Lake Roberts sometimes. He joined the 4H group and went camping with them at Hillsboro until he was kicked out for smoking. I took him to hunt for fossils when he was studying them in school."

Simon remained silent. With a deep breath, Conchita seemed to gather her emotional strength. She looked into his eyes and said, "I told a lie when I met you. You see, Rayaldo's father did not die. I am not a widow. She paused, but Simon did not interrupt. "A young man and I ran off when I was sixteen. We never got married. We moved to nearby Nuevo Casas Grandes where he worked on a ranch. We lived in the bunkhouse. He left me shortly after I became pregnant, still sixteen years old." She took another breath before adding more detail. Simon waited.

"I went home to my parents who were not welcoming. They told me they would help with a midwife but expected me to be on my own soon after his birth. They offered to keep their grandson, but I refused and took my son. It was 1936 and the depression did not end for Mexico as quickly as it did here.

"After a few months, I made the journey from Casas Grande to Ciudad Juarez. Rayaldo and I slipped across the border to El Paso with a coyotaje. I began working at Marcak Farms then. As you know, we met a few years later, and I owe you and Las Cruces my life." When Simon saw tears welling in her beautiful brown eyes, he regretted bringing up the subject.

"Concha, I am sorry I brought this up. Let's put it aside and ..." She seemed not to hear what he said and continued talking.

"He does mean well, but he must have his father's temper pent up inside him. His father was a young Mexican ranch hand when I first saw him in a rodeo and was swept away. We left town that weekend. I ran away from home without telling my parents and never wrote. Can you imagine coming home to strict Catholic parents after that? And pregnant?"

Conchita, tears flowing, continued to explain as Simon listened silently. She had never opened up to him before, and he didn't want to discourage her. In the last few minutes he had learned more about his mistress than in the past decade of their relationship. She had been through a lot but weathered it well.

"I know that Rayaldo can be a bully, but I think he learned that early from school. When he was growing up, the white kids bullied him, ganging up on him and beating him with a baseball bat, then telling the Anglo authorities that it was Rayaldo who chased and beat them. So Rayaldo learned not to trust white people, and he learned how to stay alive by intimidation. You remember when he was expelled. He could have turned out differently if only ..." She stopped, overcome. Simon took the white handkerchief from his breast pocket and placed it in Conchita's hand.

When Conchita buried her face in the handkerchief, Simon did not know what to do. This was all new for him. For all his social dexterity, his interpersonal skills were absent.

"Simon, this night is so beautiful. Please forgive me."

"Nonsense, Concha. It's I who should apologize. I am sorry. I only brought it up to suggest ..." He didn't finish his thought because he was not sure how it would sound right now. In fact, he was never sure how to say it.

"What, Simon?" Her face registered equal parts curiosity and pain. "Please finish."

"Well ... I was wondering ..." He set his knife and fork on his plate. "How would you feel about moving in with me? You and Ray Junior." She dropped her hands that still clutched the handkerchief, revealing a face filled with disbelief. He continued.

"I have three bedrooms, Concha. You can have two of them. You can save rent and be in a better community. For me, you would always be available for ..."

He couldn't finish the sentence. Not because of the unintended sexual inference but because ... well ... he wasn't sure *how* the arrangement would help him. He just wanted her ... near him. He wanted her company. That's it. He had to tell her before—

"Simon, I am overcome. I have never had an offer as generous as that." She wiped her eyes, and he saw her working to regain composure. "Before you come to your senses, I accept your offer. If it wouldn't cause a stir in this restaurant, I would come over there now and kiss you."

He gathered strength to finish his thought, "Concha, I need to be near you." His head was downward in the prayer position as he continued. "You give me strength. I feel comfortable around you." Now he raised his head to look into her eyes. "Concha, I care for you. I only brought up your children because I wanted you to know that they are as welcome as you are. The past is over. We have only the future, and I want to spend my future with you and your—our—children." With that, she stood, walked around the table and gave him a tender kiss.

They enjoyed a delicious dinner and later, spent a beautiful night together.

The next week, Conchita and Ray Jr. moved from the rented shanty on the southern side of town, using a box truck that Rayaldo normally drove for Simon. The moving crew included Rayaldo and two of his friends.

Conchita Kouris, she daydreamed one day as she worked at her new kitchen sink. The name would probably never be hers, but she didn't need that—not really. She had a comfortable house with an attractive man who loved her and her sons. She was home. And that's what mattered.

***

The day after Conchita's move, Simon did two things. He made an appointment with his doctor and set up a meeting with his lawyer.

Simon listened to David Janis MD announce his condition. "I see that life is treating you well, Simon. You have a thriving business. You look good. Your blood pressure is a little high, though."

"Doc, I get these dizzy spells every now and again. I am worried about my heart. Does high blood pressure cause dizziness?"

"Could be. Let me get an X-ray and you come back in two weeks. Whenever it feels serious, take one of these pills, but only if you think you might be having a heart attack," Janis insisted. "Then, call me right away. The pills will help you if it's a heart attack but can cause other damage, especially if it's something else."

Simon got the message. He took the small vial of the tiniest pills and examined them closely. "What is it, Doc?"

"Nitroglycerin."

Simon was aghast. "And they're safe to swallow?" He had heard the term referred to explosives, not medicine.

"There is a very small amount in each pill, and you can see how tiny they are. The nitrates will dilate your arteries and increase blood flow letting the heart rest," Janis explained. "The chemical is very stable. You won't blow up. Trust me. No one ever has."

Janis signed some forms he was holding and opened the door for his patient. "Remember. Come back in two weeks. Don't forget to go to the hospital for the X-ray. I'll call and tell them what we're looking for. Good day, Simon."

***

George Small was a tall, rotund, white-haired lawyer with an equally large reputation. He knew people. He was the guy who could pick up the phone and something on the other end would happen. Simon Kouris was willing to pay for the very best. Small had influence, and Simon respected and needed that.

In large part, Kouris' success was due to the influence of those who could make things happen. Small was a former New Mexico State Senator from Dona Ana County. The Democratic Party had sought him for the governor's race in the 1940s. He declined the governor's position due to health issues. The truth was that he was sick of the political process even though, for the last three decades, he had used that same political leverage to achieve a legal outcome that favored his clients.

"Simon … Come in, my Greek friend and have a seat. My time is yours. What do you need?" With both thumbs, Small stretched the suspenders already straining over his crisp, starched white shirt.

"A will, George. A last will and testament, just in case."

"You're not planning a trip anytime soon are you, Simon?" Simon knew the English language well, but he didn't catch the nuance in Small's question.

"I'm not planning a trip at all, George. I just think a man my age should be prepared for any eventuality."

Just then a knock on the door interrupted Small's next question. "Mr. Small. Excuse me but the mayor is on the phone." It was Mary, Small's receptionist/legal secretary. "Can I confirm the two of you for a meeting at Town Hall next Wednesday at 5:00 pm?"

"Yeah, tell the bastard I'll meet with him, but not at 5:00 unless he wants to pay double my fee." She started to close the door. "No, wait Mary. Tell him 5:00 is fine." Then he added quickly, "He's got as short a temper as I do. I don't want him to misunderstand my meaning." The door closed and the conversation resumed.

"Now Simon, where were we? A will, huh? So, who gets your fortune? And what do they have to do to get it?" Kouris didn't mind Small's candid demeanor. After all, it had helped him make his fortune. That's just the kind of man Simon liked on his side. No nonsense.

Intimidating, smart, reliable, and loyal.

After a half hour of note taking, Small turned to Kouris and shook his hand. "I'll have the papers drawn up this week. Come see me Monday next to sign your life away, Simon."

Kouris stood and turned to leave the office when Small's booming voice stopped him. "And please don't make me have to earn my hourly rate for this anytime soon, okay?" His style was legendary, and he was as respectful to a client as anyone, especially one as well-heeled as this client.

"Thank you for always being there for me, George. I'll see you Monday."

-19-

NEW MEXICO, 1957

In his private office, Simon Kouris read and re-read the invitation bid for the high-rise building. He had lost the bid to a man who tricked him. That was true. But he noticed something in the document that made him curious. He had never seen it before.

It was in the section marked: Conditions of offer of the bid notice. It stated what Simon needed to make things right. Condition Eight stated:

> *If the bidder is successful and later unable to perform as stipulated in the contract, the bid will be rescinded and granted to the next sequential bidder at any time during the contract.*

That's it, Simon reasoned. There were only two bidders on the project. Valles won, yes. But if he cannot perform, then I can take over, and at my original offer. The project will be mine.

He was still in the fight. Now he had to find a way to make this Valles character unable to perform.

Simon was sure he knew the way.

"Rayaldo, come into my office and close the door." He found Rayaldo reclining on the office couch in the foyer. "I need your help on something.

Are you and your friends available tonight?" he asked the young Hispanic man reading a Superman comic book.

***

Conchita could tell that something was up. Rayaldo wasn't his usual self. Her son did not come by the home on Maple Street just to visit. Was it to get a meal? she wondered. She would certainly feed him— anytime. He is a man now, she reminded herself, recalling his many brushes with the law. At 21, he must face the legal system as an adult. Conchita was still worried about Rayaldo's three curses: fighting, booze and money; but at least the episodes of legal problems had diminished since her benefactor hired him. It was surely Simon's influence that kept him out of trouble.

"Mama, que tal?" he asked his mother by way of greeting.

"Fine Rayaldo. And you? How is work going?" From his fidgeting, she knew he was troubled by something. Small talk never suited Rayaldo. He had no time for it. Small talk with his mother was the worst. He endured it out of respect. Conchita knew that he was being considerate to her. She also believed she was the only one he had any real respect for.

"Estoy bien. Tango un trabajo hoy. Un mal gente." He replied that he was fine and that he had an assignment from his boss … a bad guy to deal with. "Estamos a matar a el y su esposa (We're supposed to kill him and his wife)."

"Rayaldo, cuidado (be careful). Puede ser peligroso." She reminded him that there could be danger.

"Nooo, Maaa. Yo Puedo manajer las cosas peligrosas." He responded that he could easily handle himself in any danger. Then, he asked about Ray Jr.

"He's fine, son. Doing well in his new school now," she answered, aware that Rayaldo knew the whole story about his half-brother.

Rayaldo understood the deception his mother had perpetrated about Ray Junior's paternity. He agreed to keep her secret out of respect for her.

Reassured to hear that his mother and Ray Junior were doing well, Rayaldo grabbed the sandwich Conchita had made and left, waving his left hand over his head as he held the sandwich with his right hand. "Hasta luego, Mama."

"Ser seguro (Be safe), Rayaldo." Then she called after him, "Please come see me tomorrow, when it's over."

"Bien." And he was gone.

That night, Conchita spent time with her rosary at the handmade altar in her room. Her prayers were for her eldest son.

***

Bartolome Valles sat in his burgundy leather chair facing the stone fireplace of his wood-paneled den. He was holding his infant daughter, Jordan, who was a bit over a year old. The hour was late.

The Seth Thomas clock on the adjacent wall read 11:30 pm. A single chime sounded the half-hour mark, and for a second, stole his attention. Bartolome knew the clock was accurate. He prided himself in adjusting it every day and winding it on the first day of each month. It was a thirty-one-day clock that had been handed down from his father and mother before their passing last year. This late November night, the clock would mark an ominous incident.

Baby Jordan was asleep, but just barely. Named after the Jordan River where John baptized Jesus, she had worn out her mother earlier in the evening. Bartolome took over the night shift in his infant's newest malady. She wasn't a sickly child but had recently become colicky, causing her parents concern. Since Jordan was their first-born, they regarded every illness as serious. Lately, when she was sick, she cried from her crib in their bedroom. That meant little sleep for either parent, so they slept in shifts with the other trying to comfort her in the den. Tonight, it was Bartolome's turn.

Bartolome was twenty-five and very fit. At five foot ten inches tall and weighing 150 pounds, he looked like a teenager. At an early age, his father had taught him the value of hard work. His arms rippled with muscles developed over a decade of heavy construction work.

He rose at 4:00 am daily and worked through lunch, quitting at 5:00 pm only because his crew quit. He had been in scuffles as a kid, but nothing ever serious. He was strong enough to lift two heavy adobe blocks by himself, but he had never been in a life-or-death struggle.

Bartolome did not expect the assault that was headed his way but was not surprised either. The day before while returning to the job site, he had narrowly avoided danger when two men nearly ran him off the road. He put the incident aside, blaming the spirits of the nearby watering hole and the men's ineptness at self-control. But he remembered a note on his truck last week telling him to leave town or else. Now, it became clear that these two incidents fit a pattern of increasing intimidation.

He heard the crunching of leaves outside the double jalousie windows on the north side of the house. It came from the backyard. He could make out at least two distinct strides of footsteps in the dead leaves of the single cottonwood tree.

He was the target for an assault. He knew that now. As a father taking care of his infant daughter, he considered his priorities briefly. Defending his life and that of his family replaced the need for nursing Jordan's colic.

There could be more attackers, maybe coming from the front as well. He had to think quickly and act to protect himself and his family. Or else, all of this—his life, family, home, and business—would be gone.

Would Kouris stoop that low? He didn't need to open the door to confirm that these were not neighborhood kids playing a prank. The nearest neighbor would have to walk almost a mile down a dirt road to reach his house from any major road. No. These were bad guys. Simon Kouris had sent them.

Bartolome knew Kouris was not a new arrival to this country. He had lived in the area for more than thirty years, but he was from the old country. For him, the closest thing to family was business. If you crossed either, this Greek marked you for retaliation. Bartolome suspected he had crossed Kouris' line. It wasn't complicated. His action had been deliberate. He had known what he was doing when he seriously underbid Kouris on a construction project. He reasoned that Kouris would eventually accept him into the profession and see that business must change just as life and nature changed.

Bartolome was a good builder. He had acquired a contractor's license and built several new homes for the locals and even some smaller commercial buildings. He wanted a taste of commercial work and began bidding on larger projects, which most informed contractors in the area understood were to be left to Kouris. Bartolome knew Kouris wasn't happy but did not predict a violent reaction.

Now something one of his workers told him came back to him. "Esos malo gente (These are bad men)," Enrique told him when he returned to a jobsite after his near collision. Enrique Garcia was Bartolome's chief mason and best friend. Enrique and his sons witnessed the incident from the construction site.

Enrique then told his best friend that Kouris had run a competitor out of town the year before, but no one could prove it. Two of Kouris' thugs first threatened him with firearms then, instead, gave him a beating after the man agreed to leave town. Bartolome was the second target in as many years.

Now it was clear to Bartolome that he had made an error in his judgment of this crusty competitor. Kouris seemed to be deadly serious about protecting his territorial claim from young upstarts like Bartolome Valles. The deadly part was outside in his backyard right now.

Peeking through the white lace curtains, he saw the men were carrying guns. He couldn't allow them to steal the lives of those he loved or to end his life. His family needed him.

The expectation of violence was enough to shock Bartolome into action. Surprise was his only defense. He had two weapons in mind. But first, he must free himself from cradling his infant. With one sweeping movement, he pulled himself sideways, depositing his daughter on the leather chair. Thankfully, she had fallen asleep.

Bartolome grabbed the wood ax mounted over the fireplace mantel and took three quick paces in his sock-feet toward the roll-top desk near the door to the large central hallway. The desk was open, and he found the second weapon tucked in a cubbyhole. He stuck the five-shot antique revolver in his jeans pocket. He had no choice but to leave his sleeping daughter, his most precious gift from God, to defend her life. At her birth, he had promised God to keep her safe, to preserve her right to live a full life with all its joy, love, pain and sorrow.

He felt a surge of adrenaline. He must be victorious.

Energized, Bartolome turned and entered the dark foyer. Across the large hall from the den was his master bedroom where his beloved Catarina slept. He could hear her tussling in bed trying to find a better sleeping position, awaiting his return. The foyer also opened onto a rear porch that he had enclosed to become Jordan's future bedroom. The solid-core wooden door had a keyed lockset handle. Although the hallway was dark, light from the first quarter moon allowed him to count at least two thugs through the small window beside the door, but with no lights on inside, he knew they could not see him.

The doorknob turned. They were testing the lock. It would be easy for them to break it and enter where he was standing. He had calculated that he was facing two men, but there might more waiting behind them.

Bartolome considered his options. He had little time to decide on a defense, but he knew stealth was his ally. The door would open on its hinges even with the lockset destroyed. He angled himself behind the door, giving him the advantage of surprise.

He expected the first man would use the butt end of his shotgun to break the door latch and move inward with the gun aimed forward, while the second would enter aiming a handgun in the same direction. If he was correct, the surprise from his first blow would stun any other intruders into momentary indecision. That would be his edge.

The two men were whispering loudly outside. They were Mexican. Or at least they spoke Spanish with a natural accent. One's name was Rayaldo. He knew this because the second gunman used his name, asking if they were both ready. "Rayaldo, estamos listo?"

Rayaldo responded with impunity. His inflections, even in whisper, were unmistakable. This helped Bartolome assess his first target. Rayaldo was the man giving orders. He heard Rayaldo call out numbers in Spanish, "Uno ... Dos ..." Bartolome readied himself for what was coming. "Tres ..."

He shook when he heard the butt end of the shotgun knock off the doorknob. It was now or never. The waiting seemed to last minutes. Time was distorted. Then it happened. In an instant, the door flew open, stopping only when it slammed against Valles' left leg and foot. In what seemed like slow motion, the second gunman tripped and fell to the floor with the shotgun in his hands. He used the gun more to brace his fall than for the reason he had brought it.

Rayaldo started to vault over his partner. When he placed one foot on the floor, it was just past the threshold. His trailing foot swung even farther into the room.

Except for the dim firelight from the den, it was still dark. Bartolome remained hidden only inches behind them.

-2O-

NEW MEXICO, 1957

Bartolome swung the ax toward Rayaldo with such force it didn't stop until it sliced through neck bone and tissue then into the edge of the door. Rayaldo's head pivoted on neck muscles, the blade engaged the cervical spine and slammed into the door, stopping it from completely severing the man's head. His limp torso, lacking support from legs, hips, and back fell slowly toward the floor on top of gunman two, who apparently didn't see what happened in the commotion.

Bartolome released the cleaver from the door and raised it over his head for a second downward thrust. Gunman two looked around just in time to see the blade that would end his life. Bartolome did not hold back his rage. It seemed to him that his strength came from beyond. Within the space of a few seconds he had ended the lives of two bigger, stronger brutes.

It took several more seconds for the would-be killers to stop moving. Remarkably, Bartolome was clear on what he had done. But he knew there might be more … somewhere.

The commotion woke the infant in the next room. Jordan's cries, in turn, awakened Catarina who rolled the covers back and without a robe, headed toward the soft glow emanating from the den.

She had taken four steps out of the bedroom, crossing the threshold into the large central hallway when Valles saw his wife's feet leave the ground as her neck was caught in the tight grip of a third assailant. She wore a St. Catherine medallion that was now pressing into her throat. Her father had given her the medallion when she received confirmation in the church when she was twelve. Would her patron saint be the instrument of her death?

Gunman three had entered through the opposite side of the house, soundlessly unlocking the front door with a knife, wedging the latch to release it. He must have entered the kitchen then proceeded to the bedrooms in the rear.

For an instant, Bartolome saw confusion on the face of the third gunman when, in a beam of moonlight, he spotted the crumpled bodies on the floor. But he held his grip on Catarina's neck.

Fear filled Bartolome as adrenaline pumped through his body. Aware that a struggle had ensued in the hallway, he realized his wife was in danger. Now Jordan was crying at the top of her tiny lungs. Bartolome could hear Catarina struggling to move toward her crying baby, dragging her abductor with her.

The advantage Bartolome had over the man was that this was his house. He could pace the house in the dark without bumping into anything. After all, he had built it himself. His wife had carefully placed every piece of furniture where it rested. Even in pitch blackness, he could navigate well without giving away his position.

The baby's cries along with Catarina's desperate whimpering screams seemed to make the intruder nervous. Bartolome maintained a death grip around the wood ax. Filled with rage, he wanted to inflict pain on this would-be assassin, not just kill him. The man had invaded his home and threatened his family. He remembered the pistol in his pocket.

Bartolome released his clutch on the ax to grip the cold handle of the Smith/ Wesson .38 revolver. Resting his right thumb on the back of the hammer, he prepared for the next step. He could tell Catarina had reached Jordan whose cries had switched from the piercing shrills to rhythmic sobbing. But where was the intruder? Shadows from the flickering fireplace gave him his answer. The man stood behind the chair, facing the open door, no doubt waiting for him to enter. He had pushed Catarina to her knees, still gripping her neck. She was clutching Jordan to her bosom and gasping for breath. Bartolome had to time his next move with accuracy.

A sudden pop from the fireplace provided the distraction Bartolome needed. When the gunman turned toward the explosion, he released Catarina, and

Bartolome crept up behind him, placing the muzzle of his revolver within inches of the man's head.

Turning to face the barrel of Bartolome's weapon, the intruder dropped his gun to the floor. The gunman was not a brave man. Like most bullies, he was a coward. That's when the man's bladder suddenly released its contents, leaving a puddle of urine on the hardwood floor that Bartolome and Catarina had carefully laid a few years earlier.

Bartolome's rage escalated as he realized how close he had come to losing everyone he held dear. He slapped the man as if challenging him to a duel causing him to lose his balance and fall against the open fireplace.

Desperate to escape the fire, the assailant vaulted toward Bartolome, his hands reaching for Bartolome's face and neck, his own face right where the .38 revolver was now aiming. As he leaped, the 40-grain slug discharged from the revolver and stopped his effort.

The shot rang out, stunning Catarina and Jordan. Breaking the assailant's nose, the bullet entered his skull then fragmented into smaller, more lethal shards of lead. He fell backward with his left arm now resting on a burning log in the large masonry fireplace. His shirtsleeve caught fire and the smell of burning flesh began to pervade the room.

-21-

NEW MEXICO, 1957

"Bartolome, Bartolome, what has happened?" Bartolome tried to collect his thoughts when he heard Catarina yell his name. At first, he looked at her, his face devoid of emotion. He had just saved his family. His wife was screaming his name and running toward him with their daughter in her arms. He could only mutter his observation. "Catarina, you're bleeding." She felt her throat.

She was, in fact, bleeding from the amulet pressed against her neck. In the firelight, Bartolome could see that the wound was only superficial and not arterial, although it was dripping onto her nightgown. She would be okay.

Little Jordan didn't have even a bruise from falling off the chair and being jostled by the incident. They were lucky. *He* was lucky! If he hadn't been awake trying to spare his wife another sleepless night, his assailants might have been successful.

"Dios mio," was all he could muster. "Dios mio." He was hugging Catarina and Jordan as they stood mere inches from their would-be assassin's burning flesh.

"Who are these men?" Catarina demanded. "Why have they entered our home with guns?"

Could more hit men be waiting outside? Bartolome wondered. What should he do now? How could his family move on from this horrific night?

***

Simon Kouris relaxed in his vintage rust-colored leather chair, enjoying a nightcap and the late-night fire in his den. His live-in housekeeper and son were already asleep.

The child who just turned six years old had developed a mixture of ethnic characteristics both Mexican and Greek, confirming an obvious but unacknowledged truth. But there was something about publicly admitting that he was living in sin with his housekeeper and their bi-racial child that seemed more immoral than their current arrangement.

Simon wondered if Conchita knew where her elder son was tonight. He tried to be patient in waiting for his team to report success on their assignment. He could not imagine the consequences of the assault gone wrong. At first, he wanted the young upstart, Valles, out of his town, but Bartolome had not heeded his warnings. It's his fault for not getting it, he reasoned. Violence was the only way to get what was rightfully his, the high-rise contract.

***

Husband and wife stood consoling each other by the fireplace with three dead bodies in their home. Whatever they did, they must deal with the bodies. Questions would be raised when these men turned up missing. Kouris had sent them and would be expecting them to report back to him tonight. He might let them enjoy a few drinks together at his bar, the Red Fox Inn, to celebrate their success, but he would expect them back after a few hours.

Bartolome tried to think. His body was still pumping adrenaline and he was shaking. Holding Catarina and his daughter as a crutch to stay upright, he knew he had to deal with Kouris' hit men and then with Kouris' attempt on his life. Darkness was the best time to dispose of the bodies. With dawn coming, his window of time was short.

He had pulled the third assailant's body onto the hearth, but the man's clothes still smoldered and the skin on his arms had melted around the bones.

"The jobsite. That's it," Bartolome exclaimed suddenly, pushing away from Catarina who had been sobbing into his shoulder. "That's... it," he repeated, as if saying it again with assurance would gain him the strength he needed.

"Que paso eposo mio?" Catarina asked. "What are you thinking, my husband?"

He was right to be concerned. Kouris could have the police there in a few hours. He would twist a story to make it look as if these men had come to welcome the newcomers and Valles killed three innocent young men. He could not risk telling the police who would be on Kouris' side.

Everyone knew Simon Kouris was a ruthless bastard in business in this small town, but he was *their* ruthless bastard. Valles knew he could be convicted of murdering his would-be killers ... but not without bodies. He would drive their car to a nearby tavern and park it, making it look like the men had simply vanished.

We'll bury them, he decided. With no bodies found, there'll be no questions to answer.

But how could he prevent the cold-hearted bastard from trying again to kill him?

Catarina had managed to get Jordan calmed down by rocking her. She turned her face away from the carnage as if that would make it disappear.

Bartolome put out the fire, and as he stared into the ashes the answer came to him. "Ashes," he muttered. "That's it! A message to Kouris." He stood and turned to drag the body out of the room.

"The fire ... yes, the fire." Bartolome muttered. "Ashes," he added. Catarina stared at him, dumbfounded.

"Fuck with me and my family and get your hired help back ... in a jar." He said it in a tone Catarina had never heard from him. She loved this man to whom she had pledged her life in marriage, yet his unexpected display of rage frightened her.

Now thinking clearly, Bartolome dragged the corpses outside, one by one, hauling them into the bed of his construction truck that he had lined with a canvas tarp.

The sight of Rayaldo's dangling head, connected only by tendons, made Catarina shudder. She pulled Jordan close, hiding her face the way a young girl might cover her face in a horror movie. But this was no movie. This was real and it happened in her home, the center of her world. Her faithful husband had built this house as a shrine to her and their future family. It symbolized their love and the promise of a good life together. Three dead bodies being dragged through her home represented a repugnant desecration.

Hiding her face was a vain attempt to make it all go away. Looking up, she spotted the La Santa Muerte medallion dangling around the neck of one body. She wondered who had given him the medallion. His mother? Girlfriend?

"How could such a murderer wear the sacred ornament of a saint?" she nearly shouted. When Bartolome heard her, he stopped, bent down and pulled the medal off. He was about to hand it to his wife for safekeeping when he realized the mistake in that gesture. He stuffed it in his pocket and continued to carry out his mission.

With Jordan now asleep, Catarina helped her husband get all three bodies into the truck and covered by the excess tarp before he heard the clock strike one. A single hand exposed from the brown canvas caught his eye. A finger on this hand wore what appeared to be … Yes … a gold ring. Perfect. He removed it and stuffed it in his pants pocket. Pulling the tarp back to reveal Rayaldo, the leader, he declared, "This will work."

Bartolome knew the bars closed at 2:00 am. It would be good if at least some patrons saw the car parked there. He must hurry, but first he collected the shotguns and pistols, then rushed to the kitchen and gathered three empty Mason jars. Instructing Catarina to put Jordan in the truck cab, he scooped ash from the fireplace into each jar and tightened the lids. Before securing the last one, he included some burned skin and reached into his pocket for the ring. This would send a clear message to Simon Kouris.

Minutes later, Bartolome drove the car along the lonely stretch of road from his home toward town. Except for his wife behind him in their 1948 Chevrolet pickup, he was alone on the road. Their home was about a ten-minute drive from any real settlement, but at least the bar was on this side of town.

He would park the Kouris team's 1951 Studebaker in the rear parking lot of the Red Fox Inn, a favorite hangout of the drinking class. Almost two hours had passed.

So much had happened in those two hours, yet he seemed to be in a race with time. He saw lights and heard music and raucous laughter as he approached the restaurant parking lot. The bar would not be closing on time tonight, not with the crowd there now. He parked the car at the back of the lot, suggesting a late arrival. That would be consistent with Kouris' expectation of their celebration.

He turned off the lights, coasted into the parking lot and maneuvered toward a parking space. Pulling the handbrake with gloved hands, Bartolome pivoted to get out, first making sure the shotgun and pistols were in plain view on the seats. He pulled himself out of the car and saw his wife a few hundred feet down the road, the brake lights a signal that she was there. Before closing the door, he stopped, remembering something. He reached into his pocket and grabbed the La Santa Muerte medallion and suspended it from the rearview mirror.

Bartolome eased the door shut with little noise. He ran toward Catarina, who by now had turned the 48 Ford pickup around and was waiting for her husband. Trusting him, she had become his partner in this deception. Bartolome opened the passenger door and pulled himself into the cab next to Jordan, who was lying in a baby carrier. She was half awake, nursing a bottle and content for now.

Catarina followed her husband's directions to the construction site, even though she knew the way. They arrived at the project area around 2:15 am. She parked where he pointed, next to a rectangle of forms awaiting concrete pouring promptly at 6:00. That was less than four hours away.

Grabbing a hand shovel, Bartolome began digging one grave wide enough for three bodies under what would become a deep pier footing. The crisp November morning kept him from sweating, but he was hot inside. When that portion of the pier footing was six feet deep instead of the normal three feet, he stopped, exhausted from the effort and climbed up the wooden ladder where three bodies lay on the ground. One at a time, he heaved them down to the bottom of the pier footing. Rayaldo was the last to be placed in the makeshift grave. Catarina's job was to remain in the truck with Jordan but also to keep a lookout, ready to douse the headlights if she saw any cars approaching in the distance.

Bartolome climbed down the ladder again and arranged the corpses side by side. Resisting the urge to turn them upside down on their faces, he covered them with the canvas tarp. He then filled the hole, tamping the dirt solid as he did. It was work he never would have chosen, backbreaking and horrific, but he knew it had to be done.

***

Kouris continued to warm himself in front of his massive stone fireplace, now sipping some sherry. It was after midnight. He expected the trio back within the hour.

By 3:00 am he could wait no longer. He got in his car and drove toward the tavern that was now closed. He noticed the empty parking lot, except for a single car … his.

Where was his team? Drunk? Arrested? He feared the worst when he looked in the car and saw all the weapons, unfired. Did they even go on his mission? Or did they chicken out? Then he noticed the La Santa Muerte medallion hanging from the rearview mirror. He knew it belonged to one of Rayaldo's friends. He had seen it around the punk's neck more than once. But where were they?

***

Bartolome wiped his brow, now soaking wet after his ordeal that had taken more than an hour. He had dug one grave for the three, buried them, and backfilled the footing with a decent degree of compaction. He threw the shovel up over the three-foot embankment and climbed the ladder, pulling it out from the top and leaning it against the shed, from where he had borrowed it earlier. He got in the truck, tenderly kissed his wife's cheek and brushed his sleeping daughter's face.

Bartolome was physically spent but ready for the message part of his plan.

He knew where Kouris lived. He had attended a party there when he first arrived in town. The party, it seemed clear now, was intended to convey a message to Valles that Kouris owned this town. It would make Bartolome's message to him even more meaningful.

He drove within a block of Kouris' home. Collecting the three Mason jars from the floorboard of the truck, he ran up the winding street along a newly installed concrete sidewalk to the massive iron gate surrounding the Kouris mansion. The gate was open, revealing an empty driveway. Bartolome guessed that Simon was out looking for his gang.

Bartolome stacked the Mason jars two on the bottom, one on top like wooden jugs at a county fair. He had turned to join his wife, who was waiting a few hundred feet down the path, when he heard the 1957 Cadillac coming from the other direction. Choosing concealment, they hid behind bushes planted around the circular driveway and waited until Kouris rolled into the driveway. Seeing his expression would be a bonus.

***

From headlights shining on the front door, Simon could see the jars at his doorstep and wondered what had been left and who had left them. He grabbed the revolver from his glove compartment. Was someone waiting for him? Did he miss seeing the jars when he left an hour before? Not likely. He walked up to the front porch as gingerly as one would approach a rattlesnake. He saw that the containers were filled with a dark gray powder.

He had left his car lights on and put his pistol in his coat pocket. He knelt to look closer at the jars. When he unscrewed the lid of the top jar, the rancid smell of human flesh filled his nostrils. When he realized the ash was laced with residue of skin, he dropped the jar, stood and backed away, releasing a guttural sound. The jar broke on the concrete step revealing a gold ring within the ashes. It rolled toward Kouris until it hit the toe of his boot.

Instinctively, Simon backed away even farther. Perplexed, his mind raced to connect the dots. Could this be his crew? How? How could one man kill three of his best muscle who came unannounced? Had he underestimated this Valles character? What would he do now?

Consumed with rage, Kouris retrieved his pistol, pointed the revolver into the air and squeezed off six rounds into the early morning sky. Then, out of ammunition, he shouted Greek profanities, as if the words had the same effect as the lead slugs. He dropped to his knees and cried out as the car lights trained on the two Mason jars still standing.

*****

It was after 3:30 am when the young family got back home. They had been through a harrowing experience, and now it was time to clean up the mess. Evidence remained that could lead to questions by any authorities. A broken door, blood, skin, torn clothing, and even urine must all be purged from their home.

They began in earnest as soon as Catarina put Jordan in her crib, fast asleep finally. By 4:30, they were both in need of coffee. Catarina plugged in the drip coffee maker and they took a much-needed break.

"What have we done?" Catarina uttered under her breath.

"We did what we had to do," answered Bartolome. He didn't like how the answer sounded. So, he added, "Oiga me, mi esposa, (Listen to me, my wife). We had no choice. They were going to murder us ... even little Jordan."

She knew. They both knew. They just needed to console each other. Bartolome used words of reassurance with relief that it was over. He hoped it was over. He expected one last volley from Kouris, but he was ready. The weapon, still in his pocket, was missing only one round.

With Bartolome's promise to send two of his crew to guard the house, Catarina agreed to stay behind, make breakfast, and finish cleaning up while Bartolome attended the duties that got him into this fix. "I'm going now, Catarina. I'll be back after the concrete pour is finished. 8 o'clock or so. Keep the doors locked." He kissed his wife's forehead and turned toward the front door.

"Cuidado mi esposo. Be careful," she said.

"I will," he replied as he closed the door and headed for the truck.

***

Taking care not to wake Concha, Kouris collected the broken jar and ash.

Reverently, he placed the ashes in a vase and fingered the gold ring as if it held the secret to a meaningful response. He placed the ring in his pocket.

During the light of day, he would hatch a sinister plot.

***

The pre-dawn hours found the project site bustling with activity with Enrique Garcia supervising his crew, issuing last-minute instructions for the concrete pour. This building was large compared to others in the community. A rust-red 1948 Chevy pickup was pulling into the construction site. Garcia turned to greet his boss and best friend who was now out of the truck and walking toward him.

"Buenos dias, Patron. Que te hacienda?"

Bartolome thought carefully before replying in English. "I'm good, Enrique. And you?" He hoped Enrique couldn't see the strain in his face and the fatigue that surely showed in his eyes. He had to maintain focus. He was determined.

"Seguro. Estamos listo a hoy." Enrique told his boss that he was great, adding that he and his crew were ready for the day.

"I know you are, Enrique. Thanks for getting here early. I had some trouble at home."

"Patron, I am glad we came early. We found some soft soil in part of the footing we must have missed yesterday. Luis is compacting it now with a tamper. We'll be ready. We still have an hour. It is only a few feet. It's like someone dug it out last night. Yo no se."

Bartolome felt tightness in his chest as the lump in his throat burned. Determined not to involve his best friend in his is deeds, he managed to maintain his composure and close the conversation. "Enrique, maybe have your steel crew add some reinforcement in the area. Just don't add water to the mix when it gets here. I want the footing strong." Enrique gazed at his boss, without a reply as Bartolome walked away.

Enrique Garcia, the masonry foreman, assigned his nephew Luis to tamp the soft soil in the footing trench with a plate tamper. His older brother was above him spraying water occasionally to help consolidate the soil that Luis had just tamped. They were both satisfied with the job. The ground felt solid.

"Tio Enrique, nos listamos. It's firm," Luis said to his uncle. The job was done. They were ready to pour the footing.

"Luis, tu y su hermano traeme varilla aqui." Enrique asked his nephews to bring reinforcing steel to the footing they had just tamped. The nephews knew how to install rebar and did so quickly. After sending two workers to guard his house, Bartolome spent the hour looking at other parts of the job. "My wife thinks she heard noises last night. It'll make her feel safe until I return." Nervously, he glanced at the soft soil site, anxious for all evidence of his earlier activity to be covered over.

About 5:45 am all the workers transitioned to their concrete-pouring attire. Removing their work boots, they put on rubber boots and rubber overalls. The crew even wore hard hats, a recent innovation used in high profile projects such as bridges. Both Bartolome and Enrique wanted to keep their workers safe.

They put on gloves, grabbed their tools and positioned themselves around the worksite. Enrique was now telling the crew the sequence for the concrete pour. "Aqui es la primera lugar for el concreto entonces otro rincons singuiente." They would begin the pour where Enrique was pointing, followed by moving the concrete trucks in sequence to each corner. They were ready.

When the trucks arrived, Bartolome and Enrique greeted the first driver whose clipboard held the concrete order. The two men studied the order for confirmation of the mixture strength and the total amount needed. The strength was designed to be 3500-psi (pounds per square inch). This was more than the 3000-psi strength typically used.

Although there was no building code yet in Southern New Mexico, those who considered themselves professionals, abided by the empirical standards of the time in addition to the contract standards. Both Bartolome and Enrique were satisfied with the paperwork and directed the driver to the first pour location. Work began.

Around 7:15 the last of seven concrete trucks departed the job site. The fourteen members of Enrique's crew were busy leveling and finishing the footing. The experienced masons employed rakes, shovels, screeds, trowels and other concrete finishing tools.

For now, the concrete would be left to harden in the best way known, with patience. Enrique often joked with his general contractors that his work and materials were one-hundred-percent guaranteed against fire, wind and theft. Having shared that saying for the umpteenth time, Enrique still raised a smile from both contractors.

Bartolome reached a point around 7:45 where he could relax and appreciate the humor. He left the jobsite a few minutes later for breakfast at home. Construction work usually started early and finished early in the New Mexico desert because of the summer heat. For consistency, the same work schedule continued through winter. The only exception was during really cold weather when concrete and other construction materials were at risk of freezing. But this November morning was cool and dry, perfect weather for concrete.

***

"It's done, mi esposa. Yo me a acave," Bartolome told his young wife. The unspoken message was that the three bodies were covered beneath twelve cubic yards of concrete, now curing in the New Mexico sun.

"Gracias a Dios! Sienta te, mi esposa. El desayuno esta listo." Obediently, Bartolome sat at the table waiting for Catarina to bring breakfast. Jordan was awake and sitting in a small, sparsely cushioned aluminum highchair at the corner of the table between her parents. She was picking at the remains of the Cream of Wheat her mom had made earlier.

Jordan was delighted to see her daddy, giving him coos and goo-goos and blowing kisses. Then to get his attention, she put her forefinger inside her cheek and tried to make a popping sound, something Bartolome had taught her much to Catarina's chagrin. Bartolome returned the gesture. "Good morning, miha. How are you this beautiful morning?" Bartolome asked his daughter.

Catarina stopped mid-stride, unable to imagine his calmness. How could he be so relaxed about all this? "Mi esposo, is everything going to be all right?"

She served her husband four eggs, four strips of bacon and two slices of toast along with black coffee then sat to let him say the blessing.

"Bendícenos, Señor, y bendice estos alimentos que por tu bondad vamos a tomar. Por Jesucristo Nuestro Señor, Amén." Each made the sign of the cross and ate breakfast.

Bartolome finally answered. "Yes, of course it will. God is with us. He saved our lives last night. How can we question him?" She wanted to believe him but had her secret doubts.

"The concrete is installed. No one knows but you and me. No one will ever think to consider what happened to three thugs with criminal pasts."

But Catarina couldn't stop worrying about her husband. Had it been an act of self-defense or had he committed murder? What if the intruders were only trying to scare him into leaving, like the incident a year before? No. They broke into the house with weapons drawn. Surely Bartolome had a right to defend his family and property. She tried to set her doubt aside … for now anyway.

***

After Ray Jr. headed to school on the bus, Simon sat at the dining room table while Conchita brought breakfast, huevos rancheros. The two ate in silence.

Sometimes Simon was broody in the morning, but Conchita could tell there was something bothering him today. She knew from experience that it was better if *he* broke the silence. She would wait. She was almost tearful, imagining his petulance had something to do with Rayaldo and the tidbit of information she had received the day before. Conchita grew impatient. "Simon, I thought I heard gunshots last night. What happened?" His one-word answer was the only thing he said all morning. "Coyotes."

Simon left the table without another word or even a farewell gesture. Conchita heard his car engine start and he pulled away. She went out the front door just in time to see his car pull onto Maple Street and he was gone. The fastidious housekeeper noticed what looked like a pile of dust on the front step. She went to the pantry to get the broom and dustpan.

***

Simon stopped before turning left on Pine Street. He needed a moment to collect his thoughts. When he looked in the rearview mirror, he noticed Conchita cleaning up the ashes on the porch. He sped on with a lump in his throat and a tear forming in his eye. But soon, his sorrow turned to wrath.

He started fuming from the events of the early morning, oddly energized despite his lack of sleep. He was not heading toward his office.

It was 9:00 am when Simon drove by Valles' construction project. The one that should have been his. There was not much activity, a few Mexican laborers around the site cleaning up after a concrete pour. Valles' truck was not there. No doubt he was at the Las Cruces County Courthouse scouting new public construction projects to steal from Simon.

Simon was not sure what he would have done if Valles had been there. He didn't know what he would have said. Without a plan, he dismissed the idea of a confrontation. He also dismissed the idea of using the authorities to clean up the mess he had caused.

But what was he going to say to Rayaldo's mother? "Concha, the ashes you swept up on the porch this morning; that was your son. You see, I sent him to kill my competition last night and well … things didn't turn out the way I planned." She would never forgive him.

He kept searching for possible explanations. Perhaps he could say that Rayaldo just left town. He continued to consider his options.

Aside from money or alcohol, the only other motivation for Rayaldo to do anything was a woman. Concha would believe her son might disappear for a lover without telling his mother.

He had no choice. Admitting that he knew a man killed Rayaldo would lead to questions. The man's answers to the police would lead to him. Answers to the authorities would be complicated and because of his reputation, he wouldn't survive scrutiny.

***

"Chief Haas, I have something to report to you," Kouris announced sitting across the desk from him at Police Headquarters.

"Hello, Simon. What can I do for you?" the chief asked. He knew all about the rumors ... about Simon's muscle and how he used it. He had heard about the contractor who Simon ran out of town ... out of state, in fact. This man seemed to have a lock on the town's large-scale construction projects though he had never been able to prove anything. And then there were the political interests. Simon knew every influential elected official and had donated most of their campaign money. Haas would have trouble making any charges stick unless he found Kouris with a smoking gun and a dead body.

"A man I hired is missing. I just wanted to report it," Simon said. "His name is Gonzalez, Rayaldo Gonzalez." The chief was taking notes, and with a soft grunt, urged Simon to continue.

"I don't know where he went. At first, I thought he was just hung over and missed a day's work. I went by where he lives. The landlord hasn't heard from him either."

"Where does he live?" the chief asked.

"Over near Bell School. As I said, I don't know what happened to him. After several days, I got worried. I know his mother. I asked her. She hadn't seen him since last week either. We both saw him with a girlfriend from Mexico the weekend before. At first, we thought he might be trying to get her citizenship but, as I said, we haven't seen either one of them since last week now."

"When, exactly?"

"Thursday, around noon. I paid him his weekly salary and asked him to keep an eye on the construction yard over the weekend. You see, I just bought a dump truck and haven't got the company stencils on the door yet."

After a half hour of questions, the chief announced that he would open a missing persons case for Gonzalez.

"Thank you, Chief. Please let me know if you find him or if anything turns up. His mother is quite worried." He left the building.

Chief Haas filed the report and alerted the adjacent cities of Lordsburg, Silver City, Hot Springs, Deming, Hatch, Roswell, Carlsbad, Albuquerque and El Paso of the missing person. He also alerted his only detective.

Detective Starnes was a lifelong Las Cruces resident and had seen drifters come and go. He recalled breaking up a bar fight at the Red Foxx Inn involving Gonzales and some Anglo tourist headed to see Old Mexico. He shared his sentiment with the chief that he was happy to hear of another troublemaker out of his hair.

Chief Haas dismissed the incident, and after six months, Gonzalez was officially listed as missing.

-22-

New Mexico, 1958

Simon Kouris had waited a whole year for the right time. He knew one bank vice president who owed him a big favor. According to plan, when no other bank manager was present except for Karen James, he unwrapped the gold ring one last time and studied it while waiting for James to complete her business with a customer. Oh, he would see the ring again ... when he finally told the police. He would tell Chief Haas that he had learned through the grapevine that Valles had killed Rayaldo and then tell him about receiving the ring. He would also suggest that the chief search for the ring and drop the hint about the bank safe deposit box.

"Hi Simon. What brings you in on this beautiful day?" Ms. James greeted the major client to whom she was indebted.

"Good morning, my beautiful and favorite vice president." Kouris kissed her hand. "May I have a private word with you, my dear? After following her into her office, he closed the door and ensured that the blinds were closed as well. "Karen, I need you to do something for me. Something that will pay your debt in full."

After Kouris left the bank, James waited. Then with a small red pouch in her hand, she secured the only master key for the safe deposit boxes and entered the bank vault by herself, closing and locking the interior safe room door. She opened deposit box number 908, removed the box and placed it on the newly installed central laminate table. Next, she opened the box with the second master key and carefully placed the red jewelry pouch inside, at the bottom, near the back corner.

She noticed that the box contained some cash, what looked like life insurance documents, a birth certificate, and some other legal documents. Resisting the urge to snoop, she closed, re-shelved, and locked the box using the master key that she returned to the exact location in the bank president's top middle desk drawer.

No one would question the actions of a vice president entering the vault room unescorted. She had done this before, although for less nefarious purposes.

At least Simon had forgiven her $10,000 debt, her only solace for the trivial criminal act she just committed. She wondered why Simon wanted that ring placed in the safe deposit box. She would never find out.

-23-

SOUTHERN CALIFORNIA, 1970

Southern California always seemed overcast. On a cloudy March morning, Zachary Martin waited in dress greens to be awarded a combat medal at the Marine Corps Air Station at El Toro, California. He didn't learn about it until the night before. He called his parents, who turned out to be on vacation in San Diego. He managed to get through to them in time for them to start out at daylight. Oliver and Hazel Martin drove the ninety miles from San Diego to El Toro and saw their son receive the Bronze Star for heroic actions. He hadn't bothered to tell them about the incident when he was on leave in New Mexico. The commanding general (CG) of MCAS El Toro delivered the star in a huge ceremony. The unit commander, Martin's colonel, read the citation and handed the medal to Martin. The CG shook Martin's hand and gave him a personal message. It seems that General Adams was a friend of newly promoted Major Newman.

General Adams conveyed Newman's admiration for this young forward observer. Both Captain Drake and Captain Newman had submitted separate nominations for the medal. As a result, Martin was given the Bronze Star along with a Combat V and a Combat Promotion to E-5 Sergeant. His service record would reflect that the Fifth Marines Regimental Commander, Colonel Geston had suggested raising the award to a NC (Navy Cross) but that request was ignored by Marine Corps brass. Martin wondered if the use of the acronym, NC was misunderstood by staffers at the Commandant of the Marine Corps who had to approve any such request.

***

Six months later, Zachary took advantage of an early discharge from the Marine Corps so he could start college. By all appearances, his future should have been bright. He was young, strong and good-looking. He was a decorated war hero ready to start his life by earning a degree in engineering.

Zach's family owned three farms and a ranch near his hometown. He had saved his combat pay from Vietnam and was ready to buy a new car. A 1971 Pontiac Firebird suited him. While others went for the Camaro Z-28 or Mustang, he liked the lines of the Firebird. He bought a bright yellow one at the dealer in Deming, New Mexico. The car matched his personality.

Despite the awards for his courageous rescue under fire, Zach would never totally recover from that moment in 1969. He would be plagued by this act for a generation.

Many years later, he met someone who had developed a similar black hole in his heart. As they shared their experiences, they began to understand that the personal consequences of their actions were unavoidable. It was then that the healing could begin.

-24-

New Mexico, 1957

Simon Kouris drove from the bank to see his attorney George Small. He knew it would be prudent to wait a while before the next step. The memory of witnesses in the bank seeing him and Ms. James together needed to fade. A week or two would be enough, maybe a month. There was something else he had to do first. He entered the law office across from the county courthouse where Small earned most of his considerable wealth.

"Good morning, Mary. Is the senator in?" Kouris asked, knowing the answer after seeing the bright red 1957 Cadillac parked out front. "Mr. Kouris, good morning to you. Yes, he is. Let me see if he can see you." Simon knew full well that the senator would see this client, one who always paid for legal services on time with no excuses. "George, here's a personal letter for you to deliver when my will is read," Simon said to his attorney after they exchanged greetings. "No one sees this but the recipient and not until that time, okay?"

"Of course, Simon. You have my word," responded Small. Simon knew that his word was absolute.

***

That night, Simon Kouris had his usual glass of wine by the fireplace. He felt overly tired, as if he had done manual labor all day. But as he reached for his tulip wineglass for the fourth sip, he noticed something he could not explain: sharp pain in his left arm leading to his shoulder and neck. He tried to speak but noticed a shortness of breath. He would have to see the doctor about this tomorrow. It's an aggravating annoyance, he thought, as he stood to walk it off … still nursing his wineglass.

The pain in his left arm now enveloped his jaw. He felt nauseated and wondered if the wine he drank was bad. Now his breathing difficulty became more pronounced and he was sweaty. His entire chest felt as if it were being squeezed by a giant hand. His face turned cold and the heart palpitations in his upper chest rose to his nasal cavity. Now he was dizzy, almost losing consciousness.

Where was that vial of pills? "Concha! Concha!" he gasped. She was behind closed doors in her bedroom, saying prayers before getting ready for bed. Ray Jr. was already asleep in the third bedroom. Simon gasped for breath. His shoulder blades ached with the residual pain in his arms and chest.

The room closed in around him. He could still see but not with the peripheral vision to which he was accustomed. It was as if looking through a long, narrow tunnel with darkness enveloping him. His balance shifted and his legs buckled. Red wine went everywhere staining the white mohair rug in front of the fireplace.

***

The funeral was large and attended by notable civic figures, elected politicians and friends. Simon had no real family that anyone knew about. He often claimed that Las Cruces was his family. Conchita Gonzales was listed as Kouris' next of kin on the death certificate. Dr. David Janis had determined that Kouris died of a massive heart attack. Conchita sat on the front row with Ray Jr. They would return to Kouris' home and continue to live on Maple Street where they had lived since Simon invited them.

Neither Conchita nor Ray Jr. was in tears. In fact, no one cried. While they may have attended to honor the deceased, most had heard the pejorative gossip about Kouris' temper and the alleged intimidation to remove rival competition. Simon's illicit relationship with his maid was also an open topic of conversation.

Many forgave Simon but viewed Conchita with scorn. In fact, Arturo Baca was the only reason she was sitting up front near the casket. With a similar heritage, Baca felt sympathy for her and recognized that her relationship with

Simon qualified her as Kouris' common law wife.

***

Later in the month, Simon's attorney, George Small, called Conchita to arrange the reading of Simon's will. She and Ray Jr. were the only ones named as beneficiaries. Conchita would own the home, but there was more. She also now enjoyed a sizable fortune in stocks and bonds and a respectable bank account.

Ray Jr. was given something even more valuable: a name. Simon had accepted the fatherhood of Ray Jr. and even signed papers that recognized his paternity. The young boy's name was now Ray Kouris. Additionally, the boy would get $25,000 on his twenty-first birthday if two conditions were met: he must serve in the US Marine Corps, receiving an honorable discharge and his mother must agree to Simon's bequest when the time came.

There was one more article from Simon for Conchita. It was a letter sealed with wax in a slightly faded envelope. She broke the seal then hesitated before reading it. She re-sheathed the letter and drove home. As she rounded the corner, Conchita was rife with curiosity about the letter and not focusing on the intersection. She never noticed the small blond boy chasing a cat into the street ... until ... her car was almost on top of him. "Mierda!" she screamed and hit the brakes.

At five years old, Timothy Anderson hadn't started school yet. Conchita would never forget the sound of tires screeching to halt her car within inches of the child as he held his hands to his face like that would somehow stop the car.

Mrs. Anderson was already running out of the house scolding young Timmy for playing in the street. "Mrs. Gonzales, I am so sorry Timmy gave you that scare. Are you okay, dear?" As neighbors, the two had spoken regularly, and on occasion Conchita had volunteered to clean her home for social or holiday events.

"I'm fine, Libby. I am so sorry myself. I wasn't paying attention. I apologize. Is Timmy okay?" By this time, Timmy was up, holding the cat in his arms and shivering as though he were cold. He was also sniveling, trying to hold back tears.

"Conchita, he's fine. He learned a lesson. That's for sure."

"Timmy, do you see why we tell you to *never* play or run into the street?" Her tone was demanding. "You could have been hurt ... or killed!"

Conchita, who had regained a bit of composure, said, "Timmy, I am going to bake some cookies this afternoon. Will you come over with your mom later and have some?" Timmy was all smiles now.

The mailman had just made a delivery to the Anderson's front door drop. Libby turned to address him. That action marked the end of the event that could have been far worse for everyone.

Still shaking, Conchita virtually crawled home in the 1955 Chevy that had been Simon's car until last week.

Now parked in the circular driveway, she collected her belongings from the bench seat of the Chevy and walked around the car, for the first time looking at the front of the car from a child's perspective. She then heard a familiar, young voice.

"Muh-ma, I'm home." Ray Jr. had his arms raised in triumph at the feat. He had walked the three blocks home from Bell Elementary.

"Ray. Welcome home, miho. I have some news for you, and I'm going to make some cookies for you and Timmy down the street."

"Why Timmy?" He looked at his mother quizzically.

"Well, he had a real scare this afternoon," she said. "And it's the neighborly thing to do. So, go get changed and show me what you did at school today."

Their life was now idyllic in Conchita's eyes. They owned a fine home and had resources that her family could never have dreamed of. They had friends and neighbors in a good community. They were respected and acknowledged at St. Anne's Catholic Church where she took Ray Jr. every Sunday.

But their life would take a different turn as a result of forces not yet seen by either. One of those forces would arrive this afternoon in the form of a letter from the grave.

While Ray Jr. changed, Conchita indulged her curiosity. Sitting at the kitchen table, she read the letter that George Small had given her, the letter she was thinking about when she nearly hit her neighbor's child:

My Dearest Concha,

I am beyond myself with grief with what I am about to tell you. I did not have the courage to tell you face to face as you deserve. I am sorry to tell you this way. Please forgive a shameful man.

Concha, I am certain Rayaldo is dead at the hands of a man I held in contempt for business reasons. I sent Rayaldo and two of his friends to 'put a scare' into the man and chase him off. He was stealing jobs that were meant for me. Anyway, I sent him out the night he and his friends disappeared, and they never came back. I never knew what happened but there was a 'message' sent that same night with

Rayaldo's ring left on the front doorstep. It was as if he said, 'You sent him. I killed him. Leave me alone.' Bartolome Valles is the man. I am sure that he somehow killed all three since all of them disappeared the same night.

I tell you now so that you will know the truth of the matter. I have felt guilt ever since that night. I accept responsibility for putting Rayaldo in danger of such a vicious killer as Valles. I leave my name and a legacy for Ray Jr. in hopes of avoiding that outcome for him. Please take special care of my son, Concha. Tell him I have loved him since the day I met him on your return from El Paso. Keep him true to my honor.

My love will always be with you and Ray Jr. I wish I were still there to share the future with you.

Simon Kouris

The letter was on two pages from Simon's stationery and bound in an envelope that bore a large stylized K on the back fold. The printer's mark was unaffected by Simon's crude attempt to place wax on the flap.

Conchita had suspected this all along. She had given a greater life to the incidents that may have led to the avowed conclusion. It was somewhat of a relief to know the truth, and yet she knew the man who killed her son would not be held accountable. How can I? … How can I go on from here? she thought. What can I do?

Was the part about being sent to 'rough them up' the truth? Or were the words from Rayaldo to her that afternoon more of the truth? A loud 'ding-dong' shook her into present awareness.

Timmy and his mother rang the doorbell, one that she had repaired herself after years of being inoperative. "Come in, Libby and Timmy. Ray, a friend is here to see you," she called.

Still apologetic and trying to be gracious, she sent Timmy into Ray Jr.'s room and asked Libby to join her in the kitchen. Libby started to help Conchita make cookies for their kids.

"Libby, you heard about Simon, I know. Well, I was at the lawyer's office today. He read Simon's will." She paused for several seconds searching for the composure to finish her announcement. "Simon gave me his estate … including the house."

Elizabeth Anderson released a noticeable sigh of relief that gave Conchita some emotional comfort and assurance that Libby was indeed a true friend.

Conchita added, "So, it looks like we'll be your neighbor for a while longer."

"Oh Conchita, we were so saddened by Simon's passing, but I am happy for you and Ray Jr. I am so relieved for you, Conchita." The two hugged and squeezed hands as if to seal their friendship.

"But there's more. I always told everyone that Ray Jr. was my grandson. He's not. He's Simon's son ... and mine." Conchita watched Libby's face for a reaction. When there was none, she continued, "Incredibly, in the will, Simon acknowledged that he was Ray Junior's father. He already had drawn up papers that changed Ray Junior's name to Ray Kouris. I needed to tell you first, as my closest friend and neighbor."

"Praise God and bless Simon for being a man," Libby responded. "Have you told Ray yet?"

"No. I don't know how. I don't know how he will take it. I have withheld calling myself his grandmother in front of him except for school. What do I do? How do I ..." Her self-questioning trailed off.

"Honesty is the best policy, right? He is a child still. Make him proud of his heritage; Greek wasn't it?" Libby asked.

-25-

NEW MEXICO, 1958

Several months had passed since Simon's death. Conchita tilted her wineglass all the way up to get that last little drop in the bottom before she ambled off to the kitchen for another glass. This would be her fourth this evening, but … who was counting?

Ray Jr. was in his usual position for Friday night at 9:00 pm, glued to the TV and ready to watch "Twilight Zone," his favorite show. After the episode was over, probably to avoid being sent to his room, he started asking his mother questions.

"Mama. Why is the earth round?" he asked. Then before she could answer, he posed another equally ludicrous question. "Mama, why was I born?"

Conchita looked up, above her bifocal glasses, from reading her *True Life* magazine. "You were a gift from God, miho," she said, then added, "You are here to live your life like all the rest of us."

Then he asked, "Mama, do I have brothers or sisters?" She was stunned. She had downed the better part of a bottle of wine, and it was not 10:00 pm yet. She could tell her responses were affected by the alcohol. She would not remember all the words she then uttered.

"You had a brother, miho. You are named after him. His name was Rayaldo. He died a few years ago. You used to call him tio, remember?" Then before she knew it, a secret fell out of her mouth in her inebriated condition.

"A man killed him."

Ray Jr. whipped around from his prone position on the floor. Now sitting cross-legged, he faced his mother with rapt attention.

"What happened?" he asked, stone faced.

"It's a looong story, miho. He was always a troubled soul, but this man killed him for no reason."

"Who, Mama? Who?" he begged.

"A man ... from this town. His name is Valles."

Conchita would never remember giving this name to her son. Ray Jr. would never forget.

"It's time to go to sleep, Ray. Get your pajamas on. Give me a kiss." She would only vaguely remember saying this to him, as she staggered toward the kitchen with her wineglass and deposited an empty bottle in the waste bin.

***

"Padre Juan, I need to talk to you. Es importante." Padre Juan had been the priest at the church she called home since 1936. She opened the conversation properly with a Catholic Profession of Faith and a sign of the cross. "Padre Juan, you see, I learned something from Simon after he passed away last year. In a private letter to me, Simon said that my son, Rayaldo, was murdered. Murdered by a man who still lives here ... in this town. Worse, Padre, he attends this church. You know him." From her chair, she leaned forward trying to exclaim the import of her statement.

She showed him the hand-written letter that had been in her possession for the last fifteen minutes. The priest read, then re-read the letter and lowered his head.

"None of this makes sense," Padre Juan said. He knew the man named in the note by Kouris was a family man who attended Mass regularly with his wife and baby daughter. He had known Bartolome since he was seventeen years old. He recalled meeting him and Catarina in the church's flower garden. He knew Bartolome could not be a murderer, but he needed proof.

Conchita waited for the priest to acknowledge her revelation. He didn't. "Padre Juan?" she asked through her tear-stained face. He simply looked at her, staring beyond her eyes.

The sun shone through the stained-glass window into the rectory office attached to St. Anne's Church. The two were sitting across from each other on opposing couches designed for pre-Cana counseling held before marriages. The setting worked well for occasions like this, for consoling a family member when a loved one died, for a parishioner wanting a face-to-face confession, or even where a marriage was in trouble.

"Padre, there's more." Conchita's tears reduced to whimpering in preparation for what she was about to say. "Padre, I am tormented by my actions, too," she started. "I knew what was happening with the two men in my life, and I did nothing to stop it."

At this confession, Padre Juan adjusted himself forward in his seat and gestured with his hands urging his guest to continue with her honest admission.

"First, Rayaldo came to see me the afternoon he disappeared. I could tell something was up. He was fidgeting like he did whenever he had something to hide ... except he wanted to tell someone. Well, he finally told me. Simon ordered him to break into the man's home at night and kill them." Covering her face with her hands, Conchita cried while Padre Juan waited.

Recovering, she continued, "Father, I told him to be careful ... to be careful ... not to refuse to go ... not to refuse to kill ... not to quit and find another job. *To be careful.*" She broke down again, sobbing.

The release was good for her. She had to get it out. It all made sense to her now. It wasn't murder as she had decided when the conversation started. It was self-defense. Valles had defended his home and family.

But there was more inside that needed to come out.

"Conchita, El Dios te ama." Padre told her that God loved her and added, "Tell me more, my child."

"Padre, I ran away from my home forsaking my family. I lived with a man without the sacrament of marriage. I gave birth to a child and lied to everyone about his heritage ... twice. I have failed as a mother to keep my children from evil. I held my tongue when I saw things these men in my life were doing wrong. Mea culpa. Mea maxima culpa. Padre, mea culpa. I am responsible for my son's death."

Now she was sobbing bitterly with her head nearly on her lap, her small hands covering her ears as if she wanted to hear herself no more. Padre Juan seemed to accept her story without question. She had been conflicted about Bartolome Valles, but that was before she started retelling the story. She had reasoned out the actions of Kouris and Rayaldo and was coming to terms with the consequences of her inaction.

That inaction to prevent a crime was something the legal system called nonfeasance. But her confession would remain private. Public exposure would serve no useful purpose and would probably ruin many lives. Padre's duty was to heal … not harm lives.

"Conchita, I'm a priest. I serve you as a messenger from our God. He loves you and me and Simon and Rayaldo and everyone involved in this situation. He only wants our peace. He gives us all His love. You have removed a boulder blocking His love from entering your heart. Be joyful, my child. You are forgiven and you are loved."

The slightest hint of a smile crossed Conchita's tear-stained face. Padre had reached her heart and she was listening. She would be fine now.

"Conchita, as I said, I am a priest. I am *your* priest. In accepting your confession, I must ask you to perform a penance." Conchita repositioned herself on the couch, scooting closer to the front edge.

"My child, you believe that you have sinned in all the things you confess here and now. Whether you have or not is between you and God. However, in order to receive the Sacrament of Forgiveness you must do the following: First, you must love yourself more than you have ever done. Not a self-centered love but a love that is like our Father gives us, unconditional love. You must love yourself without the expectation of anything in return."

He continued, "Conchita, God made you, and God lives as a presence within you. Your love for yourself is an expression of your love for God. We are commanded to do so in many parts of the Scripture, remember? There is even a guide for what I am instructing you to do. The charge Jesus gave us was 'Love the Lord your God with all your heart and with all your soul and with all your mind.' Your heart, your soul and your mind are *you*, Conchita. Love your God by loving your heart, soul and mind.

"Here's what you must do, my child. Sit still once a day and feel love for yourself. Feel blessed and give thanks for the life you have and for all the people who fill that life. Count the things that blessed your day, every day. Be grateful. Have a gracious heart and see everyone in terms of this love.

"Second, you must *forgive* yourself and everyone involved in this incident for all the same reasons. You cannot love yourself if you harbor ill will toward others. Remember, God is living within them as well. Forgiveness is the most important part of your penance. You see, God's love is much like a water faucet. You control the faucet, but the water is pressurized and comes out when you decide to open it. Forgiveness is essential to allow love to flow; it opens the faucet. When you withhold forgiveness, you turn off the faucet. The faucet can be on all day and all night if *you* decide so. The water … or rather, the love will never run out. That is the grace you are given as God's child."

Listening attentively, Conchita regained her composure and, with the help of a silk handkerchief, dried her tears. She had observed every movement, gesture, and inflection of her priest, whom she judged wise beyond his years and station. But she also believed that his unspoken sentiments were the same as hers. Rayaldo got what was coming to him. It was self-defense on Bartolome's part. She just had to say it.

"Padre, I do know that this man was defending his family. His actions were justified, even if it meant the end of my son's life." Her tears started again. "I forgive him. He was right to defend his family. I would tell my son that if he were here now. My son was wrong to follow the order Simon gave him. He was *wrong*.

"Simon was a hard man, made harder by a wrath that started before we met and grew stronger without anyone to temper his emotions. He had no wife to do that for him. I forgive him for all he did, even for his dishonesty about my son. He defended all his actions, which he thought were justified. He might have thought, in some vain way, that withholding the truth would protect Ray Junior and me.

"Padre Juan, I feel like a failure. With all the things I have done wrong, my son, Ray Junior is now in trouble in school and was even expelled for a week for smoking and cursing. I don't know where my life is going. I feel like it is falling apart.

"It is hard to forgive myself for my sins." She gestured toward her chest. "I am … in here … with the sorrows that I caused. How can I forgive myself? How can I love myself when I deserted my family and failed my firstborn? And now, not keeping my second born out of trouble?" Trailing off, she added, "When I could have done something."

"Conchita, those actions are done. They're gone. They don't exist. They cannot be changed, improved or eliminated. You can do nothing about them. However, you *can* leave them behind and live your life in the here and now."

"You have been living both in the past and the future, worried about your sins and how to fix them. In doing so, you have missed the beauty of today. I think this is the message of numerous verses throughout the Bible such as in Isaiah when it says, 'Forget the former things; do not dwell on the past. See, I am doing a new thing! Now it springs up; do you not perceive it? I am making a way in the desert and streams in the wasteland.'

"Or in the New Testament in Matthew: 'Therefore, do not worry about tomorrow, for tomorrow will be anxious for itself.' Each day has enough trouble of its own."

Taking Conchita's hand in his, he summarized. "Life is for the living not the dead. The past is dead and will never return if we let it stay there and don't carry it with us every day of our lives. Your past is dead. Let go of your grip on the past, Conchita. Let go."

Conchita stood, perceiving that her allotted time had long since expired and this priest surely had work to do. She had work to do as well, now more than ever.

Walking her out of the rectory and through the garden to the parking area, Father had one last message to impart.

"Conchita, most people think that it's those things we do right or wrong … the successes we have or our mistakes that make us who we are." He paused, stopping to face his parishioner.

"My child, it is more what we *feel* about what we've done that affects our condition. It's how we feel about our wrongdoing that makes us who we are … how we react to our actions with thoughts of guilt, remorse and shame. Instead, receive the forgiveness of God and freely embrace the life unfolding for you every minute. You have the power of forgiveness simply by accepting this blessing. Be forgiven by the grace of God."

Conchita's face froze, staring at Padre Juan. She found no words appropriate for a meaningful response. Turning away, she entered her car and drove home.

-26-

New Mexico, 1959

After he endorsed it, Bartolome gave the check to Catarina for bank deposit the next day. Oscar Whitesmith had paid him for some construction work completed the prior week. Then he thought about the conversation they had about a new pickup for the company.

Their 1948 Ford pickup had more than 100,000 miles and was now experiencing regular breakdowns. First the brakes needed replacing, then a water pump sprang a leak, now an oil leak in the engine crankcase had developed. They needed a new or at least newer truck to remain competitive.

"Catarina, could you get the title for the Ford pickup from our safe deposit box? That way, we can save time if we pick out a truck this weekend." She answered that she would, of course.

***

Upon receiving the key for Box Number 908 Catarina opened it to search for the title. She found the title and something unexpected, a small red pouch in the corner. She opened the pouch, quickly dropped it, and lurched back to the wall behind her as if a rattlesnake surprised her. The ring landed in the box undamaged.

A bank clerk heard the commotion and poked her head in. "Is everything okay, Mrs. Valles?"

Little Jordan, who accompanied her mother, had just turned three years old. She danced in circles, twirling her full skirt as she sang all the words to a popular song. "Mama is fine," she announced, stopping mid-twirl. The clerk was obviously amused at the antics of the precocious child, albeit a Mexican child.

Recovering from the shock of seeing the ring, Catarina took it and the title and closed the box, asking the clerk to please return it to the safe.

That night, Bartolome returned from his day's work, and after dinner Catarina brought out the truck title and the red jeweler's pouch and announced to him, "Look what I found in the safe deposit box." Her husband had not seen the ring since he placed it in the jar of ash early that fateful morning.

"Madre de Dios! How did this get in our box at the bank?" he asked as he gazed out the kitchen window, attempting to reconstruct his actions that unfortunate night of the attack. Then he tried to recall the last time he had been in the vault. It was to place Jordan's birth certificate in ... 1956! "We haven't been in the vault since before the events that night. Someone put the ring in our box," Valles said. "But who? And why?"

"Someone has invaded our private possessions," added Catarina, incredulous. "To give us something of value. It doesn't make sense. For what motive?"

After a moment of silent contemplation, the two turned from what they were doing and looked at each other with faces as cold as the heart that contrived the idea. Bartolome spoke first. "Kouris. He did it to accuse me. To connect me to the disappearance ... and ... perhaps foul play."

He failed to say the word "killing" but continued to explain. "A person disappears, and the authorities are led to our safe deposit box with a tip that something incriminating is there. And it would be there, right in our box," Bartolome said.

"It had to be Kouris. But how did he get it in?" The box was supposed to be off limits to everyone, even the bank staff. "Did he have that kind of influence?"

"When did he do this?" Catarina asked.

That's when Bartolome put the parts together. Standing, he retrieved his hat from the hook by the door. He was no longer addressing his wife. "He died before he could accomplish his plan. But he had to have an accomplice in the bank. Who was it? Did someone else know? Or suspect?" They were rhetorical questions spoken in a loud enough whisper that Catarina could hear. Lines on her forehead conveyed the worry she felt as her husband walked out the kitchen door.

Bartolome took the ring and hid it in a remote part of the garage, placing it high on a nail hook in shelves behind some canned fruit.

-27-

New Mexico, 1960

Bartolome swallowed hard. His throat was dry and filled with a lump, the kind that comes from internal conflict. He had felt conflicted for maybe three years now. Oh, the evidence was gone or at least hidden. Kouris was gone—dead—of natural causes that Bartolome had nothing to do with. But he still remembered, and it was the remembering that haunted him.

His place in line for confession was behind a little Mexican woman who could have been his mother's age. What could she have to confess, thought Bartolome, compared to my moral offense?

Now it was his turn. How would he begin? He had been asking that question for months. His cupped hands cradled his damp forehead. He removed them when he heard the confessional curtain open. He looked up to see the older woman leaving the confessional booth, walking away silently, her fingers gently rubbing a plastic rosary and her mouth forming Hail Marys.

Sitting in the booth, his palms sweating, Bartolome pulled the curtain for privacy even though he was alone in the church. He noticed the triangular-shaped wooden kneeler and wondered if he should kneel. He read the Act of Contrition printed on the kneeler, mouthing the words.

Without warning, the sliding screen snapped open and Bartolome heard Padre Juan say, "My child, God blesses you for your act of contrition and confession, a blessed sacrament. Please make the sign of the cross and begin."

Bartolome genuflected, repeating the still familiar words. "In the name of the Father, the Son and the Holy Spirit. Forgive me Father, for I have sinned. It has been a very long time since my last confession. I have sinned against my God, my family, and my humanity," he said, recalling the traditional words of the sacrament.

He then told the story in its bare truth, as one would do after-the-fact and knowing the lessons learned, clearly having remorse. The confession lasted a long time. At the end of Bartolome's story, the priest was without words for several grueling seconds.

Then, Bartolome listened as Padre Juan began slowly, parsing his words with scripture. "My son, I know you believe you committed a great sin. I am not convinced that protecting one's self and one's family is a sin, but rather a blessing and a service to your family. However, your relationship with God is what is most important. Believing that you sinned, you would be committing an even greater sin to reject God's forgiveness. You might detest what you've done and even detest yourself for doing it. But God still loves you and yearns for you to return to his house.

"Remember that Jesu Cristo forgave even a murderer, Saul of Tarsus, who became the Saint Paul. Saul was responsible for ordering many Christians to their deaths. In Acts, he said, 'I persecuted the followers of this Way to their death.' God forgave him and changed his life, and the same can happen to you. You do not need to feel guilty any longer. I give you this penance only for your sake. I have never given a harsher penance to anyone. But I know you are worthy of this great blessing.

"First, you must do at least one good deed for someone every day for the rest of your life. Second, always love your enemies as you love your friends. Make it an act of contrition."

When it was over, Bartolome felt a huge weight removed from his chest. Now his heart pumped fresh blood because of the purity he felt inside. He read the act of contrition on the kneeler aloud: "My God, I am sorry for my sins with all my heart. In choosing to do wrong and failing to do good, I have sinned against You, whom I should love above all things. I firmly intend, with the help of Your Grace, to sin no more and to avoid whatever leads me to sin. Our Savior, Jesus Christ, suffered and died for us. In His name, may

God have mercy."

Padre Juan then prayed the prayer of absolution: "God the Father of mercies, through the death and resurrection of His Son, has reconciled the world to Himself and sent the Holy Spirit among us for the forgiveness of sins. Through the ministry of the church, may God give you pardon and peace. I absolve you from your sins, in the name of the Father, and of the Son and of the Holy Spirit.

"God has forgiven you of your sins. Go in peace, my son, and sin no more."

Upon exiting the confessional, Bartolome stopped at the entrance to the church to take the sacrament of the church's holy water. He knelt, facing the chancel, and genuflected with his forefinger. Silently, he made a note to visit another troubled parishioner, one who lived on Maple Street over by Bell School … sometime … sometime.

-28-

NEW MEXICO, 1960

Sometime came sooner than Bartolome expected, and the visit happened at an unexpected place ... at least for Conchita and Bartolome. Not for Padre Juan. After all, he had arranged the meeting. After three months, the time was right.

Padre Juan asked for an audience with his two parishioners by sending each a simple note on St. Anne's stationery. The note summoned the recipients to attend a private counseling session that was not to include other family members. Neither Conchita nor Bartolome suspected the true circumstances of the meeting.

More than three years had passed since the incident. Jordan was now four years old. Ray Jr. was eleven and in the fifth grade. Bartolome was successful in his business, engaging in many fruitful commercial contracts.

Conchita was recovering ... slowly. However, both Bartolome and Conchita still carried the anguish of their actions. Neither had told anyone except Padre Juan.

Spring had arrived, and April held no weather surprises. Easter had passed but only by two weeks. Padre Juan's garden beamed with color and expressions of joy from the flowering shrubbery. It was filled with bright yellow sunflowers, deep red roses, white yucca blossoms, and the orange of barrel cacti. It was a propitious setting for a private meeting. The sitting area in the courtyard amid the Father's carefully tended blooms was the perfect place for this important encounter. Enrique Garcia, a stonemason and member of the church, had donated his work to St. Anne's. The three semi-circular granite seats formed a triad facing each other, about five feet apart. The triad represented the Trinity: Father, Son and Holy Spirit. Garcia had also carved a stone figure to accompany the benches that rested on crushed stone.

Saint Anne, the namesake of the church, was the mother of the Virgin Mary and the grandmother of Jesus Christ. Garcia's artistic skills were impressive for a stonemason. St. Anne's benches and sculpture were beautiful works of art but served another more pragmatic purpose. Garcia had crafted a base for the statue. The perimeter of the half circle had twelve carved notches denoting daylight hours. The statue was positioned on the base, facing north using a compass so it served the practical use of a sundial. The shadow from St. Anne's raised right hand served as the hour marker, noting the time. It was almost 9:00 am, the padre noticed. It was time.

A car door closed, and footsteps approached the garden along the gravel path. Padre stood, holding the half-size Biblio Catolico in both hands, and greeted his first arrival.

"Padre Juan, to what do I owe the pleasure of our visit today?" the woman inquired.

Before he could answer, both heads turned toward the sound of a second car door. Conchita turned back to face Padre Juan. "Padre, what did you do?" she asked sharply.

"Something each of you should have done years before," Padre Juan said.

The wrought iron gate, an entrance to the garden, opened then closed and latched. With his head bowed, Bartolome walked reverently toward the central garden. An unexpected sight stopped him. The two parishioners held each other's gazes for a few seconds.

"My children, please sit," Father said. They did, one on each bench. Bartolome knew the benches and carved figure since Enrique, the creator, was still his best friend. He remembered seeing them on a wooden table in Enrique's home shop during the shaping process. He also knew and loved the garden since it reminded him of his beautiful wife, Catarina. It was where they met. He thought he saw Conchita relax ... just a little when he smiled at the memory. Padre Juan sat on the remaining bench and placed his Bible at his side.

Padre Juan began. "Each of you has a heavy burden that we have talked about privately. Normally, I would not discuss parts of a confession. That is private and meant to be between you and God. But I know you want to do this with each other and that you both need some encouragement. Am I right?" He held his unclasped hands upright in a sign of openness. He observed ever-so-slight nods that signaled agreement.

"Good. Now you need to speak about things for which you are sorry… not for the purpose of trying to make the other feel better but rather to help each of you embrace the truth. Bartolome, would you like to start?" Valles shuddered and held his head upward, toward Padre Juan. "Bartolome, do you remember the proverb in John that says, 'The truth shall set you free'?" Bartolome looked at his hands then slowly raised his head to observe Conchita. Their gazes met again.

"Señora Gonzalez …" he began slowly. "Señora, I … am … responsible … for … your son's … death." He spoke haltingly, parsing his words with care. "In fact, I …" Now his downward glance studied the ants crawling along a path in the crushed-stone gravel. Looking up again, this time directly into her eyes, he faced her as a criminal would face a presiding judge about to pronounce sentence. "I was the one who took his life. I killed your son, señora."

There was a long pause as Bartolome gazed into Conchita's eyes for an answer to the burden that he had carried these many years. Then his head dropped abruptly. But this time he didn't notice the ants. He was watching tears drop one by one onto the stone between his work boots. His own tears. He held his gaze on the ponding tears until he had the courage to look up again.

What he saw surprised him. He saw forgiveness in Conchita's eyes, and his heart melted. It gave him the courage to finish what he needed to say.

"In fact, I am responsible for the death of the other two with him that night. I took their young lives as well."

Conchita spent the next half hour listening to Bartolome's account of the activities that led up to the actions causing his anguish these last three years. She was withdrawn as if still recovering from denial, yet attentive to Bartolome's account of her son's actions. He told her everything, omitting only the most gruesome parts.

He mentioned the ring. He told what he had done with it initially and why. He withheld where Rayaldo was buried, and she didn't ask. When he was done, she shifted, moving closer to him yet still on her bench. Her thirteen years of seniority gave her the authority to address him in familiar Spanish.

"Gracias por tus honestidad." She thanked him for his honesty. "Y tambien, yo tango un confesion." She uttered that she too had a confession and glanced at Padre Juan who encouraged her.

"You see, I learned about your role in my son's death through my son himself before he came to your home that night. He was instructed by his employer, my younger son's father ..." Her voice trailed off as she lowered her head.

"Simon ordered him to kill you and your family."

This admission brought tears for what she had been so ashamed to say out loud.

Padre Juan, sitting across from her, moved beside her and put his hand on her shoulder, which seemed to give her strength. She turned to face Bartolome and continued.

"I knew about the plan, and I did nothing. I should've said something to my son. What he was told to do was wrong. He knew it! But his life had been hard as an immigrant, and Simon Kouris was the only one who ever stood up for him. Rayaldo wanted desperately to please him. I am the one who is guilty. Mea culpa, Señor Valles, mea culpa." She rested her head on Padre Juan's shoulder.

***

Bartolome let the words sink in. How different life might have been if Conchita had stopped her son. But could she have stopped him ... really?

Conchita related all the things that had plagued her about the incident. She held nothing back. She told Valles about Simon's note and the ring, confessing to Bartolome that Simon had the ring. His suspicion had been correct. Her confession confirmed that Kouris had somehow managed to get it into his safe deposit box.

After an exhaustive hour of listening to his parishioners expose their innermost secrets and fears, Padre Juan took over.

"My children, there are wounds in your hearts that are now clean of infection. But you will need to heal and be kept free of contagion; the contagions of hatred, anger, fear, guilt, and worry. Keep your hearts focused on love instead. I am giving both of you the following penance." With that, he handed each of them a small laminated card with a quotation written on parchment.

He explained, "The Chinese call this a koan. They use a brief saying like this to remind them that love is the answer to all the questions we have."

The calligraphy of the koan made it difficult to read but the message was simple: "My heart is filled with love."

"You are to keep this with you wherever you go and look at it regularly. As you inhale say the first part, 'My heart is filled ...' As you exhale, say the second part ... 'with love.' Let it become a part of your day. Memorize it. Say it like the rosary. The intent is the same." With that, Padre Juan left the two alone.

The meeting ended with Bartolome and Conchita walking side by side in silence toward the parking lot. When they had cleared the gate, Bartolome was the first to speak.

"For all my actions, I ask forgiveness. I am truly sorry that you have lost a son. I wish it were not so."

Then, it was Conchita's turn. "I forgive you from my heart. You did no wrong. You did what had to be done. You have nothing but love and honesty in your heart."

Politely, they shook hands. Neither saw Padre Juan smile as he watched the exchange from his rectory window.

-29-

New Mexico, 1971

Conchita was outside St. Anne's church in her car waiting for her appointment with Padre Juan. She had her hands on a moneybag from the Farmer's and Merchant's Bank fattened with her son's inheritance from his father.

Earlier she received a call from the mother of a young woman her son had known for a few months. It seems that the woman had given in to Ray's seductive solicitation with promises of marriage. After several intimate times together, the young woman pushed Ray to fulfill his promise.

It was then that Ray skipped town and moved to Anthony, New Mexico, leaving no forwarding address. Conchita had spoken with the young woman who was pregnant by Ray. Her parents urged their daughter to have an abortion, to avoid ruining her life, which she did. With that revelation, Conchita went home, tore up the honorable discharge papers her son had previously presented when he had asked for ... no ... demanded his inheritance. She would never tolerate that behavior from any man, especially her son. Her own life was forever changed when she fell under the charm of a similar young man about Ray's age.

It was time, she noticed, looking at the car's clock. She left her car unlocked as she normally did and walked stridently to the rectory entrance of St. Anne's, where Padre Juan would be waiting, probably reading the Bible or writing a homily for Sunday Mass. Twice she struck the black iron knocker on the door. That door reflected the Moorish influence on the Spanish architecture in Northern Mexico, conquered by Spain in the 1500s.

Inside, she heard Padre Juan walking toward the door. He opened it and greeted her. "Bienvenidos, señora." Conchita knew her face couldn't hide her troubled mood. For Conchita this was not a social call. She was in pain. Secretly, she hoped Padre Juan could tell. She needed his consolation but was hesitant to ask for it.

"Padre, I need to give you something ... something that will help the church." She started to explain but couldn't get enough words to string together. His silence urged her to continue. "This money was supposed to be for Ray Junior after he got out of the service, but Simon insisted that I approve the gift.

"I am sure that Simon wanted me to evaluate the character of our son at age twenty-one and decide if he deserved the inheritance. He does not." Again, Padre Juan waited in silence.

"Ray has always been a troubled child," she continued. "First in school he almost got kicked out like his half-brother." Padre Juan ushered her inside and closed the door.

"I read his USMC service record from his separation papers. He was barely issued an honorable discharge because of his lack of discipline. In fact, Ray didn't earn the ribbon they would ordinarily give for good conduct because of problems with his superiors both in Vietnam and before his discharge from the service at Camp Pendleton."

Before Padre Juan could lead the troubled woman to a chair, more of her story spilled out. "After his discharge, Ray fell in with a group of young men here in Las Cruces who were a worse influence on him. He escaped arrest for robbery a few months ago because he was not caught and the other two did not report him to the authorities. There is honor among thieves, I suppose."

Conchita adjusted her posture and sneered to express her contempt for her son's actions. "But the worst is that last week, I found out he had promised marriage to a young woman of a different faith. She gave in to his advances on several occasions and became pregnant."

Conchita, who moved next to the rectory window, hesitated before finishing the story. She turned away from Padre Juan's inquiring face and, never removing her gaze from the bird feeder outside, she tried to gain the strength to admit the worst consequence of her son's behavior, "Father, she had an abortion."

Feeling weak and spent, Conchita approached the settee and sat, clutching the moneybag. Father Juan held her elbow, steadying her then took the chair opposite her. After a deep breath, she continued, "My son did the same thing to that girl that happened to me." Now she lost her composure and let tears fall into the palms that covered her contorted face.

Standing suddenly, she thrust the bag at Padre Juan and announced, "Here's his inheritance ... for St. Anne's. I know it will be better used through your wisdom." Conchita turned and strode to the door, ready to depart. She opened the door and stepped out before Father could react.

"Is there more you want to talk about, Señora Gonzalez?" he called.

"Thank you, Padre. Please find the money a worthy home," she said over her shoulder and walked toward her car. Padre followed her, trying to keep pace in a gait undignified for a Catholic priest.

"Señora," he called. "If you need to talk more, I have the time. I want to help you in any way I can. We're all in this world, struggling together. God wants us to be here for each other." Conchita stopped abruptly and turned to face him.

"Father, I cannot talk about this anymore. I need to give you this now and follow the guidance you gave me over ten years ago." A pause gave her a chance to swallow the lump in her throat. "I should have done this before now. I put it off then and I don't want to put it off anymore. Thank you, Father."

With that, she was in the car slamming the door. Padre Juan stood on the gravel parking lot watching her drive away.

-30-

New Mexico, 1971

Ray was down on his luck. He had lost another job and was in the employment office doing two things. He was applying for unemployment benefits and looking for another job that might last longer. Losing this last job wasn't his fault, he justified. His self-pity was interrupted by a deep, female government voice from the other side of the counter.

"Mr. Kouris. Just fill out this form completely and bring it back with the last paystub from your former employer. Be sure to bring some sort of termination notice too. And I'll need proof of your application for three of these job vacancies." The rotund, middle aged, Anglo woman looked over her pink-rimmed reading glasses.

The New Mexico Employment Commission's office was on Alameda Street in Las Cruces. The way the woman enunciated her words slowly and distinctly convinced Ray that she thought he would not understand English. It was another way that white people conveyed disrespect to Mexican Americans. It was just one more thing to ruin his day.

Las Cruces had been Ray's home all his life, except his mother always reminded him that he was born in El Paso ... because the hospitals were better there. Las Cruces was where he worked and lived. Well, where he used to work. He was now without a job ... again and living in Anthony, New Mexico.

The woman gave him a list of three job opportunities in his field. He would have to prove that he applied for all three if he wanted to have unemployment insurance payments of $59 a week. He would take the list even if it did not lead to a job. He needed the unemployment checks.

What would my mother think? he ruminated as he left the office building where others still waited in line. He uttered an expletive out loud. "So what? Puta Madre!" Everyone within earshot turned toward him.

He had not told his mother about being fired Tuesday morning for backing a dump truck into the rear of a motor grader, snapping the water line of the grader's water pump. No one told him the driver parked the grader adjacent to the road. Where was he supposed to wait until a front-end loader filled his dump truck? ... and the grader was not there when he drove up. "Ese!" he said to himself.

Ray was walking to his 1955 Chevy, the car his mother had given him after he returned from Vietnam. Humph ... a gift, huh? A seventeen-year-old wreck! What about the gift his father had left him?

Blaming others for his mishaps was a well-worn pattern for Ray. But while others around him could see it clearly, he was blind to the fact that the circumstances of his life belonged to him. It was not something anyone ever confronted him about. His universe of friends was generally like him, down on their luck and more willing to blame their failures on something or someone else. In Ray's case that someone was generally Anglo or any privileged class.

"Chinga te madre." Inside his car he issued a profanity toward the old white man who had just cut him off in traffic. "Fuck the Anglos," he added, waving his hands in anger.

At least his car was in basically good shape and it was the envy of his friends. They all wished they could have a mother like his. Little did they know what she was really like.

Conchita had withheld the gift Ray's father promised him, using some fancy white man's legal tricks, he decided. If only he could have that $25,000. How much better his life would be. He tried to dismiss his anger at his mother and focus on the matter at hand: a job or at least an interview.

Ray drove into the construction site the employment office gave him as a job lead. He would have to explain what had happened on his last job. He would have to keep the issue of the broken grader to himself.

"Good morning, señor. Is this BeeVee Construction?" asked Ray.

After thirty minutes grilling Ray about his experience in block laying, the man told him he needed more experienced masons.

Upon leaving the site, Ray noticed the yellow sign at the entrance that said: "Another quality project from BeeVee Construction, New Mexico License No. 230024. Bartolome Valles, Owner." He studied the owner's name and then gazed back at the trailer. He thought about the man who had interviewed him. Then he remembered something his mother told him when he was around ten years old.

Ray felt empty. His mother had more-or-less disowned him after he confronted her about his inheritance, for the dozenth time.

He had $113 to his name. He was living in a garage of his cuñado's home in Anthony. Oh, he wasn't a brother-in-law exactly. In fact, Ray had no living siblings. But his friend had a hot-looking sister.

The term, cuñado, was Mexican slang used to taunt a man with an especially attractive sister, implying that he was having relations with her. He would never say that to Anthony's face though and jeopardize his rent-free housing, albeit in a garage.

Ray's unemployment benefits would run out in a couple months. His food stamps would end, too. They were helpful, but you couldn't buy beer with food stamps.

-31-

NEW MEXICO, 1971

Ray, Jr. was headed out to ask for a job with framers at a Dale Bellamah project. Bellamah was a large firm that built hundreds of homes every year in Las Cruces. He had applied with them and been turned down before because they subcontracted their wood framing. So, this time he would ask the framing subcontractor for a job.

"Como esta cabron?" Ray greeted the figure he recognized from four years before in a different setting. Zachary Martin was on a stepladder nailing two wall frames together, wearing protective goggles and holding a Paslode nail gun attached to the hose of an air compressor. The man turned to see the source of the Spanish profanity slung toward him. His old acquaintance reacted with glee.

"I'll be go-to-hell. It's Greek! How the fuck are you, man?" he shouted above the compressor noise, stepping off the ladder. Ray was diminutive compared to Zachary Martin whose tall frame approached him.

"Como esta?" Ray asked, his hand outstretched to greet a war buddy. The two exchanged pleasantries before Ray announced the purpose of his trip. He was desperate for work, any kind of work.

"Have you ever framed a house, Greek?" Zach inquired.

"Si, a un otra vez con mi amigo en Belen," Ray answered, remembering that Marty could understand Spanish. His answer that he had helped a friend one time seemed weak.

He could see Martin thinking about his answer. He wondered if their time together in Vietnam would help him secure at least a temporary job.

"If you can carry lumber, I can use you for a week or two. Is $1.75 an hour okay with you? As an independent contractor?" The minimum wage was $1.60 and had been since 1968.

Ray tried not to react too quickly to Martin's offer. He knew that the reference to independent contractor meant Martin would not have to act as an employer and deduct taxes, etc. To Ray, it also meant he would have no deductions and his work would be essentially 'off the books.' He could still draw unemployment benefits ... and food stamps. It was the best of both worlds. Of course, he would take the job.

"Gracias, cuñado." Ray expressed his appreciation in street jargon.

Then Zach asked him, "Could you do me a favor, Greek? Could you not call me that? I don't have a sister anyway."

"Claro, que si." Ray answered that he understood.

"... And you know my name is Ray, right?" Ray countered. "Greek was just a nickname used in the 'Nam.'"

"Glad to know that ... Ray. You got it." Zach responded as they clasped hands. Zach had learned how important it was to use a person's name. Last year, he had attended a free Dale Carnegie course, learning that and several other useful interpersonal skills. "You can start now if you like. Got a tool belt?" Before Ray could respond, Zach followed up. "If you don't, I've got an extra you can have. It's in the truck. Let me get it." Together they walked toward Zach's father's pickup.

"What have you been doing since getting out?" Zach asked.

"Just odd jobs, you know ... I did janitor work for a while. I even worked in the circus once when it was in town. I worked for A&M Construction for almost a year when they had layoffs." Ray withheld the tractor incident.

"Well, this is only a two-week gig, you know. I'm not sure what we'll have after that. And I'm not exactly an employer. I'm just like you, an independent contractor. When we finish this house and the next, Bellamah doesn't have anything for at least a month."

Ray was putting on his new, used tool belt. He noticed Martin looking at him quizzically. "What's the matter, ese? Am I doing it wrong?" Ray asked. Then he noticed that Zach's tool belt was on differently than his with the latch in front.

"Naw, man … some people wear it that way." Martin's answer seemed condescending to Ray.

At 11:00 am, the day was already on the downside. Ray learned that the crew started at 5:00 am and usually ended by 12:00 to allow Zach to clean up and get to his afternoon classes.

Zach explained. "Ray, we start framing at 5:00 and stop at noon. Will that work for you?" Seeing an affirmative nod from Ray, he continued. "We usually stop for the burrito truck around 8:00 and have what we call 'lunchfast.' We gobble that down then hit it hard until noon."

"You could work longer, getting the site organized for the next day. We've got to watch our tools all the time or they'll be stolen …."

Ray sensed that Zach wanted to finish the thought "… by some mojados selling them to the pawn shop." But Ray misunderstood.

Zach finished his thought. "There are some guys from the framing crew next door who 'borrowed' some of my tools when I went to get sodas one day. I never knew until I saw my framing square on the roof after they left."

That comment, coupled with memories from three years before, led to Ray's next question.

"Hey bro, just like the old days, huh? In the 'Nam'? Fighting for our country? Killing people? … Covering it up, ese?" Now Ray was wearing a sly, knowing grin. He could see he had hit a nerve. He saw Zachary Martin stunned for the first time, ever.

Regaining his composure, Martin announced, "Let's get to work. I've got to finish this corner before class." Zach turned to walk his new hire back toward the job site.

"Are you still in school, man?" Ray thought that Martin's comment meant he was finishing high school since Ray lacked a diploma. He realized that couldn't be the case as soon as he spoke. This white boy was in college; that was something else he despised about Martin … and all white people.

Zach replied, "Yup. I'm studying to get an engineering degree … halfway finished. Just two more years and I can quit this manual labor gig."

Ray felt gut-punched. As it was, he could not quit this "manual labor gig" in the foreseeable future. He withheld a response.

***

The two weeks were eventful for Zachary, who was now more convinced about Ray's lack of integrity. He was wishing he had never hired him when he saw Ray drive up to the work site at 7:00 Thursday morning. The framing job was almost finished, no thanks to Ray who had been late for three of the last seven days on the job. While they took Sunday off, Zach expected the crew to work twelve hours every Saturday to compensate for the time he took off for classes Monday, Wednesday and Friday afternoons.

During the last seven days, Zach had been the focus of sharp barbs from Ray. Monday, Ray appeared to be intoxicated or at least recovering from a hangover. He arrived late, of course. Then around 8:00 when the burro wagon drove up and the crew stopped for lunchfast, out of character for him, Ray sidled up close to Zach which made him feel uncomfortable.

"Hey man. Do you remember all those things we did in 'The Nam'?" Ray asked Zachary, who privately detested any use of the abbreviated term, 'The Nam.' It wasn't the abbreviation as much as ... well, it sounded like someone's attempt to brag about being there. He couldn't put his finger on it exactly, but the term wore on his psyche.

"I remember it all, Greek ... I mean Ray," he said, looking at him with anxiety mixed with expectation. What's he driving at? Zach wondered, but deep inside he knew.

"You know, the time that guy was shot, and you took out the whole village? Remember that?"

Before Zach could answer, Ray added, "And they pinned a medal on you too, ese ... y los mujeres y los ninos?" Now shaking his head, Ray appeared almost courageous, delivering the slanderous accusation about the dead women and children in the village.

That brought Zach to a halt, standing in a mud puddle in his green jungle boots, the only part of his uniform saved from those days. He turned to look at Ray.

Zachary Martin was a foot taller than Ray Kouris and his stature alone should have been enough to stop Ray's thinly disguised blackmail. But before Zach could utter a word, Ray delivered the punch to the gut.

"It would be a real shame if anyone ever found out about that, huh? You know ... war crimes and all." Ray left Zachary standing as he continued toward the line for the burrito truck.

Then there was the time Ray extorted money from Zach. That was yesterday. He didn't want to face him or even see him again. It was for that reason and not his nailing job that he looked away from the arriving 55 Chevy.

Ray got out, holding his tool belt and with his peon shuffle, sauntered toward the jobsite. He grabbed a couple two-by-four wood plates and brought them to the central part of the job and lobbed them then returned to the pile for more when Zach corrected him.

"Ray, we're done with the wood plates. Can't you see? The trusses are set. Those are going back to the lumberyard as excess. You can bring the truss bracing that Mike has cut over there and hand them to me. I'll be walking along the top plate and you can hand them one at a time," Zach said.

Ray shifted his posture as if to challenge the lead framer's direction. He acted as if he wanted to say something defiant. But instead, he turned to get three two-by-four blocking pieces that Mike had cut to the right length. He brought them back, climbed a stepladder, and waited until Zach needed the next one.

"Ese..." Ray said in a low voice to convey privacy between the two. "Ese, primo, I need some ... some extra money today. My rent's due and the landlord will kick me out if I don't come up with five hundred by tonight."

"Five hundred dollars?" Zach asked, pushing his goggles over his forehead. "That's pretty high for rent. I pay a hundred twenty-five, and I live in a nice apartment. Do you live in Telshor now?" he asked, referring to a high-rent district.

"No ... ese ... I live with a friend. But I've been out of work for a while and ... well, it's been more than a month since I paid rent." When Zach stopped to consider the request, Ray added more. "Even if you could help a little, bro'."

Although Zach suspected he was being a sucker, he found himself taking off his gloves and pulling out his wallet to see what he had.

"Thanks, bro'. I mean ... I really appreciate it." Ray was more supplicant than ever. That posturing gave Zach hope that he would be more attentive to his work hours.

"Look Ray, all I have is two hundred seventy-three. I'll give you two-fifty. That's a month's wages you're going to owe me, okay? And remember the start time is 5:00 not 7:30, right?" Zach tried to make the terms of the loan clear.

"You got it, bro'. Gracias para ti." Then he added, "By the way, that thing about the 'Nam'... My mouth is shut." Ray looked at Zach with a cold stare as he put the $250 in his hip pocket.

Zach was stunned into silence. Had he just paid hush money to this con artist? What the hell? Ray was off the ladder and getting more blocking.

Three days later, after the house was framed, Zach knew he would be happy to be rid of Greek or Ray ... or whatever his real name was. The crew was gone by 11:00 am, leaving Zach and Ray alone together. Zach was putting tools away as Ray cleaned up the construction debris, dumping trash into the dumpster at the site.

Zach looked around, puzzled. "Where's the Ramset? he asked under his breath. Then, he spoke aloud, "I had it out to set the base plates and thought I set it over there at the front door."

Every carpenter packed up and stored his tools in a specific order to prevent misplacement when he left the jobsite. Zach was following that protocol when he discovered he could not find a very expensive tool.

Ramset was a brand name for a powder-actuated gun that fired a .22 caliber charge, driving a zinc-plated concrete nail with a washer through wood into concrete as a fastener. It cost several hundred dollars but was worth more in timesaving from driving traditional cut nails into concrete. It made a stronger connection as well. A single trigger squeeze could replace the time it took for a dozen or more hammer swings, not to mention easing the fatigue from all the swings.

"Where is that Ramset?" he asked again. "Ray, have you seen my red Ramset?" Zach was now searching the bed of his truck.

"Are you accusing me of stealing something from you, bro'?" Zach was not implying that anyone stole the tool. He just thought it might be hidden under something around the job site. He did not expect Ray's response.

Ray became unhinged. "I come here every fuckin' day at 5:00 am to work seven damn hours for your ass and you accuse me of stealing?" Zach saw that Ray's head was shaking and his eyes squinted in feigned disbelief. With arms outstretched, he added, "How could I steal something from you? I haven't left the jobsite since I got here?"

He was right. Except … Zach remembered that earlier today it had been his turn to get cold Cokes from the Circle K down the street. Could Ray have taken the Ramset then? Could it be in his Chevy? For an innocent man, Ray's tirade seemed extreme. Zach suspected that searching Ray's car would make the situation worse.

But it was an expensive tool. As much as Zach wanted to check Greek's car, he backed off. The tool was gone. He could go to the police. Or he could go to a few pawnshops tomorrow and inform them, but— Ray interrupted his thoughts. "So, you lose your expensive tool and the first thing you do is blame the fuckin' Mex'can. You haven't changed a bit, pendejo (stupid)." He wasn't finished.

"Just because you're a big man with your own company and going to school to be a pendejo engineer, you think you can keep ordering me around like your brown Mex'can slave. And blame everything that goes wrong on me." Ray kept tearing into Zach, challenging his sense of personal honor and respect for human rights. Zach froze, stunned by the false accusations.

"Forget you, pendejo. Fuck your dollar seventy-five an hour labor job. Fuck you as well. I quit!" Ray flung both arms in the air then quickly dropped them. He unbuckled Zach's tool belt and, throwing it at him, walked toward his car.

Then he dealt the crushing blow.

"… and you know what? I might just remember a little more about that incident in the vill' that night … over a beer with a reporter from the El Paso Times."

With that, he slammed the driver's door to the 55 Chevy and accelerated the engine a few times as if to add non-verbal profanity before he raced away.

He left Zach leaning, face-forward on the bulkhead of his father's pickup wondering what could have precipitated the whole ugly incident and what was at stake if Ray carried out his threat.

***

Zach pulled off the highway at Exit 79, a business exit for the town known as "T or C." He was parched and needed a Dr. Pepper. He was headed to Albuquerque to pick up his father who had been there for a week, receiving treatment for emphysema. Oliver's emphysema had worsened after Zach's mother passed away earlier this year.

Oliver needed more medical help than his family physician could provide, and the doctor suggested the Lovelace Respiratory Research Institute in Albuquerque. "They're doing some sort of testing of a new drug with a trial group of emphysema patients," Zach remembered the doctor saying at Oliver's last office visit.

Last night his father had called and asked Zach for a ride home. He sounded despondent, like he had given up already.

The travel took two and a half hours from Las Cruces. That gave Zach too much time to think about the recent episode with Greek. He couldn't get out of the habit of using the nickname ascribed during their time together in Vietnam and he couldn't get the disturbing incident out of his mind.

Greek knew something that only a few knew. Zach hadn't even told his mother or father. It was just … too much … to … explain. He thought about how they might react. Telling the truth was always a religious expectation in his youth. His father linked honesty with good character and expected it of his son.

Beside the highway, Zach noticed the same sign he had seen for the last twenty-one years of his life. The town was originally called Hot Springs after the natural hot springs in the area. But an offer from a popular NBC radio program that later became a television show caused the name change. In 1950, the year Zach was born, Ralph Edwards, the host of the NBC quiz show announced that he would air the program from the first town in the United States that changed its name to the name of the show. "T or C" was an abbreviation. Hot Springs won the honor of being named Truth or Consequences.

Truth or Consequences loomed large for Zach about then as he focused on the incident with Ray. The truth was painful to keep inside but revealing the truth? What would that mean? Ray seemed to be insinuating that Zach did have something from his past to hide. His obvious intent was to motivate Zach to consider that he also had something to protect: his future.

The My Lai Massacre occurred in 1968, a year before Zach was in Vietnam but didn't come to national attention until after he had returned to civilian life. In My Lai, hundreds of innocent civilians were killed by wanton acts of revenge by Army units, resulting in a highly publicized trial in 1970. Lt. William Calley had been found guilty and sentenced to life imprisonment for killing twenty-two civilians.

Yes, he did have something to lose, Zach realized. His freedom and his future.

***

Zach returned to his Las Cruces apartment late Sunday afternoon after getting his father home to Deming the day before and tending to Oliver's dwindling herd of registered Herefords that were more than cows to Zach's father. They were Oliver's lifeblood now. He had developed champion bulls and heifers over the last two decades. His father was well known in those circles, even selling one prize bull to John Wayne's ranch in Arizona, south of Tucson.

Zach walked toward home, carrying the NVA (North Vietnamese Army) backpack. It was one of his few reminders from his Marine Corps days. The backpack was filled with textbooks and the HP 35 scientific calculator he had just bought. He spent $395 for that tool. It was expensive, but worth it for the time it saved and the accuracy it gave him in engineering classes. It would replace the slide rule he had been carrying around the past two years.

He had salvaged the tan backpack from an NVA stronghold in the Arizona Territory that his unit had destroyed. Besides his jungle boots, the backpack slung over his right shoulder, was his only physical reminder of Vietnam; it was the only thing he brought back from the war that he still used.

He did so for practical reasons. It was the best-built backpack he had ever seen. He guessed it was made in China and designed for the long hikes along the Ho Chi Minh Trail from North Vietnam, through Laos, along one of several trails into northern South Vietnam. One trail led directly to the Arizona Territory.

Upon returning home, there was a note on his apartment door with an ominous message. After reading it, Zach shook his head in disdain. How could he do that?

Money. He wanted money, Zach thought, answering his own question.

"Your friend came by earlier today and asked about you," Helen, his landlady, said. She had heard Zach come in and opened her door into their common hallway to deliver the news.

"Thanks Helen."

He laid the note open on the table at the entry to his apartment under an electric lamp his mother had given him. The lamp was a conversion of an oil lamp altered by his grandmother forty years before. The note, now visible from the light read:

> *"Bro,*
>
> *We can make a deal and your secret is safe with me. Meet me at O'Malley's tonight at 6:00.*
>
> *-You know who I am"*

Zach stared at the clock. It was already 5:00. Wondering if he should go, he used the bathroom then splashed water on his face trying to rinse away the thoughts racing through his mind. Slowly drying with a white towel, he attempted to regain composure from the anticipation of another shakedown.

***

Zach pulled into the Mesilla Valley Mall parking lot looking for Ray's 55 Chevy, which was nowhere to be seen. He waited in his three-year-old Firebird for fifteen minutes before getting out. As he opened the door, he noticed something puzzling.

Near his car, another driver seemed to be waiting for someone. The car was an older non-descript sedan with Texas plates. The occupant, who wore an unusual suit for a mall visitor on a Sunday, seemed to be watching him.

Zach went inside and sat at the booth in a restaurant adjacent to a window that would give him a clear view of cars approaching the parking area. His seat selection also gave the occupant of the waiting car a clear view of Zach, who assumed the driver was just the curious type.

A flash of light distracted Zach from reading the textbook he brought with him to study for a structural design test he had the next day. The light reminded him of his days in The Arizona, especially since Vietnam was foremost on his mind right now. After a brief scan of the parking lot, he saw a car pulling out of its spot and another glint of light. He dismissed it as an anomaly.

***

Dan Thomas, investigative reporter, removed the Nikon F2 from its case on the seat and adjusted the settings while it was still below the windshield. After ensuring that the settings were adequate, he raised the camera and clicked off several pictures using the motor drive mounted to the base of the camera. He then lowered it to limit visibility by anyone, especially the subject.

Where is this Ray guy? Thomas wondered, still sitting in his car. It was 6:15 and past time for the scheduled meeting.

Earlier, Thomas had gotten a call from a Ray who promised him the "story of the century." The subject of the story was a tall guy who looked like Kwai Chang Caine driving a yellow Firebird. They were to meet at the restaurant at 6:00 and discuss bribe money for this other guy's silence about a war incident.

Now, only Kwai Chang in the Yellow Firebird showed up. He was curious but losing interest. He had left El Paso in the morning to scope out the alleged meeting site and drive around Las Cruces. But now, his entire Sunday seemed wasted.

At 6:45 when the Kwai Chang guy left the restaurant, he didn't look worried. Thomas had to conclude that his private tip was bogus. He started his car, jerked it in gear and raced away.

Upon arriving at his El Paso home, Thomas removed the film from the Nikon and carefully installed a new roll. Whatever was on the roll had no value or significance. He threw it in the trash. It would be a waste to even develop it, and he wanted to be ready for the next day with a fresh roll. He adjusted the camera settings for the ISO of 100, which was good for daylight shooting. Then he put the camera back in the El Paso Times bag.

-32-

New Mexico, 1971

The steel door slammed shut with violence. The jail cell was wet and nasty. He avoided sitting on the bench since it had been soiled with sputum or something worse.

He tried to find an empty corner to stand out of the way. There was none. Five men were packed into this holding cell designed for one inmate. The county justified its overcrowding to the fire marshal by saying it was only temporary quarters for those arrested and awaiting arraignment. They said the time in the cell together would 'probably' be limited to a few hours.

"No me moleste," Ray said to the imposing figure gesturing with his lower front torso toward Ray's rear end. "Leave me alone, man. Get out'a here," he added in English in case the man did not understand Spanish.

"Aw come on, sweetie. Just relax. You'll love it," answered the burly white man with a shaved head the size of Ray's chest. "I promise I'll make you squeal with delight," the man added, laughing and smacking his lips.

"Settle down, both of you. Keep it civil in there or I'll give ya somethin' to whine about," commanded the duty jailer at the Dona Ana County Detention Center.

Damn white cop, Ray thought. Why did this always happen? He kept one eye focused on the man with the shaved head as he reflected on the incident. He was speeding for sure, but reckless driving? And the insurance thing? I can't afford insurance. I can barely afford gas.

The wreck was not my fault. The other driver should have seen me coming from behind and not swerved into my lane. He was driving on Interstate 70/80 West toward Las Cruces near Moongate.

It was a Sunday afternoon after a few drinks at the Moongate Bar at Summit Pass where the road transitions over the Organ Mountains. The descent off the mountains partly accounted for the 110-mph speed clocked by the state police who only caught up to him after the wreck, five miles before the I-25 exchange.

The driver of the 1965 station wagon was pronounced dead at the scene. A widower and father of two grown girls was a contract worker at White Sands Missile Range. Christopher Bonner had spent twenty-five years as a civilian contractor driving to and from work along this road but had chosen Sunday to catch up on a project while it was quiet. He was headed home after ten hours of work that resulted in completing the project.

"Jailer, when can I get out'a here? It stinks. I've got someplace I have to be at 6:00," Ray pleaded. It was already 4:00 pm and he had an urgent need to keep his appointment, a monetary need.

"Kouris, you're liable to be in there for some time to come. The guy you hit is dead. Did you know that? You were drunk and ran him down at a hundred ten miles per hour. Did you know that? Or were you too drunk to understand your rights when you were arrested? You disgust me," the jailer proclaimed to Ray in a voice loud enough to be heard by all occupants of the cell.

Other inmates awaiting their arraignment started giving unwanted attention to the newest arrival. After a couple hours of standing, Ray grew tired enough to endure the sputum and sank on the bench with his head cradled in his hands. The 6:00 pm meeting was now secondary in his mind. He wondered if this offense meant jail time.

He used his one phone call that resulted in a visit but not bail.

***

Ray talked to his mother from the other side of the transparent wall. "Miho, what happened?" Conchita asked sitting in a folding metal chair with her arms leaning on a ledge. She spoke through the stained Plexiglas window with nine quarter-size holes forming a circular pattern, hoping his reply would convince her that the authorities were wrong in telling her the circumstances.

"Mama, I had a wreck, but it wasn't my fault," he insisted, pleading. "It was that white guy. He swerved right in front of me ... in the left lane, ese." She cringed every time he used that term with her. Although it was gutter slang and intended for talking with a male, Ray insisted on using it with his own mother.

"But surely the police would have seen swerve marks, miho? Did you say anything to them?"

"No Ma. I didn't talk. I wanted to see you first. What should I do? How can I get out?"

His head was in his right hand now and he was sobbing. "I didn't mean to do it. I didn't mean to...." Ray's words trailed into the oblivion where he felt he was headed.

Raising his head, he saw the disbelief in his mother's eyes. "Miho, you must learn to—"

Before she could finish, he half stood and almost shouted at his mother through the holes in the Plexiglas.

"To stand up. Right? To fight like a man. Right?" Then motioning around at his new accommodations, he added, "Or now that I'm in jail, do you want me to bow to the white cops and do whatever they tell me to do?"

Without waiting for an answer, he continued his rant. "I've followed your rules, ese. They don't work. They don't lead nowhere, Ma." He lowered his head again and whimpered pitiably.

"Miho, I'll call a lawyer. I'll see what he can do." When Conchita stood, Ray could tell the visit was over. He observed her stance then hung his head again. "My life is over." He cleared his throat and scrutinized Conchita through the murky Plexiglas. Their gazes locked.

"I doubt I'm worth it. Don't waste your money. I'm done."

"Don't give up, Ray. You're still young. You have a whole life ahead of you. Neither your father nor I ever gave up on our circumstances. You persevere.... You grow.... You embrace life in all its glory and all its trials. You think I have never had problems?" She paused, then continued.

"I have had plenty of problems. I never spent time in jail, but I was pregnant with your brother and alone at age sixteen during the depression in Mexico with nothing to my name and only two friends. My parents kicked me out when Rayaldo was born.

"I found a way. I didn't fight my circumstances. I saw them as lessons. I learned from them. So did your father. He built an empire, and despite his flaws he provided for you and me all those years. He felt empty. He felt depressed. But mostly he was exhausted.

"Life has kinks, miho. They're there to make us better. But it only works if you let it. You're running away, Ray. You're hiding from life and the truth. You blame your failures on others or bad luck. You'll never get anywhere like that. Face up to what's right in front of you. Lift your head up. Be a man, miho. Be a man."

Ray was not moved.

"All right, Kouris … Gonzalez whatever your fuckin' name is. Time's up. Let's go," the guard announced. That gave Conchita the opportunity to leave. She watched as the guard ushered her son out of the visiting area.

Ray turned and gave her one last look, one that conveyed disdain. It was a look of rejection, like from an abandoned dog at the pound, searching for an explanation. Before the door shut, she was consumed by her son's expression.

***

The judge slammed his gavel with authority to get the attention of everyone in the courtroom. Judge Galvan had been in this chair for a few years now, and there had been no serious disruptions in his courtroom until last month when a bitter divorce case got out of hand. The attorneys couldn't control their respective clients. It might have been okay if it had been confined to yelling. But it wasn't.

Judge Galvan noticed sudden movement in front of him as the bailiff hurriedly approached the plaintiff's table. The husband, a former Recon Marine who knew how to hold his fists for close quarters combat, now walked stridently toward the petitioner's table.

A swing by the man revealed the reason for the bailiff's sudden movement. His right fist was headed for his wife. At the last minute, the bailiff used a defensive move he had learned in Army Special Forces to wedge his forearm as a shield protecting the woman against the assault. He saved her, and the Recon Marine was imprisoned after that. It was the next day that Judge Galvan bought the Colt .45 he now kept under his seat on the dais.

The prosecutor presented Ray's case. "Your Honor, the state of New Mexico brings a charge against Ray Gonzalez Kouris for voluntary manslaughter, reckless driving, driving under the influence, intentional disregard for human life and numerous other New Mexico motor vehicle operator statutes. The defendant has been held without the ability to post bail awaiting this trial. He waived his right for pre-trial conference. Last month, you ordered jury selection and set a date for the trial."

"How do you plead to these charges, Mr. Kouris?" Judge Galvan asked.

"Not guilty, Your Honor," said Christina Rodriguez, Ray's court-appointed attorney. Rodriguez, a recent graduate from the UNM Law School, having passed the New Mexico Bar, had been practicing in the Public Defender's Office for almost a year. Although she was a capable attorney, this was her first serious defense case.

After the jury heard the attorneys' opening statements, testimony proceeded through questioning of witnesses, including an expert witness in psychology from NMSU. Cross-examination by opposing counsel was routine. Evidence included a room filled with large pictures of the wreck and opened beer cans recovered from Ray's car. The testimony revealed that Ray had consumed eleven servings of beer or other alcohol less than thirty minutes before the wreck.

Evidence also revealed that Ray was angry at the white bartender for not serving him more and had left the bar hurling some Spanish profanities toward all white people, vowing he would get back at them for what they had done to him. A witness saw him weaving across the median on several occasions with his arm outside and his middle finger gesturing toward a dozen white drivers. All witnesses testified that he was agitated and unmistakably infuriated at them for no reason.

Ray was stoic during the testimony, periodically turning around and sneering at both his mother and the family of the man killed in the wreck. The jury took notice of his contemptuous behavior. More than once the judge had to warn Ray's attorney to restrain her client.

Dr. Doris Henderson, a youthful psychology professor at NMSU testified as to the probable mental state of Kouris before the wreck. She answered several questions from both the prosecution and defense and held her ground when the defense attorney challenged her trustworthiness as a witness because she had a bias toward Hispanics.

Her reply refuted that allegation when she revealed that she had been married to a Hispanic man for more than five years.

Henderson had a professional interest in making a good show. Earlier, she had convinced the judge to let her bring a few exemplary psychology students to observe the trial during her testimony. A star student, Jordan Valles, watched intently and took copious notes from her seat near the back of the hall.

The gavel came down with even more authority than when it first started three days before. The jury delivered its decision to the judge. The verdict was guilty on all charges, including voluntary manslaughter. The racially mixed jury reflected the socio-economic makeup of Las Cruces, and was unanimous in its verdict. With sentencing set for next week, Ray was facing prison time.

***

Conchita buried her head as she had done every time Ray let her down. She was sobbing this time. One son killed, another in prison. Convinced she had been a failure as a mother, she remembered the words of Padre Juan and again tried to forgive herself.

She watched Ray's use of gang gestures, flinging his hands and arms in the air. This will not help his sentence, she realized. She noticed the dignified elation among the dead man's family members. After several months of waiting, they would now be granted justice.

Ray had been led into the courtroom in leg and hand shackles, no doubt to validate the scorn he deserved from the judge and courtroom. He had wantonly killed a man and put many others in danger. He was a menace to society and needed to be portrayed as such. Stanley Haas, the police chief for more than twenty-five years, agreed with the district attorney that the shackles would remain attached to his arms and legs over his bright orange jumpsuit.

***

Four weeks later, Ray's attorney was waiting at the table. The bailiff made a public display of securing his shackles to the steel hook embedded in the concrete floor near the defendant's table. Rodriguez offered a kind smile. She had been cleared by the bailiff to bring Ray a donut.

"Just don't try to use it for a jailbreak," Rodriguez cautioned, putting the weakest smile on Ray's face.

The gavel struck hard and the courtroom became silent as the sentencing hearing began.

Rodriguez and Ray faced the judge who announced, "I will hear from both the prosecuting attorney and the defense attorney and finally, the victims will have an opportunity to speak. District Attorney, you're up first."

The court stenographer recorded both attorneys' statements. Now the victims had a chance to speak to the judge. Two young adult women were near the front of the seating area waiting to be called to speak. Both had prepared remarks they read from the witness box.

The two sisters stood together, sobbing. Their testimony was akin to a relay race where one daughter who could not go on, passed the baton to the other to continue the race. It was effective and noticed by everyone except Ray. Even his mother was moved by the loss of the two young women.

When testimony concluded, the judge closed the hearing and cleared his throat, preparing to speak. Everyone was silent, awaiting what would be a momentous decision.

Judge Galvan spoke, "The matter before this court today is the sentence to be imposed on the prisoner who has been convicted by a jury of his peers. The criminal act of voluntary manslaughter is a third-degree felony in New Mexico. The remaining crimes hold various mandatory minimum sentences. When any criminal act results in the death of one or more persons, the court may add these sentences consecutively to determine a combined sentence. Reaching that decision is based on the court's perception of the prisoner's lack of contrition. That was the basis for my decision.

"Bailiff, please have the prisoner rise and face the court."

The bailiff spoke, "Mr. Kouris please stand and face the court." Ray and Rodriguez stood together.

"Mr. Kouris, you stand convicted of seven counts of violations of New Mexico Motor Vehicle Law as well as the crime of voluntary manslaughter. A unanimous jury decision found you guilty on all counts on all charges. Do you have anything to say before I pronounce sentence for these crimes?"

"No, Your Honor. Let's get on with it. Toss the damn Mex'can in jail. Throw away the key."

"Mr. Kouris, you got it!" Galvan cleared his throat again.

"Mr. Ray Gonzalez Kouris, I sentence you to a total of thirty years in prison at the La Tuna Correctional Facility in Anthony, New Mexico." A hush saturated the entire courtroom before the judge continued. "The aggregate of thirty years is based on fifteen years maximum sentence for manslaughter and the remaining fifteen years aggregated from half a dozen remaining charges including reckless driving, reckless homicide, driving under the influence, reckless endangerment, driving with an expired license, driving without a valid driver's license, and drinking alcohol while operating a vehicle." The judge paused before continuing. "You will serve this sentence that cannot be reduced for any reason and may not be commuted except for cause. You are not eligible for parole at any time during your sentence."

"Mr. Kouris, you are a menace to society. From where I sit, thirty years isn't enough to pay for the crime you committed against two young ladies here in the courtroom today and against the citizens of the State of New Mexico. But it's all I can give you. I've done the math. Your disregard for human life, even your own, is tragic and shameful.

This court has noticed your contempt for these proceedings and for the family of your victim. Your conduct has been reprehensible both before the wreck and during this trial. Mr. Kouris, ya got what you asked for and ya got what's comin' to you. Now get out of my courtroom and the presence of these respectable citizens."

***

Conchita did not race to the front of the courtroom and embrace her son. Rather, she walked slowly to the small cluster that had gathered around the two daughters, leaving her son to be led out by the bailiff. Conchita waited her turn and introduced herself as Ray's mother and then, when a hush fell over the group, she addressed the sisters.

"You two have endured unspeakable pain over the past few months. I want you to know that I am very sorry for your loss, especially since it was my son who caused it. Please accept my sorrow for what my son has caused." She paused to calm her racing heart. She was now the subject of verbal scorn by half a dozen friends surrounding the sisters. Nevertheless, she regained her resolve and continued.

"I learned your father was Catholic and a member of our church only after he died. I want you to know that I donated in your father's name to St. Anne's. I made the gift when this first happened. I also attended your father's funeral."

The women looked shocked but remained silent. "Because of the donation, there will be a stone memorial erected in the small garden beside the church. It will honor your father's Patron Saint, Christopher. I learned from Padre Juan that your father had chosen St. Christopher when he was confirmed into the church as a young man in St. Louis.

"The carved stone memorial is complete and will be installed next week. You and your entire family are invited to attend a formal Mass in your father's name to be held in the church garden."

Conchita, who had managed to stem her tears, handed each woman an envelope then quickly turned and left the courtroom. The sisters stood in silent awe. It was apparent they could find no words to respond to the mother of their father's murderer. They could only embrace each other and let the tears flow.

-33-

NEW MEXICO, 1973

The massive pecan trees on Horseshoe Field at Hadley Circle on the NMSU campus had yielded fruit. The term, horseshoe, referred to a U-shaped road built at the original college site in 1888. The wide semi-circle surrounding the large open field was lined with buildings. Pecans from the overloaded trees dotted the median between the two roads.

It was the fall semester of 1973. Jordan Valles had started college at age seventeen. In addition to starting young, she entered as a sophomore by passing several college level entrance exams. Now she was in her junior year.

Zach's engineering classes were mostly in the area around Jett Hall. Jordan's psych. classes were close but on the upper part of the horseshoe in Science Hall.

Jordan sat on the ground, leaning up against a large pecan tree with her knees forming a desk for her Psych 301 textbook. She was reading, holding her book with the left hand and taking notes in a notebook with her right hand propped on another text on the grass.

The morning was warm for late fall. Although Jordan was engrossed in her studies, she kept glancing furtively at the young man crossing her field of vision as he walked toward Jett Hall. Slung over his exposed muscular right arm was what looked like a military backpack. He returned the clandestine glimpses, unsuccessfully avoiding detection.

"Hi." Zach broke the ice as he moved within earshot of the attractive young woman. She looked up.

"Hi." Returning the greeting, she let her gaze last long enough to convey modest interest.

"I'm Zach. Zachary Martin. I am in engineering," he said.

"Jordan Valles. I'm arts and science, majoring in psychology." She added that part, hoping to allay the common ridicule ascribed to arts and science majors … that they're airheads.

"Oh, you're a doctor," Zach replied.

His comment grabbed her attention. He had paid her the first compliment she received for her degree choice. "Well, no. Not yet anyway," she replied, laughing. "I've got to finish this class and another year and a half. That looks like a military backpack," she added to keep the conversation going and maybe learn something about this guy.

She had dated some young men over the last year, but no one really piqued her interest. Zachary Martin had possibilities written all over his trim, muscular physique. She hoped her body language wasn't too obvious then realized she was touching her hair nervously. She stopped. "Yeah, I was in the Marine Corps. I am back from Vietnam a couple of years now."

Jordan sensed he wanted to get that fact out front before he went any further. She knew that many young women were turned off by the war and by veterans for their participation.

"This is an NVA pack I found while there. Theirs were better than ours."

She acknowledged the comment with a nod and said, "Thank you, Zach, for serving our nation. You must be brave." Her voice reflected both empathy and sincere respect.

***

Zach would always remember the moment as the first one where Jordan got his attention. She wasn't like other girls he had met. She was clearly Hispanic but spoke English with no appreciable accent. She dressed modestly and did not flaunt her shapely figure with short skirts or form-fitting clothes that could double as a swimsuit. He thought her glasses made her look intelligent. Later he would learn she didn't conform to the popular image of an arts and science major.

She was not only smart, but also drop-dead beautiful. As Zach edged closer, his eyes and slight smile conveyed his interest.

"Thank you for saying that. Jordan, I'm glad to meet you. I am headed to an engineering lab for a two-hour class. I saw you studying out here all by yourself and I just wanted to say hello. Maybe later we can grab a burger and you can tell me about psychology."

"Yeah. I'd like that," she said. She hoped her quick response assured Zach of her interest.

"I get out at 11:30. Can I meet you here and we'll go to Blake's?"

"Sure, Zach. I have an exam and should get out about then too. I look forward to 11:30."

***

Zach's two-hour lab ended a few minutes before Jordan's test. Seeing that Zach was already at the tree waiting, she walked across Horseshoe Field, and the two made eye contact while still a distance away.

She smiled, noticing that Zach's stare was transfixed on her. Feeling awkward, she switched her gaze toward a group of ROTC cadets drilling in the field.

Zach's late model Firebird was parked at the curb on the north side of Horseshoe Road. As they approached, the pair immediately felt comfortable with each other.

"A yellow car," Jordan proclaimed.

"Yup, my favorite color." Zach opened Jordan's door and held it for her. She thought back to her dating life and realized this chivalrous act was another first.

They both ordered green chili cheeseburgers from Blake's Lottaburger, a drive-in on Valley Drive, a few miles from campus. They talked about things like education, hopes, dreams and aspirations—as much as their short class break would allow.

Within an hour, Jordan could tell that Zach thought their future was sealed. Jordan would need a bit more persuading.

When they arrived at the lot where Jordan had left her car, Zach saw another reason for their compatibility.

"Right here," she said, pointing at the yellow VW. "That's my car."

"Really?" he responded with zeal. "You drive a yellow car too?"

"Yes, my father bought it for me when I started college. It was a reward for getting an academic scholarship. Yellow is my favorite color. As a psych major, I learned that it means I'm cheerful, enthusiastic, optimistic and confident. I'm all those things, Zach. It also means I am sometimes overly critical and judgmental," she added, her demeanor turning solemn.

Immediately she smiled again. "And you probably have all those characteristics too, if you like yellow as much as I do." She leaned over to give him a peck on the cheek and then slid out, but not before stuffing a small note in his shirt pocket. "Here's my number. Call me."

He did.

-34-

New Mexico, 1973

They had shared four dates: a local movie, a dinner, the Alamogordo Zoo and once to White Sands National Park on a Sunday afternoon. Meeting the parents was a special event, though. It was Thanksgiving and Jordan got her mother to persuade Bartolome to let her invite a special friend to their family dinner.

Earlier Jordan had told her parents that Zach spoke fluent Spanish. Of course, her father wanted to know his name and where he was from.

Jordan greeted Zach at the front door. He noticed her parents standing inside. "Buenos tardes," he said.

Bartolome welcomed Zachary into their home using familiar Spanish and wished him a Happy Thanksgiving. "Bienvenidos. Feliz Dia de Accion de Gracia." He introduced himself and his wife. "Soy Bartolome. Ella es mi esposa, Catarina. Y tu conoces Jordan (and you know Jordan)," he added.

Zach felt the handgrip of a man who knew labor and could easily take care of himself despite his diminutive size. His brown hands were rough with permanent callouses. Zach saw lines on a russet brown face that seemed derived more from wisdom than age. Jordan's father was young and strong in spirit but gracefully old with experience.

"Buenos tarde ustedes. Con mucho gusto, señor y señora." Zach returned the greeting but replied in more formal Spanish to convey respect. Jordan's mother, noticing that, winked at Jordan as Zachary moved past them.

Bartolome studied the tall young man and saw immediately why his daughter was attracted to him. He was sturdy in bearing, not easily intimidated. He was comfortable with the Mexican culture, speaking fluent Spanish. Zach had looked straight into his eyes and spoken formal Spanish with the accent of a native Mexican. He also spoke with confidence, and more importantly, respect.

I like him already, Bartolome thought. He also gave Jordan a wink and she beamed at her dad with a joyful smile.

The table was huge with more than four place settings. Bartolome led him past the dining room and motioned for him to sit on the sofa across from his chair. Jordan sat beside him.

"We have another guest coming, Zach. My good friend, Enrique Garcia and his family are joining our little fiesta. We've never done this before.

"Enrique is an old friend I have known since I was a child in Anthony. I hear you are from Deming. You grew up on a farm. Is that right?"

"Yes, sir. I was born on that farm in 1950. I lived there until I turned eighteen when I joined the Marine Corps and got to see the world."

"And I hear you are a war hero, too." Zach was dumbfounded. He had not even told Jordan about that.

"I talked to some friends of mine in Deming. They say you rescued several other Marines under fire … risked your life." Bartolome continued heaping praise on the former Marine.

Jordan looked stunned. She never knew this part of Zach's past.

"And you knew about this?" she asked her father.

"Your friend is a hero, miha." Her father turned toward her and winked again. No young man that she would bring for Thanksgiving Dinner would escape a background check by her protective father.

"And I remember your father, too. A good man," Bartolome said. "I bought mesquite roots that he dug up with his Caterpillar for firewood. We were regular customers back then. I used to get a load every year for cooking venison at the church fiesta in Apodaca Park."

Again, Jordan looked at him with a bemused smile. "So, Dad, you're saying that Zach and I are almost cousins?" she asked, tongue-in-cheek winking at Zach. The question did not elicit an answer.

The doorbell rang again. It was Bartolome's best friend, Enrique Garcia, his wife Mariana and their older child, Fernando. Although Fernando was twenty-three, he was autistic and not capable of independent living. His parents tried to introduce him into social settings like this to acculturate him into society.

Sitting at the table, the group exchanged brief greetings and quieted for a prayer spoken by Bartolome.

"En el nombre del Padre, el Hijo, y el Espiritu Santo. Gracias a Dios por nos familia y amigos y por sus bendiciones. Gracias a Dios. (In the name of the Father, the Son, and the Holy Spirit. Thanks be to God for our family and friends and for your blessings. Thank you, God)." Everyone, even Zach, gave the sign of the cross.

As they ate the delicious meal prepared by Catarina, small talk permeated the conversations, some in English, some in Spanish and a mixture of each. Nicknamed Tex-Mex this combination of English and Spanish in a conversation was not uncommon but considered an inferior dialect.

"Enrique let's speak in one of the other languages," urged Bartolome at one point. Catarina nodded in approval and Mariana poked her husband in the ribs.

"This is not a construction site," she said to him under her breath.

It was then that the conversation focused on construction. Enrique asked Zach if he knew construction, "Tu sabes construer, verdad?"

Zach, responding in English, said, "Yes, I do. I feel like I was born into it on the farm. But I've been working my way through school by framing houses for Dale Bellamah during breaks and on the weekends. Things are a bit slow now though."

"We should use him on some of our projects sometime, primo," Enrique suggested to Bartolome, using the Spanish term, cousin, as a moniker for his close friend. "We have plenty to do, and he needs the work."

"I am close to an engineering degree … about a year away," Zach explained. "It's not that I don't want to do construction work. I love it. I just found something I like even more … engineering design. It seems to come easy for me and I can do it well."

Bartolome leaned back in his chair to absorb the idea. He had been considering hiring an engineer and providing a different kind of service for his clients. Every time he got a large job proposal, he had to hire engineering and architectural services for design work which was expensive. He estimated that their work cost him as much as twenty per cent of his bid price. Anything over that ate into his profit margin. "If you could hire a full-time engineer who really knew construction, you could grow the business and improve the bottom line," Enrique said.

"Enrique, that's a good idea," Bartolome said. "Zachary, when you graduate, do you want to work for your girlfriend's father?" He grinned slyly at Jordan.

***

Only three months into their relationship, Zach said the 'L' word to Jordan. It was the Christmas season when Zach and Jordan attended Sunday morning Mass. Jordan was becoming more assured about their future together. Zach was locked into his decision.

"Jordan, can we go for a drive later? I wanna show you something." She looked up into his eyes and responded positively, as she always did to his invitations.

"I'll be back to pick you up after I change clothes. Let me get dressed in something more casual than a suit."

Although Zach was not Catholic, he would gladly go anywhere just to be with Jordan. Before Mass, she had schooled him on some Catholic protocol. He was always eager to take the lesson.

Taking Zach's cue, Jordan changed into casual Sunday-afternoon attire and waited, catching up on some weekend homework.

Soon they were walking along the meandering pedestrian path to the museum. They held hands in the cool, New Mexico winter. Behind the building ahead, blue skies framed the purple Organ Mountains that seemed to have caught and held onto white clouds that couldn't escape the towering peaks, clustered tightly together. During a clear day, the peaks grouped together resembling a pipe organ, hence the name.

The emblazoned sign as they entered the museum grounds announced their destination: The New Mexico Farm and Ranch Heritage Museum.

"What are we doing here?" asked Jordan who had never been there before.

"You'll see," Zach answered with a knowing smile.

Inside the museum, Zach fit right in. Cowboy boots, Wrangler jeans boasting a championship rodeo buckle on a western belt, a plain white shirt and a ball cap, typical modern ranch-hand attire.

Zach paid for their tickets and they wandered around, soon passing through the kiddie area where a slide protruded from the second story of a large red barn. Next, they walked through the dining hall toward the exhibit rooms. There they saw displays for farms and ranches. Zach stopped abruptly when he came upon the reason for the trip. He gestured toward some pictures on the far wall.

"Jordan, you never got to meet my parents. But here they are," he announced.

"That's my father holding the Grand Champion bull and the trophy he won, and that's me holding the end of the halter lead, helping him. I was five years old.

"And here's my mom. She's showing off a purple Grand Champion ribbon at the same Luna County Fair for knitting and crochet work she did regularly.

"And here is my Uncle Herb with a Reserve Champion steer he raised when he was in FFA in high school … a long time ago.

"And here's my brother … well … really my half-brother more or less."

"Your brother?" she asked, incredulous. "Your brother? Zach, the little boy is black. You're white. Your parents are white. How could he be your brother?"

"I should have said, adopted brother. We grew up like brothers. We even cut our palms one time when we were ten to share blood with each other—to be blood brothers—something we picked up from Daniel Boone or somethin' else on TV."

Jordan stood still, listening, as if any movement might stop Zach's flow of words.

"My parents adopted Billy when he was five years old, just about my age. I was an only child when he ended that role. Billy's parents and Lynda Jo, his older sister died in a fire in their home in Deming. He and I were inseparable, growin' up. We always regarded each other as best friends. We were even in Vietnam at the same time, just in different places, and he was in Force Recon. It was a lot more dangerous than what I did.

"We always keep in touch, like brothers. But I still consider him my best friend. You'll have to meet him some day, Jordan. He's working and living in Albuquerque now. He got a scholarship to UNM. Go figure! But he's always been a big part of my life."

"What were things like when you grew up together? Was there any racism or …?" Jordan didn't know how to finish the question.

"There was no racism in our hometown because everyone knew us and knew the circumstances. The citizens of Deming never looked down on black people. They had an incredible tolerance for multi-cultural mixtures. Just like Las Cruces, there were plenty of mixed marriages between Anglos and Hispanics. But in Deming, even for blacks, it was nothing like the events elsewhere in the country."

"What do you mean?" she asked.

"Well, Deming had a reputation that was like that. There was one incident in high school we all were given as a lesson in humanity. The football team had traveled by school bus to Silver City for a Friday night game. The band came too but in a bus behind us. Billy was in the first bus because he was quarterback of the football team. Another black student rode in the second bus because he was in the band.

"The buses stopped at a restaurant so we could eat dinner before the game. Everyone went in and sat down including Billy and Tom. That's when the trouble began. The waitresses hadn't even taken our orders when we began to hear commotion near the entrance. The manager of the establishment told the team coach that he would gladly invite everyone to eat except 'those two,' pointing at Billy and Tom. He said he would not serve them, and they had to leave. Billy didn't know what to do, but he and Tom tried to exit the building when the band director stopped them at the door, put his arm around Billy and Tom and led them back to where the manager and the coach were still arguing."

Jordan was transfixed on the story. Zach told it like he was there. In fact, he was there, seeing it all again. While Billy was the quarterback for the team, Zach was a linebacker.

"Well, the manager wasn't budging and all of Deming's forty-two students were already seated and watching the exchange. None of them had touched their drinks. They waited nervously for the outcome of the exchange.

"After the coach and the band director huddled for the briefest time, Coach Firkins made an announcement to the entire restaurant. Looking at the manager with pity and shaking his head, he said in his loudest coach's voice, 'Everyone get back on the bus. We're leaving and finding another place to eat.' The entire crowd cheered, including me, and we all scampered toward the bus.

"Once we had boarded the bus, cheering erupted again."

Zach had cleaned up the ending a bit for Jordan's benefit. What Coach Firkins said to Deming's football team and band was more akin to, "Let's dump this shithole and the asshole that runs it. Get on the bus, everybody." That's why everyone cheered. Not only did he speak to the students, he spoke their language.

"Well, the manager was livid," Zach continued. "I'm sure he thought he had a gold mine in revenue coming, but Deming High School had just taken that away. The entire student body remembered that lesson."

"Oh, Zach!" exclaimed Jordan. "You must've been so proud."

"You bet I was. Billy learned how much all the students loved him, if there was ever any doubt. But more importantly, the leadership— the coach and band director—made it a teachable moment. It was an important life lesson for all of us.

"We won the game, by the way. I think that event got our adrenaline pumping.

"My brother, a black man," Zach continued. "We always called each other brothers because we were. People who don't know us, don't understand. They think we're referring to a cultural brotherhood ... you know, being a 'brother.' But Billy and I *are* brothers."

Jordan took Zach's hand in hers, raised it to her mouth, and kissed it gently.

The display where they had stopped acknowledged the contributions of pioneers in settling nearby Deming, New Mexico. Oliver Martin figured prominently in the recognition. Zach showed Jordan more about his father. Jordan read that before he died recently, he had amassed three large farms and a ranch.

Still holding Zach's hand, Jordan turned to face him, staring into his eyes. Finally, with great respect in her voice, she asked, "Zach, what happened after your father passed away?"

"Well we buried him, of course." Zach's uncharacteristic flippant reply lightened the seriousness of the moment.

Jordan responded with an elbow in his stomach. Chuckling, Zach feigned pain. Then regaining his composure, replied, "Jordan, when my mom passed away, my father sold everything, except for our home farm. He had an attorney establish an educational trust for his grandchildren. That would be for Billy's and my children, if we ever have any," he added, rolling his eyes playfully.

"When Dad died, he left me and Billy the home farm. We still have it. We leased it out so we could finish school, but I'm not happy with the tenant. I think he has wrecked the family home, and he never pays rent on time." Looking downward, Zach shook his head.

Slowly he raised his gaze to meet Jordan's. He spoke with sincerity. "Jordan, you only know me from my present life. I wanted you to have a glimpse of my upbringing like you have shared with me over the past month. There's a lot about me that you don't know. And there are things I've done in my life that I am ashamed of ... things I wish I'd never done."

He lowered his head and her gaze followed. He looked up again. "Jordan, there's no better way I can say this...." Staring into her eyes, he held her shoulders and made his announcement.

"I love you. I love you with a capital L." Before she could respond, he touched an index finger to her lips.

"I knew I loved you almost from the time I met you. I feel like I never knew what love was until I met you." Zach felt a shiver pass through her like a tiny earthquake.

"I feel like the love I have for you doesn't originate from me but comes through me, like I'm its conduit. For the first time in my life, I feel true love … not affection, not lust, not intense fondness but genuine love. Well maybe some lust," he added, breaking the tension, and causing her to grin.

Then, serious again, he added, "Jordan, I truly love you more than I have ever loved anyone or anything. I thought you should know."

It was her turn. She put her arms around him and let him hold her. She held his embrace for almost a minute, long enough to blink away the tears forming in her eyes. Before speaking, she let her arm drop from his back and shifted slightly backward to gauge his reaction.

"Zach, as I'm sure you can tell, my parents really like you. I am happy for that.

"I care for you, but I've only known you for a few weeks. I have strong feelings for you." His head took a slight dip, now focusing on the turquoise pendant around her neck.

"I don't think I can say what you want to hear…. Right now." She studied Zach thoughtfully.

His body language was as clear as a church bell.

"Zach. I'm not going anywhere. I like where we are right now. Please know that I have enjoyed these past few weeks more than any time in my life." He looked up. His crest-fallen countenance faded some as Jordan continued.

"I was born April twenty-third, Zach. I am a Taurus. That's a bull, you know. We Tauruses are stubborn, like the bulls you rode as a youth." She was pointing to the picture of him at a rodeo on the display.

Zach glanced at the picture and grinned, knowing he was riding a steer and not a bull.

"It's just that I need time, Zach. I need time." She again moved closer and accepted his embrace. "I need time. I'm not going anywhere. I like this." She whispered the last few words into his chest. There in the museum hall with no audience to deter them, they held their embrace until—

"I can wait!" Zach declared suddenly to the empty hall, his voice echoing with the authority of a Marine Corps drill instructor.

Frozen within his embrace, Jordan's eyes popped open and she jumped as if awakened by a loud alarm clock.

"I can wait," he said again, this time whispering in her ear. They spent the remainder of the afternoon strolling and holding hands.

The day ended at Jordan's front door with a gentle kiss.

As Zach drove back to his apartment, he tuned the radio to KGRT, the local AM station and heard a song that gave him shivers. The acoustic guitar plunked familiar chords. He loved that tune by the Seekers and turned up the volume so he could sing along.

"There is always someone for each of us they say. And you'll be my someone forever and a day.

I could search the whole world over until my life is through, But I know I'll never find another you."

He passed a jewelry store on El Paseo Drive and noted its hours of operation displayed on the door.

"Valentine's Day," he said aloud. "Yes, Valentine's Day."

***

It was January and a fresh, light snow had fallen over the Rio Grande Valley. The snow glistened with reflections from a full moon. Jordan drove home from visiting Zach's apartment, their seventeenth date, not that either was counting. Zachary filled her thoughts, his scent, his clean apartment, the way he walked, his kindness. And his kisses. His kisses were divine.

Her drive home from Zach's apartment normally took fifteen minutes. Pulling up to the curb in front of her house, she realized she couldn't remember anything about the drive. She parked her VW on the street and entered through the side door using her house key. The porch light stayed on all night and it was past her father's bedtime. She hoped her mother might still be up reading in the living room.

"I think I'm in love," she whispered to her mother as she removed her coat in the hall.

Catarina responded in Spanish. "Claro que si (Of course, you are)." She smiled knowingly. "Zachary is a fine young man. And you've been in love with him for some time now, miha."

Jordan stood, transfixed on her mother who was now grinning at her. She was immobile, still holding her coat.

"You're not the only one who understands human nature. Just because you're a psychology major…." Her mother stood, approached her daughter and released Jordan's grip from her coat.

-35-

NEW MEXICO, 1974

Zach had made a 7:00 pm restaurant reservation on Valentine's Day. It was a Thursday night, and both he and Jordan had classes tomorrow, but he was sure about the timing. He had visited Glenn Cutter Jewelers and selected a beautiful half-carat diamond in a gold setting. He tucked the ring away in a jeweler's box in his jacket pocket. The restaurant had informed him the dessert menu was ready.

Jordan and Zach walked into La Posta Restaurant just before their reservation time and the hostess seated them immediately with a knowing smile.

They ordered Chili Rellenos and Tostadas Compuestas, respectively. They shared small talk and a single beer between them. The evening was special for both. It was the anniversary of the day they met just four months before, October fourteenth. A lot had happened in those four months. Jordan had grown close to this young man and spent her nights wondering about their future. Her closest confidante was her mother, who insisted that she was like a rose in bloom.

Jordan had told Zach about her love for him last month. She told him that her mother convinced her she had been in love for some time now. She knew it was her stubborn nature that delayed her admission. But now it seemed right. She studied Zach's eyes lovingly as he turned to face her.

Feeling full, Jordan resisted the dessert menu at first.

"Jordan, you must have dessert," Zach insisted. "It's not Valentine's Day without a sweet." At this urging, she relented, and the hostess brought the special dessert menu meant just for her.

She opened the menu and found a yellow highlighted box on the right fold with red lettering that read:

"Jordan,

When we met, I knew my life was complete. My vision transformed from black and white to Technicolor. My feet changed from walking to dancing. My thoughts went from words to poetry. I felt love for the first time.

You make my life brighter with every smile. I want to spend the rest of my life with you. I pledge my life to you. I love you with a capital L. Jordan, will you marry me?

Zach"

She saw that Zach had placed an open jeweler's box on her empty dessert plate while she was reading the proposal. There in front of her, in a beautiful yellow-gold setting, was the largest diamond she had ever seen. Barely able to focus, she was out of breath and her heart raced. She had not drawn a breath since she opened the menu.

"Oh Zach! Oh Zach!" It was all she could utter. She couldn't make her mouth obey. In her cupped hands, she sought refuge for her naked facial expression.

Looking back at the menu to make sure she hadn't misread it she then sought his eyes and finally summoned the composure to answer the awaiting proposal.

"Yes," she announced in a clear, distinct voice. The entire restaurant clientele, realizing what was going on, started applauding.

"Yes, of course, I will marry you, Zach. I have loved you for some time now." She reached for her new fiancé and held his head with her soft palms.

"Of course. I'll be proud to be called Mrs. Martin." That may have sounded odd for a time when women's liberation was coming of age, but she didn't care. She now knew that she wanted to be Mrs. Jordan Martin forever.

Jordan was surprised when Zach drove her directly home. She had expected they might enjoy each other's intimate company at Zach's apartment. She could see a smile on her new fiancé's face but misinterpreted the reason for his grin. She thought they were happy for the same reason, the engagement. That was true. But Zach had another surprise waiting.

Coming home at 10:00, Jordan saw unusual hints. The living room lights were on. Her parents were still up. Waiting up for her? And Zachary?

Jordan learned the reason after she unlocked the side door and her father welcomed the couple inside. That had never happened before.

They greeted Jordan's parents with smiles and a wink from Zach who followed her through the door.

"Come in, miho," It was the first time Bartolome called Zachary "son."

Jordan whirled around and addressed Zach, "You told them before you asked me?"

Her father saved Zachary. "Miha, he asked us before he asked you. He asked for your hand in marriage. He wanted to get our blessing first. Of course, we said yes but only if you did."

"We had to stay up to hear about the proposal," Catarina interjected.

Now Jordan faced Zach. "You didn't," she said, her tone challenging.

"Yes, I did. I respect your parents as much as I respect you, my future wife."

That night, they set the wedding date for November twenty-third, a Saturday. It was near Thanksgiving and the same date Zachary's parents had been married in 1930. He wanted to honor them, and Jordan was supportive of the gesture. They hoped the priest and the church would be available.

***

Pre-Cana was set. Zachary and Jordan would attend the classes required of every marriage-bound couple in the Catholic church. The classes, spread out over several months, were led by the priest along with a married Catholic couple.

The course covered many aspects of married life including spirituality, conflict resolution, finances, careers, intimacy, children, and commitment. The name pre-Cana was taken from the second chapter of John where Jesus turned water into wine at the village of Cana in Galilee.

"I called it a rata (rat). She called it a raton (mouse)," said the burley Hispanic man, with self-deprecating laughter. "The point is that each of you will have disagreements with your spouse. No one can tell if it's a rat or a mouse without a common frame of reference. We certainly had none. We just disagreed."

The man was Rudolfo Baca, a well-established attorney in Las Cruces. He and his wife, Isadora, had volunteered to serve as St. Anne's pre-Cana counselors for young adults getting married. Tonight, they entertained three couples planning nuptials. Zachary Martin and the future Mrs. Jordan Martin were among them.

Rodolfo was telling the same story he had told all who would listen in his last twenty years of service to the church. It seems that when they first married, he and Isadora had reached a stalemate when each was sure they knew what they had seen running across the floor of their humble abode in Old Mesilla. Rudolfo said it was a rata. Isadora insisted it was a raton. It developed into a squabble.

Looking back on the disagreement, Rudolfo and Isadora agreed it was a specious argument since neither a rat nor a mouse should be in the house where they were raising children. "But that is the point," insisted Rudolfo.

"Who cares what it was," Isadora added. "It needed to be caught in a trap, either a mouse trap or a rat trap."

"It illustrates that you have different perspectives on things. That will happen in your marriages. I guarantee it," Rudolfo exclaimed pointing to each couple for effect.

"Work things out. Agree where you can and respect the other's opinion where you can't," said Isadora.

"Each of you is half of your new life, the life you will share together ... as one," Rudolfo concluded.

The future Mrs. Martin turned toward Zach and in classic Spanish said, "Era un rata? O raton?"

Zach broke up the group with his response. "Ninguno. Es un perro pequeno (Neither. It was a small dog)."

***

The first part of the drive to Jordan's home was filled with laughter until Jordan interrupted the jocularity with an innocent question. "Zach, how much honesty should there be in our marriage?"

When Zachary stopped mid-laugh looking confused, she explained. "Suppose one of us did something really bad, but no one would ever find out about it unless we confessed it to the other. Should we rely on the other to maintain a confidence? Or should we keep the act to ourselves?"

Zach's thoughts went straight to the event in the deepest part of his soul where a secret was buried. His silence was deafening. He could barely drive and couldn't make his tongue work.

"Zach? Did you hear me? What do you think?"

Finally, after several seconds, he attempted an answer. "You mean things that happened before we met? Or after?" As soon as he said it, he knew it was the wrong response to give a psychology major.

"Well, I really meant things that might happen to us as a couple. But what were you thinking of just then?"

Again, he met her question with silence.

"What were you thinking about, Zach?" she probed again.

Zach was silent longer than a truthful, candid response would normally take.

"Zach? What's wrong with you tonight?" Now his tongue loosened just enough to save the night.

"I was thinking of your previous boyfriends and how I'd like to thank them for whatever mistakes they made to make you available." He managed it without hesitation and once again, laughter erupted in the yellow Firebird as they rounded the last corner before Jordan's home.

Woo-wee! That was close, Zach thought on his way back to his apartment. But she's right to ask about things like that. Should I tell her?

-36-

NEW MEXICO, 1975

The wedding was spectacular for a small town. Billy Woods, Zach's brother and best friend served as his best man.

Jordan selected Doris Henderson as her matron of honor because the woman was her mentor. Besides, she didn't want to choose a maid of honor from her four bridesmaids. They were all equally close.

Doris Henderson was older than Jordan; ten years to be exact. But she had served as Jordan's professor for many classes over the last few years and was her faculty adviser. She had also selected Jordan to serve as her graduate assistant for the coming year. Although not best friends, they were close in many ways. Jordan learned as much from their private talks as she did from other professors' semester-long classes.

Henderson, after meeting Zachary for the first time, gave Jordan a thumb's up behind his back. Jordan asked a lot of questions about marriage, those that she felt uncomfortable asking her own mother. She also asked about men in general. It wasn't just about sex, although that topic did come up. She wanted to know how men thought and what men needed from their wives. Henderson fulfilled her role well as Jordan's matron of honor.

The church couldn't be divided equally by guests, those for the bride on one side and those for the groom on the other side, as was the custom. Zach had a few friends but no real family except Billy. St. Anne's Catholic Church only held 150 people. Jordan's family and friends numbered almost that many. About 30 guests had to stand in the rear and on the side aisles.

Padre Juan administered the vows of marriage and conducted the wedding Mass.

At last, they were husband and wife and headed to a Mexican honeymoon for two weeks on the sun-drenched shores of Los Mochis. When they returned, they would move into their wedding present from Jordan's parents. The irony was that Zach had helped build it, although he thought he was building the house for a client of his father-in-law.

Their new three-bedroom home was situated in the foothills of the Organ Mountains just south of the hospital and across I-25 from New Mexico State University (NMSU) where the two had met.

"What a gift!" Zachary announced to Jordan as they rode to the airport. "And with no mortgage."

Jordan told him that she had a hunch since her mother kept hounding her about paint colors and furnishings. Catarina used the ruse of remodeling the family home and seeking her daughter's input. Zach had just graduated with a bachelor's degree and already passed the EIT professional exam. He even had a job lined up with BeeVee Construction since Bartolome had hired Zach as the company engineer. Jordan was scheduled to get her undergraduate degree in the spring and was already pre-enrolled in graduate school where she hoped to earn both a masters and a doctorate in psychology. Their married life started much like that new, popular Carpenter's song, "We've Only Just Begun" that a friend sang at their wedding. Life was good.

-37-

New Mexico, 1977

The 1974 recession had hit the southwest hard. Layoffs or job reductions were happening everywhere especially in construction-related companies.

Bartolome hired Zach that year partly because he needed a job, but also because he was his new son-in-law.

It was a fact: Zachary Martin needed a real job. There were no openings in local engineering or construction firms or any other fields for that matter. He had even interviewed for a salesman job with Maytag in Indianapolis! He was desperate. If BeeVee had not hired Zach, he would have been jobless for the first time in his life. Despite not having a house mortgage, the Martins would have no viable income. The meager salary from BeeVee was a pittance compared to what his degree would normally command, but Zach was happy to have a job, especially in this field.

Bartolome felt his gesture was the responsible thing to do, but two short years later, Zach had more than earned his salary in the newly created position. BeeVee grew a bit and was now poised to take a major leap because of a type of construction practice ultimately called Design-Build.

Bartolome hadn't realized an engineer would add so much to his company.

Reflecting, he knew it had been mostly an act of compassion on his part. His daughter was still in school and working toward a master's degree then.

"Dad look at this. It's an invitation to bid on several multi-housing projects in Albuquerque," Zach said. Bartolome lowered the construction plans he was studying to develop a take-off estimate for another project.

He looked up from his desk over his bifocals and said, "Another bid, Zach? We've got three bids out already. What if we win them all? How will we do the work? We only have a fourteen-man crew," Bartolome explained, hoping his ambitious son-in-law would slow down his project recruitment.

"I know a way we could do it if we did win it," Zach said. "We have fourteen guys. You're right. But six of them are lead-carpenters, almost supervisory level. They're eager for professional growth themselves.

"We could hire temps from Albuquerque for the grunt work and train them. Three of our guys could manage the framing and maybe also serve as project superintendents." He paused, then added, "The other three we leave here to supervise projects and train three of the other eight to be supervisors."

Bart took off his glasses, sat upright and gazed out the construction office window absorbing the thought for a moment. Could he really rely on three of his best guys to bring in an extra million this next year? Or would he lose his shirt?

"Miho, how big is that project exactly?" Bart asked while still staring out the window. Then his gaze shifted to the yellow Volkswagen driving into the yard and up to the construction office trailer. It was Jordan. He recalled buying her the car when she started college. She maintained it well and the air-cooled engine was dependable. It would last through college, he was sure.

He waited for Zach's answer.

"There are fourteen three-story buildings exactly alike on the property," Zach replied. "They each have sixteen apartment units." He took a calculator from his desk drawer and began punching in numbers, finally arriving at a total footprint of 72,706 square feet.

"They are wood frame with slab on grade," he said. "We could frame each of these in a week with a good crew … two weeks max. Piece of cake," Zach added, as Bartolome stared at him in awe.

"Except the bid is due tomorrow at 5:00 pm!"

Scratching his head, Bart paused to think about Zach's proposal. Finally, he said, "Okay, you've convinced me, miho. When you're done socializing with your better half you can work up an estimate. She's outside right now. So, go give her a kiss."

Zach jumped up and looked outside to see Jordan approaching the trailer.

"So, there are no gentlemen here," Jordan said as she walked through the door. "You just watch me walk up but don't even open the door? What's a girl gotta do to get the attention of her two closest men?"

Bart and Zach looked at each other in mock accusation. Bart spoke first. "Your husband is trying his best to work me into an early grave, miha. He wants to get BeeVee more work than we can do by putting half of south Albuquerque on our payroll."

"Thanks, Dad. I owe you one," Zach said teasing, as he approached his wife and gave her a peck on the cheek.

"Actually, honey, Zach is incredible at landing new contracts and even though we're at our limit for our current crew here, he found a project in Albuquerque that could mean over a million dollars extra profit for us next year." Bart leaned back in his chair and, resting his hands atop his head, added, "I think he has a good idea. Do me a favor, miha. Make it a short lunch. I need Zach to work up an estimate for a contract that could put us on the map. Right Zach?"

Zach, now beaming, tipped an invisible hat to his father-in-law, and ushering his wife out the door, said, "I'll be back in thirty minutes."

-38-

NEW MEXICO, 1982

It was spring when Bartolome told him. During the previous six years BeeVee Construction had amassed over $150 million in contracts. Not just in New Mexico but also in surrounding states including Arizona, Texas and Colorado. BeeVee's team of construction and engineering design had set a trend that others now called Design-Build. With Zach having become licensed as a structural engineer through reciprocity with all these states and Bartolome acquiring the corresponding construction contractor licenses, BeeVee had all the work they could handle. With a thirty percent profit margin, they were also the wealthiest in the region and Bart knew why.

"Zach, we need to talk." Bartolome instructed more than asked. "I have to finish some accounts receivable. Then I would like thirty minutes of your time, son. Can you break away soon?" He repositioned his newly acquired radiophone to his other ear for the answer.

"Sure, Dad. Just say where and I'll be there in thirty."

Bart grinned at receiving the answer he wanted. That was exactly what he expected to hear from his almost son. Zach was always loyal, ready, willing and able, always there when Bartolome needed him. The young man was smart, obsessive about quality and fixated on profit, a rare combination for anyone in construction, especially an engineer. Bartolome knew Zach was a big reason for the success BeeVee now enjoyed.

"I'm in the office, son. See you soon," Bartolome answered from inside his sleek new office building. Proudly, he gazed out at the recently installed sign announcing the new name.

The sign was only symbolic. It made the point without flair. Bartolome received the incorporation papers in the mail last week, or rather his attorney did. He and his son-in-law were now equal owners of BeeVee2 Inc. as proclaimed by the sign, their new logo, now in bright yellow.

Jordan was there to celebrate the occasion, as was her mother. Catarina had become a surrogate for Zach whose mom passed away almost ten years ago.

Although their new headquarters were still in Las Cruces, they looked more like the multi-million-dollar enterprise they had become. Situated in the new Wells Fargo Plaza, the building stood at the geographic center of the city.

Smiling with pride, Bartolome walked past the offices of four registered professionals (two architects and two engineers), a full-time bookkeeper and accountant, two office-based project managers, and cubicles for two local field superintendents, a surveyor and an office manager. That didn't include the more than thirty field employees who weren't invited to this get-together.

All the office staff gathered at the entrance, waiting for Zach to return so Bart could present him with a plush corner office the young man thought was for someone else. Aware of the office during the design and construction stages, Zach was told it would belong to Catarina.

Zach was a bit naïve when it came to family. He accepted at face value that the wife of BeeVee's owner would like her own office. But Bartolome and Catarina both knew the space was to be his. It took several months for the company's lawyers to change the name of the corporation and transfer the ownership.

"He doesn't know," Jordan reminded her mother who grinned in response. It seems everyone knew except Zachary Martin. Even his loving, devoted wife hadn't spilled the beans. Just that morning she mentioned to Zach that there was a position for chief engineer at White Sands Missile Range advertised in the Las Cruces Sun News.

Zach brushed it off with his usual response. "Can't do that, dear," he said. "You know why. If I leave the family business, your dad will ask me to give you back. I couldn't do that."

Jordan smiled at his customary pithy comeback and crossed her fingers behind her back.

They were all waiting as if expecting the return of a conquering hero. In some ways he was. BeeVee2 had just won a $5 million-bid on a high-rise engineered, designed and sold by none other than Mr. Zachary Martin, P.E.

When Zach entered the building and saw the crowd gathered in the lobby, he looked around confused. Addressing Bart, he said, "You brought the whole company down to discuss something with me? Are you going to fire me?" Then in his typical playful way, added, "Do I have to give your daughter back?"

At thirty-two, Zach certainly had options for other jobs. Several firms had come after him over the years with offers up to three times his salary at BeeVee. And those were for an office supervisory role. But Zach always turned them down flat.

"I like working half days here … only work from 6 am to 6 pm – half days!" he would explain with a chuckle as he hung up the phone, turning down one headhunter after another.

"Zach, did you happen to see the bright yellow sign as you rolled in here?" Bartolome asked.

"Yeah, I did. Have you called Neon Signs to fix it yet? There was a typo on the board. They put a 'squared' sign over the company name. Must've been smokin' something over there."

"Really, Dad … what's this all about? Am I missin' something?" That's when Jordan interjected, "My dear husband, follow me."

With the swagger of a game show hostess, she guided Zach down the hallway stopping at his new professional home. "The sign is our new company name. And here is the co-owner's new office," she said, waving her arm toward the open door.

From their first date, Zack knew his wife was smarter than he was. She was always faster on the uptake at esoteric jokes or obscure plot lines in movies. She always figured out 'who done it' in TV crime shows before the first commercial. But he wondered why such a big deal was being made over a new company sign and an office for his mother-in-law.

Now aware that his co-workers were watching his every move, Zach turned to Catarina. He knew the joke was on him, but he didn't get the joke. "Mom?"

Catarina merely shrugged. That's when Jordan pulled the office door shut to reveal the name etched on the glass in bright gold letters:

Zachary Martin, P.E. Co-Owner BeeVee2 Inc.

Zachary had never used profanity in front of his parents. Well, at least not these parents. When he had returned home from Vietnam there was one occasion where he was having dinner with his natural parents and his uncle. He inadvertently asked, "Could someone pass the fuckin' peas?" Everyone around the table stared at him in disbelief. He was so accustomed to this parlance in Vietnam, he didn't even realize what he had said.

"Pendejo," he nearly shouted, as if finding a flat tire on his work truck at a jobsite.

The word, commonly used as a profane aspersion and translated literally as pubic hair, stabbed at the crowd's enthusiasm since most of them spoke fluent Spanish. Those that didn't, at least knew Spanish profanity. While it was commonly used on the job site, the unwritten rule at BeeVee was that, under no circumstances would profanity be accepted in the office setting.

Zach slapped a hand over his mouth in embarrassment, and the crowd was silenced. A cricket chirping in a remote corner of the office emphasized the stillness.

With that, a belly-laugh from Bart signaled that Zach's transgression was acceptable under the circumstances. The entire crowd erupted with laughter and applause. Jordan kissed him, his mother-in-law hugged him, his father-in-law shook his hand, and several cameras flashed from the crowd.

One picture would run in the Las Cruces Sun News the next day under the headline:

New Ownership Sets National Course for Local Builder

"Congratulations, my son. You have earned this. You helped make this company what it is today. We can go even further with your leadership. Together we can change history. Well, we've already done that. Nice going, son."

Tears welled in Zach's eyes. "Dad, I don't know what to say. I never expected this. In fact, I don't know what you have in mind for my role here now. I'm used to just coming in and doing the work that's in front of me. Now ... I don't know ... I don't know. What I should do?"

"Nonsense, son. You're a natural leader. The work that you say was right in front of you each day. You put it there, like any good leader. You went out and got it and put it there. That's leadership, like you exhibited in the Marine Corps ... like when you went out on your own and rescued those men in Vietnam ... and under fire. Not just anyone does that. You are a leader. You can take us further than we've ever been. With you helping me at the helm, BeeVee2 can become a nationally ranked construction firm."

Zach didn't hear any of his father-in-law's words past "under fire." He was looking at the floor and re-living the incident at the village, thinking of those men and women … and children. He winced at the memory that had plagued him all these years.

"You don't need to feel uncomfortable, son," Bartolome announced so everyone could hear. "This is your firm as much as it is mine now. Here are the papers to prove it. You now own half of BeeVee2, a Design-Build Firm for the Twenty-first Century. It's yours, Zach!"

Zach felt even more emotional with that statement. It was overwhelming to him. A rare tear slid down his cheek. Jordan was the first to react, quickly embracing him. Catarina followed. By now, the entire family was in a hug-fest in front of the office crowd and a Las Cruces Sun Times reporter who snapped several more photos that would fill a library for notables from the area.

"Now we just have to work out the details of your new salary with our business manager," Bart finished with a sly grin.

-39-

NEW MEXICO, 1982

Saturday morning, six months after the announcement, found Zachary at the St. Anne's Catolico Church. He desperately needed something but could not give it a name. He had become a Catholic and attended Mass there regularly with his wife but never got the spiritual fulfillment he needed. He had heard about confession but had to study up to learn what was involved. He learned that confession was held Saturdays, usually in the evening. He was prepared at least, having called St. Anne's to check on times. The parish secretary told him that confession started promptly at 5:00 pm and it was first come, first served. He considered a private meeting with Padre Juan but decided against it because he had not talked with Jordan yet.

Despite arriving at exactly 5 pm, Zach was fourteenth in line. It was almost dinner time when he finally reached the confessional booth. The sliding door slammed open, causing Zach to be even more skittish than when he arrived.

Padre Juan spoke first. "My child, God blesses you for your act of contrition and confession, a blessed sacrament. Please make the sign of the cross and begin."

Zachary crossed himself and began, "Forgive me Father for I have sinned. I have never been to a confessional before. But I know that I have sinned against my God, my family and humanity." He began with the traditional words he learned from the booklets near the confessional.

Then, with remorse, Zach related the whole story to Padre Juan in its bare truth, as a criminal might confess to a skilled detective. The confession was the longest that day at St. Anne's. In fact, it lasted almost as long as one that Padre Juan remembered from decades before. Another deeply troubled soul.

"My son ..." Padre Juan began with what could have been the same admonition he gave to the young woman some thirty years before. "I know you think you have done something horrible and only God knows what was in your heart and what really happened. May I suggest that we meet privately ... outside the confessional to go into this more ... to help you understand your feelings of guilt?"

Zach was unfamiliar with the customs of the Catholic church, but he was pretty sure this wasn't part of the confessional tradition. On the other hand, he had never spoken with anyone about this subject. It might help to have a listening ear.

Padre Juan's last statement hit him hard.

Holding his head in his right hand, Zach's thoughts would not let him process the invitation. He wondered if speaking with another human without the cloak of privacy would help assuage his guilt for— Then it returned with a vengeance. As if a judge had proclaimed him guilty of murder, his own conscience made the pronouncement. His mind's eye saw Padre Juan sitting high on a dais with fire in his eyes pronouncing a death sentence. Guilt, remorse, and self-reproach, along with claustrophobia prevented higher-level reasoning. It was more than he could take. He yanked open the curtains and ran out of St. Anne's not stopping until he reached his truck, parked three blocks away. Climbing in the cab, his palms were damp, his breathing labored. His psyche was awash with all sorts of dire possibilities including Ft. Leavenworth or worse ... a firing squad.

The piercing sound of Zach's company beeper broke the deafening roar in his brain. He grabbed it and saw the familiar number. Jordan. Damn it! Undoubtedly, she wondered where he was. He hadn't told her where he was going ... just that it was 'business' and he'd be back soon."

Jordan was calling to remind him about their plans for dinner at La Posta. Calling her from the nearest pay phone, Zach tried to sound normal as he assured her that he would be home shortly. He hung up, walked back to his truck still filled with anxiety and wondering about his encounter with Padre Juan.

Now thinking more clearly, he recognized his stoicism for what it was. A defensive measure against self-exposure. Once again, he failed in his attempt to bring the subject out of the mental closet in which it had been cloistered for the last thirty years. Fear was his constant companion. The perfect life he enjoyed was threatened constantly by his actions in 1969. He saw no way out.

He checked his watch. 5:45. The dinner reservation was for 7:00.

He still had time.

***

Back at St. Anne's Padre Juan was flummoxed by the sudden departure and more so by the unexpected return. He was preparing to leave the confessional when the sound of footsteps stopped him. When the drapery to the confessional opened and closed again, a more submissive parishioner sat next to Padre Juan separated only by the divider and circumstances. He spoke first.

"Relax, my son. God lives in your heart. He knows what you are going through because he's going through it with you. He wants you to be free from fear and pain." The silence told Padre Juan that his message was getting through. He waited.

When Zach spoke, his demeanor was calmer. "Father, I will come to see you regularly, but just to talk."

He would do so a dozen times over the course of the next month. Time after time, Padre Juan listened patiently to Zach's story. At last, when Zach was ready to receive it, the father gave him one penance to perform. "My child, your penance is to find a person in need and help them overcome some of life's obstacles." Padre Juan remained non-specific even when pressed about what that meant. He told Zach that it would become clear when the opportunity came.

-40-

New Mexico, 1983

At first, Zach saw the man from a distance. Even meeting on the street after all these years, it was not difficult to recognize Richard. They had been friends in their youth. He was the son of his father's partner. He hadn't heard from Richard since he went to Vietnam out of high school fifteen years ago. A lot had changed for each of them. Zach's star was shining. Richard's not-so-much.

"How're ya, man?" they bellowed to each other at the same time with arms outstretched. Hugs followed and then conversation.

"We're doing all right," Richard said. Zach could tell there was more to the story and pried a little bit.

"Well, the truth is we're down on our luck, man. Harriet and I have been blessed with an adorable baby girl. Her name is Sophie. She came as a blessing but at an inopportune time," he explained, eyes lowered, looking ashamed. "You see, I was in college. We were living on the farm and Dad kept getting threats from the bank about foreclosure. He was making payments but a few weeks late each month. He didn't take it seriously, but he should've.

"One Saturday morning cars and pickups began driving in. A man with a loudspeaker quickly organized an auction, and by noon the farm was not ours anymore. We were stunned. And then the bank president told Dad we needed to be out of the house in a week. That was a few months ago. Mom and Dad moved out of state. They felt disgraced. Harriet and I are in Section 8 housing now, but we'll have to be out of that in May. I don't know what we'll do after that, where we'll go ..." His voice trailed off.

"Those assholes," Zach said, referring to the financial system. He didn't know all the circumstances but expressed outrage in support of his old friend. "Is Harriet working, Richard?"

Richard paused. Then, pulling Zach to the edge of the sidewalk to let people pass, he told Zach about her condition. "That's the other problem. You see, Harriet has been diagnosed with breast cancer and has started chemotherapy. She can't really work. She can barely take care of Sophie. I take over parenting duties and she rests when I come home from my minimum wage job."

Zach bowed his head. "I'm sorry, man. I didn't know. How's she doing?"

Richard seemed more upbeat then before. "She's doing okay. The doctor says she's not in remission yet, but he's hopeful and seems optimistic. He hasn't mentioned surgery, but I'll bet that's where we're headed."

At this point, Zach was reeling from the overwhelming struggles in Richard's life. Then Padre Juan's admonition hit him. "Look for someone down on their luck, someone trying to overcome life's obstacles, someone in need of something you can provide." Then he asked the question.

"So, Richard, you went to college, right? A degree in horticulture wasn't it? What about farming?"

"I'd really like my own farm, but I've got no money and my credit is shot because everyone knows my family's circumstances. I'd love to get back into farming working half-days." He said it in a way that led Zach to believe there was joke in there somewhere. "You know half-days ... 6 am to 6 pm." The two chuckled, both aware of farmers' long hours. Then Zach got more serious.

"Richard, what would you think about running the Martin family farm? You could live there, raise a family, grow your own crops ... your way. Make your own income; not worry about punching a time clock and deductions. You'd be doing me a favor. You'd take care of the place." Richard was listening intently, squinting in the midday sun, trying to process Zach's words.

"Are you saying lease it? I'm not sure I could handle that large of a lease. I mean you're talking twenty or thirty thousand a year for a farm that size. I don't have any operating capital to even start. I don't think I could afford something like that." Now Richard looked crest-fallen, as if he had pronounced his own economic death sentence.

Zach could see tears welling in his eyes just before Richard covered them with sunglasses.

"Sure, you could, Richard. I know the landlord. He'll make you a sweet deal." He paused before extending the offer.

"How about $10,000 annual lease ... beginning in five years; nothing before then. With that kind of collateral, the bank will extend a loan for the next year's operating capital. You can use the tractors and farm equipment we still have."

After letting the offer sink in, Zach continued. "And when you start paying the lease, you can do so directly to St. Anne's Catholic Church." Zach explained that Richard should make his lease payment to Padre Juan instead of a bank. He went on to say that the most important thing was that the place be "taken care of for posterity."

In the end, it was an offer that helped both men, although Richard Quarrel would never know how it helped Zachary. For Richard, it was a Godsend. The two would forever be close friends now. Richard would honor their friendship by sending Zach a sack of dried pinto beans every year and a large canister of freshly ground red chili at Christmas. Zach knew the old farmstead would always be taken care of as if it belonged to Richard.

-41-

WASHINGTON DC, 2001

The ornate marble columns set neatly around the monument held Zachary's gaze. From where he sat, 298 feet above the ground in Arlington County, Virginia, he had a breathtaking view of the most spectacular of all the monuments in Washington, DC, the Jefferson Memorial. It was his favorite structure.

Zach knew that the architect was John Russell Pope and that the groundbreaking ceremony was on December 15, 1938. The cost was $3,192,000. The height to top of the dome was 129 feet, four inches and from his vantage, he was looking down on the monument across the Potomac River. The materials were Indiana limestone, Danby Imperial Marble (Vermont), Tennessee pink marble, Georgian white marble, and Missouri gray marble. He had memorized these details because he loved this monument.

The statue was indeed a fitting tribute to the third president of the United States, Thomas Jefferson. This was a man who wanted to be known for three things: 1) as the author of the Declaration of Independence, 2) as the author of the Virginia law that separated church and state, and 3) as the founder of the University of Virginia. Zachary knew that his role as the third president of the fledgling United States of America was absent from Jefferson's headstone.

"What a guy." Zach's tribute was directed toward the builder of the memorial, whose name he didn't know, rather than the statue's image. Oh, he liked Tom Jefferson. He admired his contribution to American life. But Zach was an engineer and builder, not a politician nor diplomat.

And the things the builder had to go through made Zach appreciate his stamina. Constant disagreements between the historical societies, those who hated that some Japanese cherry trees were to be uprooted— some chained themselves to the trees in protest—and the architect's death during construction! He could relate to that builder, and he didn't even know his name.

A voice crackled in his headphones, "Bucket's filled and away, boss." His attention quickly shifted to his immediate responsibility, bringing up 300 gallons of fresh, mixed concrete for placement into a form for the twenty-sixth floor. No, it wasn't the normal duty of the prime contractor to run a tower crane, but Zachary wasn't a normal engineer/contractor.

He wanted to actively participate in every aspect of his projects. Sure, he could be like every other builder and stay in the air-conditioned or heated office and direct work from his desk after the morning meetings, watching reports of inspections trickle in after completion. But he couldn't be kept to that role.

No, Zachary Martin wasn't like that. He was a different sort of engineer. He loved to get in the middle of every project, from directing the delivery of forms and scaffolds to operating a tower crane. This grass roots involvement made him feel alive. BeeVee2 had developed over the last twenty-five years, and he was now a man of means. But construction was in his blood.

He was a builder because it was who he was not what he needed to do to make a living. He got high from the noise, smells, and even taste of construction. He loved walking through mud puddles and kicking chain link gates open with his boots, and even taking phone calls amid the backhoe tractor noise. This was indeed the world he would have scripted for himself if he'd had a chance. But this world fell in his lap, literally.

Of course, his affinity for building began a long time back. That was when he discovered it was fun. He acquired knowledge and skills to become an excellent engineer/builder, and loved both professions, but he had something more, a mentor. Fortunately, his wife's father had always been there to lend a hand, allowing him to learn from the master.

Life had taken some peculiar twists for Zach. He knew that. His experiences in South Vietnam had molded him into the man he was. His wife and two children molded him further yet. Zach considered his marriage to Jordan wedded bliss, and Jordan proved to be a perfect homemaker and mother. She hadn't used her bachelor's and master's degrees in psychology since the kids were born.

After the kids were in school, Jordan reasoned, she would return to her profession. That was fine with Zach, and that's what she did. Now that the kids were older, she worked as the district psychologist for the Arlington County School System, where they moved when Zach and Bart landed a big contract in the area.

Zach admired Jordan's tenacity in his zeal for construction. Moving put a definite strain on her emotions. She knew that relocating with the family business was essential, but family history was important to her. She always wanted a home where she would grow old remembering the origin of stains on the wood floors from a generation before. For that reason, they did not sell their first home in Las Cruces.

While in Arlington, Jordan made good friends and developed solid, lifelong relationships with several women near her age and one who could have been her mother. It helped that her matron of honor and faculty adviser now taught psychology at Georgetown University across the Potomac from their home on Williamsburg Avenue in Arlington.

Their children were a blessing. Billy and Christie became more than brother and sister. They were like each other's pseudo-parent, looking out for each other and correcting each other like a parent would. They were very close. Now, as they headed rapidly toward adulthood, they were ready to take on the world like their parents and grandparents had.

Billy was named for his godfather and uncle, Billy Woods. The elder Billy chose the same profession as his brother. Well, almost the same profession. He worked as the building official in Arlington. Billy was the guy who watched over Zach's kind. But he was the best; the kind of building official who explained things to contractors to gain compliance.

***

The bucket rose as Zach pulled back on the operating control lever. The bucket of concrete weighed almost two tons but climbed upward against the Washington, DC skyline seemingly without effort. His left hand began the lateral turn of the tower on its pivot, causing the crane and the bucket to follow. At just the right point, Zach stopped the leftward rotation, allowing the bucket to swing past the crane to the left. Then, again when the bucket had swung past the nadir, he engaged the right rotation to align directly above the vertical position of the pendulum swing. It was like fly casting but on a larger scale.

The bucket stopped its lateral motion and rested twenty-five feet above the crew awaiting the fresh concrete. He would now lower it so the foreman could release the concrete. Normally, that move was the sign of an expert crane operator, not the co-owner of a multi-million-dollar construction company. Zach made it his business to master the little nuances of every phase of the construction process.

He could see the lift now with twenty masons working near it, installing the twelve-inch brick veneer against the light gauge steel framing within the framework of red iron construction. This veneer would define the building. In the future, folks would refer to his work as, "that dark red brick building in central Rosslyn."

Pity, most people don't know that this veneer has very little to do with the structural integrity, Zach mused. But it had to be installed properly or it would fall; and at thirty stories above the ground, a twelve-inch brick could develop enough force to do significant damage.

"F=M(A)," Zach thought aloud, reviewing the engineering equation defining force as mass times the rate of acceleration due to gravity. He knew that brick ties must be secured with two large screws to the steel stud, and the flat portion of that tie laid in the mortar joint between courses at specified intervals.

Zach was in the act of lowering the bucket to the awaiting concrete crew when his headphone crackled again. "Miho, can you come down here?" His father-in-law had used that affectionate Spanish sobriquet since Zach asked for Jordan's hand in marriage.

"Be right there, Dad," he answered. "Let me get this bucket empty and back on the ground and I'll give the controls back."

"Jon, she's gonna be all yours again," he said to Jonathan Lee, who was listening on the same communication channel.

With the last of the concrete placed on the formwork, Zach reversed the process, setting the bucket on the ground and returning the operating controls to the primary operator. There was room for only one person at the controls of this tower crane. Zach had to unbuckle himself from the seat, remove the radio headphones then climb out of the cab and down the crane's ladder steps onto the platform before Lee could take his place.

"Boss, you're picking up that rotation routine pretty well," Lee said.

"Thanks, Jon. You're a good teacher. Now I'll turn this stuff over to the professional."

The climb down included dozens of flights of scissor-stairs, eight steps at a time. It would take him nine minutes to reach the bottom even at a brisk pace; Zach had timed himself before.

Zach wondered what his father-in-law wanted to talk about. They were on schedule, the second most important thing about this or any job. The most important being safety. There had never been an accidental death or serious injury on any of their jobs. He was determined to keep it that way.

"Safety was not the big thing. It was the only thing," he reminded his employees, paraphrasing one of his heroes, Vincent Lombardi. This project would be no different. In fact, the sign on the site construction office attested to the veracity of that claim. BeeVee2 Construction was proud of its safety record. Written in all caps a sign proclaimed:

THIS PROJECT HAS OPERATED 267 DAYS WITHOUT AN INJURY DUE TO AN ACCIDENT.

At the bottom of the tower crane, his wife and her parents awaited his descent. "What are you guys doing here?" he asked, surprised to see Catarina walking up to greet him.

"Como esta, Zacharia?"

"Oh, we just thought we'd surprise you," Jordan explained. "Mom and Dad want to take us out to a fancy restaurant. Can you break away early to get ready?"

Zach knew his wife well and could tell she expected an affirmative answer. "When two pretty girls are asking me out at the same time, I can't very well say no, can I?" Still out of breath from the descent, he struggled with the answer, then inhaled deeply before continuing. "Let me talk with Mannheim before I take off, though."

Now Bart walked toward them. "Hi, Dad. Are you responsible for this invitation?"

Bartolome Valles had earned the lines in his face, not just from the years he spent outdoors in the blistering sun, but through the way he worried about every little thing. The lines seemed to trace his worries throughout his sixty-nine years on the earth. In his third decade, he worried about making his business survive and flourish.

In his second decade, his only child's health was his worry. Jordan acquired a rare form of Hodgkin's disease. Three years and several worry lines later, she emerged as a healthy teenager with a different set of problems. But together, they worked through it all. The only facet of his life not fraught with worry was his current relationship with his family. He knew he could depend upon the love of his wife and child and now his son-in-law and grandchildren.

"I want to talk to you about something important, son. Dinner would be the best time to do it. "I have reservations at Ruth's Chris Steakhouse in Crystal City. Go get cleaned up and meet us there at 7:00."

It was a gentle order, but an order, nonetheless. It was already 5:00 pm, giving Zach little time to shower, change and drive into Crystal City, then find a parking spot and meet his father-in-law at a fancy restaurant. He would have to hurry.

"Let me go over the stripping schedule with the superintendent and make sure the test cylinders were approved by the testing lab," Zach said. "Remember, Dad, if I don't get this started, we'll lose a day."

On high-rise construction, new concrete floor levels must be poured quickly.

Lynn Mannheim served as Agent 1 for the special inspection process on BeeVee's building. His critical oversight was added to that of Arlington County's inspectors. He oversaw the actions taken by the contractor as well as the testing results for things like concrete strength, bolt tightening, welding connections, and reinforcing steel ties.

"Scheduling is everything on a construction project of any size, but more so on a project of this magnitude," Zach reminded his father-in-law. "I need to call the testing lab and speak with Mannheim and the engineer-of-record about the test results." All the written results would arrive the next morning by fax to the site construction office, but he must tell the tradesmen tonight if they were needed the next day. "Timing is everything," he added.

Turning away from the group, he dialed the number on his cell phone.

A colorful character by all accounts, Mannheim was fearless. Brusque, plain speaking, and a hard-working professional, he loved a challenge.

He had been described as a burly structural engineer with a bushy beard, a ponytail, and a sense of humor. In 1999, to stop complaints that he wasn't wearing a hard hat at the Pentagon restoration jobsite, he had a pale pink hardhat made and adorned it with a cosmetics logo and a picture of a Barbie doll and Teddy bear.... "Just to let them know what I thought," he told Zach.

Mannheim's sense of humor was balanced with a strong sense of honor. The son of Jewish immigrants who escaped from internment camps during World War II, Lynn Mannheim was the structural engineer of record and the special inspector for Zach's project. He took the call on his cell phone with his typical brusque acknowledgment, "Mannheim."

"Lynn, this is Zach Martin at 801 Glebe in Arlington. Say, how are the breaks for the twenty-first?" His tone was at once direct and respectful. Mannheim understood the question immediately. If they reached 3000 psi, they passed. If not, they didn't and that meant delays. "Good news, pound puppy. They passed! 3075 psi! Break the re-shoring. Let's get the trades into the twenty-first floor."

Zach breathed a sigh of relief. Even though he railed against the nickname Mannheim had attached to him, he was grateful for the good news. Zach wasn't one to trust or tempt fate.

-42-

VIRGINIA, 2001

"Billy Woods here. May I help you?" The voice on the other end of the cell phone call was brisk, strong, and courteous, but to the point.

"Hey, little brother. How are you? Happy Friday."

"Zach! Great to hear from you, man. How's it going on 801 Glebe?"

"Can't I call my brother without needing something from him?"

"Yeah, you might. But I'll bet my monthly government wages you didn't this time." Zach had been trapped by his own brother who knew him better than anyone.

Billy added, "If I was to guess, I'd say you were calling about the special inspection interim reports ... specifically those on the twenty-first floor."

"I didn't know your government job came with psychic abilities, Billy. You'll have to show me how you do that someday."

Now laughter erupted from within the confines of Billy's office in Arlington County, Virginia.

"Gotcha man! Truth is, Mannheim just faxed the latest interim report. I figured your call would be next."

"Awwww," Zach exclaimed, humoring his brother.

"You're good to go, big brother. Break the shoring and keep going. And Zach, you can't keep a secret from me, ya know that, right? I know where all the bodies are buried."

Stung by the ages-old adage, Zach focused instead on the hidden meaning between them. It was true they carried many secrets between them ... all except one.

"Billy, you got me. I did call you for that. But I'm smiling because my little brother is really my big brother." Although tall, Zach was dwarfed by Billy, who stood two inches taller and even with two back surgeries and three knee surgeries, at fifty, he could still bench press 200 pounds and run a 5K in 22 minutes.

"It's nice to hear your voice, Billy. I think about you a lot and miss our camaraderie. We really should get together more often. How about it?"

"Sure, Zach. Let me get this divorce thing behind me. It has me reeling right now. I have to go back to Phoenix next month for a hearing. Maybe after that."

Zach understood his plight. He would ease up on his brother. "Roger that," Zach answered. "And thanks for the go-ahead on the twenty-first. Take care, little brother."

***

Zach and Jordan arrived at the restaurant at exactly seven o'clock according to his Rolex Submariner, a Christmas gift from his father-in-law several years before. He knew Bartolome wanted him to always be on time. He also knew they would be sitting in a private corner section, the family's favorite spot.

Their choice of private dining areas had an unobstructed view of Washington's Ronald Reagan National Airport as well as the U.S. Capitol, the Washington Monument, and the Lincoln and Jefferson Memorials. This evening, a full moon rose against the horizon to add to the remarkable scenery. The evening would have been romantic if he and Jordan were alone.

"Como te vas?" Bart said as he stood to greet his daughter and son-in-law. After brief pleasantries, Bartolome, sitting next to Zach, leaned over and whispered his desire to talk business. It was Zach's cue to listen intently. After all, this man was his wife's father, his boss, and his kids' grandfather. He was the family patriarch who deserved Zach's respect and admiration. Bartolome had helped Zach become a success. He also granted him the greatest gift of all, his daughter. So, with reverence and love, Zach paid attention when the man spoke.

"Miho, I need your help," Bart began. "There's a contract for a building where we started out ... in Las Cruces. There is a building that must be demolished first though. No big deal. It'll take a couple of weeks. I need you to go with me and take charge of the demo."

He hesitated before continuing and pulled a document from inside his jacket. "Here are the details including the address, project team members, schedule and permit application. We'll take the G2 and get a jump on things tomorrow morning. Don't worry. We'll be back here for my granddaughter's graduation in a few weeks."

Now Zach was curious. Using the G2 was not unheard of; they had done so on several occasions. But for a simple demolition? It seemed like a waste of expensive resources. And what about 801 Glebe? Was the demolition a more important project? They weren't behind, thanks to Zach's diligence, but could that delicate schedule be maintained without his careful attention?

More than that, the thought of Bartolome Valles spending the major part of a month at the site of a demolition seemed ridiculous. Bart normally focused on negotiating contracts with seven and eight zeroes behind a large integer. How was this plan a valuable use of his time?

Zach wanted to ask but didn't. There would be time for questions later.

-43-

NEW MEXICO AND VIRGINIA, 2001

The Gulfstream 2 had been fueled and pre-flight checks completed when Bartolome and Zach parked the company's Ford Bronco at the Executive Flight Center of Dulles International Airport. The paint had barely dried on the BeeVee2 logo displayed on the sides of their latest 2001 model.

Suitcases in tow, the pair briskly walked around the building and past the flight line to find their ride toward West Texas and ultimately New Mexico. Bartolome was stoic, less than his normal talkative self, Zach noticed. Something serious had his partner's attention.

The G2 was a company jet leased by BeeVee2 Construction with a pilot hired as part of the lease agreement. Bart wanted to keep the same pilot. That cost a bit more but was worth it to Valles in consistency and predictability. Because of the lease agreements, the company logo was emblazoned on the fuselage of the small commercial jet, making it appear that BeeVee2 Construction owned the plane.

That helped the company's prestige and corporate visibility, but BeeVee2 surely did not own a $5 million aircraft, nor did they employ a jet-certified pilot. Zach focused on the meandering river drawn into the corporate logo. The river represented the Jordan River, after which his wife was named.

Being a co-owner, Zach never had a problem with the company name, the phonetic spelling of his father-in-law's initials, B. V. After all, the company was named well before he could lift a hammer. He was proud enough to share in the ownership … and the hard work.

Zach normally dedicated twelve to fourteen hours every weekday to his business. He reserved Sunday for church and family but would admit that he spent many Saturdays going over plans for the coming week. This Saturday was different. He and Bart were traveling to a project that seemed insignificant to Zach.

Recalling the time that he almost severed his opposable digit on a table saw, Zach's mind drew the analogy of asking a trauma surgeon to remove a splinter instead of restoring a partially amputated thumb. This trip by the company owners seemed like a waste of time and skill. Their collective talent and the professional relationship at BeeVee2 were now legend in the construction world. There was neither a Pulitzer Prize for coming in under bid nor a Nobel Prize for beating a scheduled deadline. BeeVee2 never made history playing in the Final Four or the Super Bowl for their extraordinary efforts. Their success was measured in future agreements on contract proposals based on past performance. Zach had learned from his father-in-law that his responsibility extended to more than the bottom line, though. Bartolome had taught him that they had obligations to numerous groups. First, they owed it to their family to put bread on the table. That obligation extended to the families of every employee and subcontractor who worked for them. Bart taught Zach to recognize that their decisions directly affected the families of their employees. Bad decisions sometimes meant layoffs, and layoffs created pain for an employee's innocent family.

Bart and Zach also had a moral duty to ensure the safety of everyone who worked on their projects as much as they had to the future tenants and occupants of the buildings they constructed. Their commitment went beyond building codes and federal regulations. For this reason, BeeVee2 Construction achieved and maintained a perfect safety record for the last thirty years. No one was killed or seriously injured due to an accident. Nor had any building ever structurally failed due to shoddy work.

Then there was BeeVee2's primary responsibility: to give the new building owners exactly what they paid for, nothing less and always more, if possible. That singular standard of professionalism set BeeVee2 apart from at least half the large commercial builders, ensuring they would always have work.

The G2 quickly ascended into the air and soon was on the Virginia border headed southwest. The compass heading indicated 235 degrees. The pilot would hold that heading for the next hour or so to avoid storms over Kentucky then adjust depending upon where ATC placed them to arrive in Deming, New Mexico. Deming had a longer runway than Las Cruces. Their arrival would put them closer to a part of Bart's plan.

Bart opened the plans for the building. The sour look on his face was exaggerated by lines etched from seven decades of sun exposure. He spread the plans on the table between two opposing seats. Zach sat opposite him where he could observe his father-in-law's facial expressions and body language. He could tell this project was both important and disturbing to Bart.

Zach studied the demolition plan. It seemed straightforward. They would begin by disconnecting utilities, securing the premises with chain link fencing, and staging the demolition equipment, a small tower crane they would rent for the purpose. The high lift jack would separate sections at strategic locations, disconnecting the structural integrity of the building, thus allowing for deconstruction in stages. He knew they would need to secure demolition permits from the Las Cruces Building Department first.

Zach noticed that Bart seemed to concentrate on an unusual portion of the plans, the foundation. They would excavate concrete grade beams and point load footings then remove them for recycling. Certainly, this was not the most exigent task to consider. But, still, Bart kept studying the size, weight and volume of the footings.

Finally, Zach asked the question. "Dad, is there something significant about the concrete that I should know? You're spending a lot of time looking at the foundation plan." Bartolome Valles glanced at his watch then looked over his reading glasses with a grim expression.

Zach felt a cold chill crawling up his back from his father-in-law's expression. Bartolome focused on something beyond Zach's left shoulder before looking at his watch again. Zach stifled a shiver and waited.

When Bart spoke, his words were slow and quiet. Zach had to lean forward to hear him above the G2's twin jet engines. They were alone in the cabin. Still, Bart spoke as if he wanted no other human to hear. Zach couldn't know that several hundred miles away, at Bartolome and Catarina's home on Williamsburg Street in Arlington, Virginia, a similar conversation was about to begin between his mother-in-law and his wife.

For some time, Bartolome and Catarina had planned for the revelations to occur simultaneously. Together, they scripted, re-wrote, and rehearsed their speech. It was time to be honest with their progeny, to finally tell the story of what happened more than forty years before. Both Zachary and Jordan, though separated by hundreds of miles, responded with disbelief followed by denial.

Jordan did not want to accept that her father could ever kill in such a vicious manner. But she knew her mother wouldn't lie about something like that. She swallowed hard and choked on the dry residue in her throat.

As a trained psychologist, Jordan knew there were stages of disbelief just as there were stages of grief. She recognized she was still in the denial stage. Both stunned and drawn cold by the disclosure, she blurted out, "My father's a murderer!" Her face held a blank stare to nowhere as she tried to make sense of her mother's revelation.

***

Zachary resisted the image of a younger Bartolome swinging an ax, almost beheading a would-be assassin. He had never known his father-in-law to be aggressive even in Northern Virginia traffic. He was more than magnanimous, patient and kind to everyone. He practiced tithing to his church regularly.

Many times, Bartolome and Catarina served Christmas or Thanksgiving meals at homeless kitchens. In fact, now that he thought of it, he saw his father-in-law practice kind deeds nearly every day since they had met.

Stunned by the revelation, Zachary leaned back in the leather seat facing his father-in-law. He had entrusted his children to this man. Bartolome always gave prayers at Sunday dinner for the health of their family.

No, Bart did not murder, Zach convinced himself. There was a difference! He remembered his Sunday school lessons about wars and fighting in the name of God. He thought about his philosophy professor at New Mexico State University who said, "The difference between murder and self-defense in the eyes of society is intent."

He thought about war and specifically about the issue of killing North Vietnamese soldiers. Repeatedly, he had to remind himself it was not murder.

Then it hit Zachary like a lightning bolt. He had been sitting in judgment of his father-in-law for the last twenty minutes as they flew over West Virginia and Kentucky. And now, seated across from him was clear evidence that his silent judgment caused pain and suffering.

He could see in Bart's eyes that the man was worn down by years of pretense. His courageous act of admission should have provided relief. Instead, Zach noticed lines in his father-in-law's face that reflected his own self-doubt and shame. An old, familiar shame planted in the recesses of his mind that he couldn't quite access and shame for judging his father-in-law's justifiable actions.

***

Subjects in her criminal psychology class dominated the thoughts of Jordan Martin who still sat cross-legged on the leather ottoman. She had used sound reasoning to categorize her father by one of the neat, definable descriptions within the framework of her profession. But she couldn't make sense of it. Her father simply didn't fit the profile of a murderer.

She could come up with a name for a disorder that permitted one person to kill another, albeit in self-defense. What unexpected behavior was part of her father's psyche that she never fathomed? Murder and killing were different words but resulted in the same consequence. In both cases, someone died.

Jordan recognized, from an objective point of view, that she was alive because of her father's act. Yet she couldn't grasp the reality of his violence.

As an infant, Jordan escaped the recollection of a horrible night and events that forever etched themselves in her parents' memories. She imagined how her mother must have felt that night compared to the night before. Catarina was naive and pure, a young homemaker with a baby, married to the man she loved, a man with a promising future.

Jordan tried to imagine her mother cleaning up blood and debris the next morning when the most important things on her mind the previous day were laundry and what to prepare for the evening meal.

As she let reality take hold, Jordan began to see her parents in a whole new light. They were not only the loving parents who raised her, but also the defenders of her life.

***

By the end of their conversation, Jordan's viewpoint had changed but her mother held onto the last words from her daughter's mouth. Catarina couldn't abide her daughter's judgment of Bartolome from the patronizing perch of her profession.

"I understand your shock in learning about something that happened forty years ago, something that reveals a different side of your father," she told Jordan. "It was horrific, and the scene has haunted both of us for a long, long time. But please remember, miha, you and I wouldn't be here if your father hadn't defended us and our home. Furthermore, you wouldn't be a psychologist without the education he paid for."

Catarina still wore the St. Catherine medallion her father gave her. Silently, she prayed to her patron saint for guidance. As she caressed the medallion between her thumb and forefinger, she asked for her daughter's understanding. "Miha, your father is still the good man he has always been. Please try to understand that he had no choice but to kill those men. He is not a murderer."

***

Zachary felt it now; the pain was from thirty years before in Vietnam. His demeanor changed, as did his posture. He was identifying with his father-in-law and beginning to understand something more about guilt and suffering, the suffering from private shame for actions that, at the time, seemed reasonable. Zachary recognized that he and his father-in-law now had a new bond. The bond of shared experience.

But only Zachary knew ... unless he followed his father-in-law's example and acknowledged his own past. The already strong connection between them would be even stronger if only he could share his secret. He began to acknowledge the courage it took for Bart to disclose such a confidence.

Zach could see the results of Bart's confession in his eyes. There was relief, yes, but something else. As Bart waited for his son-in-law's reaction, trepidation was evident in his face. He couldn't know that Zach understood better than anyone how important it was to be absolved of guilt and shame.

Zach saw his father-in-law in a new way. A thought crept across his mind that caused him both pride and reverence. This man had not only committed an act of violence, he was able to admit it and live with it.

His son-in-law's response stunned Bartolome. "Dad, you know I love you and always will. I'm your son. We're in this together."

Bartolome looked across the table at Zachary and beamed with pride. "Miho ... I called you that the day you asked for Jordan's hand in marriage. You became my son then. You will always be my son. Muchas gracias por tu amor y honor ... and your trust."

Now Zach understood why Bart was laboring over the plans. He needed to come up to speed, especially about where to focus on the final excavation.

The G2 started its descent into the southern New Mexico desert to land at an airport that was built in part by Zachary's real father, Oliver James Martin. Martin became a Cat (Caterpillar) skinner at age thirty and found work helping build an Army airfield in Deming, New Mexico in 1942 as part of the United States' response to the Japanese invasion of Pearl Harbor. The field was built to train bomber pilots before being deployed to the Pacific theater in WWII. That's why the runway was longer.

Deming Airfield was also where Zachary learned to fly in a Cessna 150 when he was in high school. He soloed and then learned to fly a Cessna 172 when he was only sixteen years old. He knew the field well, though it had changed a bit in the thirty years since he had first seen it from the air.

***

Jordan heard her mother's words, but she also read the lines in her forehead and caught the stern tone she conveyed when placing the teacup back in the saucer. She had called her father a murderer. That was a mistake, a gut reaction.

After thinking about it, she came to realize that the circumstances confronting her parents at the time must have been unspeakable. They had to deal with racial prejudice in the white America of the 1950s. Her father could have been imprisoned or worse just because he was of Mexican descent. Her parents' reasons for silence until now were understandable when she considered the racial prejudice of the times. "Mom, I'm sorry. You're right. I know Dad could never murder anyone. Three men breaking down the door to your home with shotguns! You must have been terrified. And guarding your secret all those years ... Oh, Mom, I'm so sorry." She stood and held her mother in a strong hug. They cried and rocked each other until finally, Catarina pushed her daughter gently at arm's length.

Catarina knew the next step was to explain where Bartolome and Zachary were going today and why. "Jordan, there's something else you should know," she began hesitantly. Jordan held her breath as she wiped the tears that streaked her face.

"After your father handled the intruders ..." Catarina paused, leading her daughter to the couch.

When they sat next to each other Catarina began again. "After your father saved our lives, we had three bodies in our home and an infant in the next room. There was blood everywhere. We knew we had done something horrifying, but at the same time we had to ... had to ... dispose of the bodies." She struggled to explain for the first time to anyone. All these years later, she had trouble controlling the shaking that threatened to overcome her.

Catarina took a deep breath and continued. "Your father was saying something about the fireplace and burial. I didn't understand. He had just defended our home and saved us. He was out of breath and shaking. So was I. You were crying. He started moving the bodies through our entry hall to his pickup truck parked out front. I saw him drag three dead men, one at a time, over the oak floor we had so carefully installed two years before. Then I saw some Catolico medal on one. It was Nuestra Señora de la Santa Muerte, Patron Saint of Outcasts. Your father removed it. I thought he was going to hand it to me. Thank God he didn't. I would have thrown it into the fireplace.

"I bundled you up, and we went with him. We drove to his jobsite where a foundation was to be poured the next morning. I helped him position a ladder into a pit or something."

She paused, shuddering at the memory. "Your father dug a grave, placed the bodies inside, and covered them up. We assumed the concrete pour the next day would cover the bodies for good."

"Oh, Mom," was all Jordan could say.

When Jordan placed her arm around her mother's shoulder, Catarina gazed into her daughter's eyes. "Now you know why BeeVee2 had to win that contract in New Mexico. The job included demolition of the older building."

"That's the building they're demolishing?" Jordan asked astonished. "Oh my God!"

Catarina's stern face transformed to an emotional release. Her 65-year-old coarse hands that had been clasped together in her lap in mock-prayer now ascended to cover her face as the tears flowed again. Consoling her mother whose head rested on her shoulder, Jordan never saw her mom so vulnerable. For an instant the mother-daughter roles reversed.

Between sobs, Catarina managed, "Miha, you ha…have no idea how h…ard it has been…to bear the se…cret…to know that we were the victims. Yet no … one would ever be … lieve us." She raised her head from Jordan's shoulder and wiped her tears on her sleeve, but they still welled in her eyes.

"… and now, the truth may come out." A more composed Catarina sat up straight and looked stoically at her daughter. "… and it may affect your family too."

Jordan stared blankly at her mom then broke in tears. The women cried together … tears of fear and grief for their husbands and what they were faced with doing.

***

The farmhouse looked much the same to Zach. The old farm was willed to him and Billy after his father passed away more than two decades before. He did not ever want to be a farmer again but at the same time, he couldn't give it away.

"Dad, look at the trees planted there." Zach was pointing to an area where the old barnyard and corrals had been torn down to make way for an orchard.

"It looks like apples, miho. Strange fruit to see here, but they're doing well."

"It's all that fertilizer where the barnyard had been," Zach suggested.

Bartolome responded with a dismissive look.

Richard Quarrel walked up to see who was paying him a visit. "Hey landlord, did you bring some muscle to collect your back-rent?" bellowed Quarrel, a fifty-something Mexican American whose small family was native to the area.

In the late forties when Zach and Richard were toddlers, their fathers were partners for a time, together owning two Caterpillars, a road grader, a large planer, a 40-yard scraper/carryall and a belly-dump. During their time in earth-moving work, the two men developed farms for others by bulldozing mesquite bushes on thousands of acres in southern New Mexico.

That income allowed each of them to buy farms. Zach's father succeeded in developing three additional farms for himself while Richard Quarrel Senior lost his farm in the recession of the early 1970s.

"Hey Richard, how are you, man? Good to see you. You've done well here. Apples in Deming, New Mexico," he said, motioning toward the orchard.

"Five years now. They should be producing soon. I was surprised too, but we planted the hardiest strain, and the wife gives them a lot of love," he continued, looking at the two men in the rental car. "I think she loves them more than she loves me."

Bart climbed out of the car and responded, shaking Richard's hand. "Well, she does have good taste in apples ... and men ... I guess. Is she doing okay now?"

"Thanks, Bartolome. Very kind of you to ask. She's doing well after that spell with cancer a few years back. We still travel to El Paso to the clinic once a month for checkups, but so far, she's cancer-free. With God's blessing we still see the sunrise together on this beautiful farm every morning. And every morning we think of you guys. To what do I owe this visit?"

Zach walked around the car and greeted his friend with a combination handshake and hug. "Richard, we have a contract locally and we need your help with something. We should talk alone somewhere. By the way, do you still have that old feed grinder I cursed at as a kid?"

The three men talked at length while walking through the orchard admiring the work of a horticulturist. Richard Quarrel had a degree from the same school as Zachary, NMSU. He applied what he learned there to his farm. Zach knew that Quarrel took pride in the farm and even though it wasn't legally his, Zach was glad he treated it as such.

Once Zach and Bart were satisfied that Richard understood their situation, they said goodbye and drove north on County Road 11 for ten miles to Deming, then sixty miles east to Las Cruces where their worksite was situated.

In the large town they made some further arrangements. They reserved large-scale equipment, bought some tools, and ordered perimeter fencing. Next, they hired security guards for the site. BeeVee2 still had an active contractor's license in New Mexico, allowing Bartolome to secure demolition permits and submit the architect's plans for review to the Dona Ana County Building Department, since the project was technically outside the town limits.

***

Three days later, Harriet Quarrel received a phone call from Harmony Travel Company in El Paso. It seems that she and Richard had won a one-week trip for two to Disneyland with all expenses paid and even some spending money … no catches.

"Richard, neither of us has ever been. We both need a getaway. This is fantastic. What fortune!" Richard listened to the tone of his wife's voice more than the words she spoke. She was indeed filled with joy, something he had not heard from her in quite a while. He knew he had to agree even though some things needed tending first. He would find a way. They were going.

The Quarrel's time away would serve the interests of Martin and Valles who had arranged and funded the vacation for the couple. Later that day, Quarrel called his old friend. Zach's phone rang and he heard a robust answer, "Hey Quarrel, is everything okay?"

"Listen Zach. I am not sure what's going on, but the missus gota call from a travel agency. It seems we won a trip. I don't suppose you know anything about that do you?" Quarrel queried not expecting Zach to admit anything.

"Hey, congratulations, Richard. It couldn't happen to a nicer couple. You deserve the time away. Don't worry about the farm. We'll take care of it while you're gone. When is it again?"

"Zach, I think you know more than you're lettin' on. I don't care what you're doing 'cause I trust you … with my life. Just be careful is all I'm saying."

Zach responded playfully, "You say you'll leave three weeks from now, right? Don't worry. In the time you're gone the chickens won't even be hatching. We know about watering the orchard. We'll take care of it. You won't even know we were there except for maybe some tire tracks in the garden and gently used farm equipment and maybe some fields plowed up."

"Now, I'm getting nervous, buddy. Naw, just kidding! Please do like I say, though. Be careful, okay?"

"You got it Richard. Have fun. Call if you wish, anytime."

***

Zach was at the site with plans in tow. He was looking at several foundation locations and critical structural joints to offset any idle speculation when the deconstruction subcontractor walked toward him.

"Mr. Martin, John Cox with Cox Construction. I just wanted to do the same thing you must be doing." Cox extended a large palm that could easily grip and hold a basketball. He was about the same size and proportions as Zach, just younger with fewer gray hairs.

Cox was wearing a worn-out Trimble GPS cap. Zach knew because he had one at home. The ball caps were functional, having a small pouch for concealing an external patch antenna for a handheld GPS system that Trimble sold.

"Zach Martin. Glad to run into you here, John. What's your plan for upper floor decon'?" Zach asked, hoping to work a little deal-making into the conversation.

"Well, we already have a source for the finish materials. I have experienced crews ready to take it apart as early as next Monday. I can come over with a prep crew on Sunday if you let me. That'd make our job smoother next week," Cox responded.

"That's great, John. Good plan. How experienced is your crew with production deconstruction this large?" Zach asked.

"Well, we've never done anything quite this big before, honestly. Most contractors are 'blow and go' guys and don't bother with the green aspects of masonry and concrete recycling like BeeVee2. But we're eager to learn. I assume you read all that in our prospectus and that's why you picked us. I hope we're still good here?"

"Of course," Zach said. "I appreciate your honesty. Cox has our business here for sure. Frankly, there aren't a lot of decon' firms in southern New Mexico either. Yours stands out with a reputation for integrity and speed. We'll take that over cost any day.

"There's just one thing we'd like to have an understanding on." Zach had rehearsed the pitch in the truck all morning. He was ready.

"We've had a testing lab set up on a farm nearby in Deming. You may know that my father-in-law built this building in 1957. It was the first high-rise in Las Cruces in fact. We want to document the integrity of the structure in specific segments." Zach cleared his throat. "We're trying for a LEED Gold Rating on the new building.

When Cox nodded, Zach continued. "But we want to make a pitch for the value of concrete in building sustainable, long-term structures that are resilient and resist wind and seismic loads. We want to use this building as a case study. That means we'll need to do some forensics and establish an argument for concrete. At certain points we'll ask your crew if we can take over for a brief period to extract and save something for testing."

Zach felt the need to buttress his explanation before Cox had a chance to respond. "You see, I'm an engineer, and our lab is specially set up to make the kind of tests we have in mind. I don't want to trust something like this to another crew or lab. I want to do it myself ... under controlled conditions. Do you know what I mean?" He was sure Cox knew that a large paycheck and future contracts swung in the balance of his reply.

"Why of course, Mr. Martin. I forgot you were the company engineer. I'd say BeeVee2 has the stellar reputation it has because of your precision work and your keen interest in the environment. Whatever you need, we'll work with you."

-44-

New Mexico, 2001

They were in a warehouse they had leased one block from the intersection of Valley Drive and Alameda. It was relatively close to the demolition site. This building was not only perfect for critical equipment storage but doubled as a construction office. They had checked into a two-bedroom suite at the Extended Stay Holiday Inn but used it only when they slept which was no more than six hours a night.

"This place could double as sleeping quarters," Zach proposed to Bartolome, "since it has a field shower and toilet." It also had a dorm-size refrigerator some previous tenant had left. "We could save some money by checking out of the Holiday Inn and staying here. All we need are two cots."

"Maybe so," Bart said, nodding in agreement. He returned his focus to the matter at hand.

While Bart had a rough idea of what to do, it was Zach who filled in the critical details. He did so in a Socratic method proposing an idea here or there with a question. "Would we be able to…" or "Should we consider …" They threw out and considered ideas together. Pressure and anxiety filled each discussion since it affected both men professionally and personally.

Zach decided they needed a break from the tension.

"Dad, we could arrange for one of the blind dump truck drivers to take this one load to the farm," he proposed without a smile, looking straight at his father-in-law. Bartolome stared at his son-in-law, mentally replaying what Zach had said.

Laughter broke the intense focus of the last two hours. Both Zach and his father-in-law decided that a cold beer was in order. The two left the warehouse for a cowboy-style bar near the corner of Picacho and Valley Drive. It was early for drinking, but they needed the break.

Zach was driving the rented Ford Crew Cab as they pulled out of the parking lot and turned left on Valley Drive. He noticed a pedestrian observing them from the side of the road. Zach could tell he was an older Hispanic man, trying to gain eye contact with them. He confirmed this when he saw the man look at their warehouse then turn back to glimpse the crew cab. "Who was that guy?" Zach said in a low voice, almost a whisper. His distracted father-in-law did not pay attention to the question.

***

Bart and Zach had contracted demolition crews to remove and salvage elements of the upper floors in sequence using a modern process called deconstruction. The difference between that and demolition was that deconstruction made a dedicated effort to salvage any usable materials prior to mechanical destruction of the building's concrete shell. They would give any reusable construction materials to companies needing them for another project. So, even though the process saved money and helped the environment, deconstruction was also the perfect stratagem for another element in their plan.

Recently a process had been developed to crush the concrete into smaller aggregate-size chunks for recycling in future concrete pours thus stretching the concrete's usefulness further. It was another green building technique that cost a bit of time but was worth it in credits for LEED and especially for their plan to extract the remains of three bodies buried underneath.

***

As planned, Zach was the foreman for the entire deconstruction project. "An engineer running the show," he said to Bart one evening as they settled on their cots. "Who woulda' thought that made sense?"

"Right." Bart said, acknowledging that in the old days, an architect ran the project, onsite.

They talked about how modern construction was more of a team concept with the architect of record and design engineer collaborating with the general contractor, project managers, site superintendents, subcontractors, material suppliers, installers, testing agencies, commercial inspectors, jurisdictional inspectors, special inspectors and myriad others.

Zach recalled the time he traveled to El Salvador on a vacation with Jordan and the kids a few years earlier and of course, he had to see what construction was like there. He was anxious to meet the contractor on a large high-rise project when he asked at the front gate. A guard stopped him and said there was no entry unless the patron (boss) agreed. In this case the patron was the project architect who finally allowed him to enter.

It wasn't just him. Anyone wanting to enter the project had to be approved by the architect who lived on the premises with his own bunkhouse in the construction office. He controlled the entire project. "What a great idea!" Zach said, admiring the concept.

"It would never happen here. Not anymore," he said to Bart. They both knew there was too much diversification in construction activities and too many special interests—and litigation, the real culprit. "The first thing we'll do is kill all the lawyers," Zach said, quoting Shakespeare. They enjoyed a much-needed laugh before settling in for the night.

***

The next day, as Zach was beginning the deconstruction process, he recalled an old witticism about true friendship. He could still visualize the sign a crusty old engineer had displayed at his work-station: *Friends help friends move. Real friends help friends move bodies.* He could only hope the moving bodies part of the project went smoothly.

The high reach machine was effective in picking apart the upper floors of the building. It was Zach's favorite machine at a demolition jobsite since it could do the work of three similar mechanical demolition tools because of its … well … high reach.

He enjoyed the feel of it as well and took over its operation. It was especially valuable in attaining recyclable-quality concrete without pulverizing it as in explosive demolition. It was also more economical although the rental fee alone was four figures an hour. With careful orchestration, Zach could keep things moving.

John Cox's team had completed the soft strip on the upper floors the week before and the lower floors on the weekend. Today, it was Zach's turn to start taking the building apart. Zach's crew had pre-weakened the structural elements, making the job easier. That would let the pieces be disassembled at strategic edges allowing twenty-foot sections to fall separately from the tearing apart by the high reach machine.

The pieces would fall into three piles on the ground where a front-end loader would pick them up and load each in one of three waiting dump trucks. Because Zach was running the high reach machine, the loading process would be out of the way of falling chunks of wall and debris. When he finished one quadrant, he would switch to the other. Monday turned into Friday with five twelve-hour days in between.

By 6:00 pm Friday, the shell was down and mostly carted off to the nearest concrete recycling center on West Picacho near the truck stop. The round-robin trip took the dumps forty minutes, allowing for loading and dumping.

The recycling firm would not pay for materials but waived the dump fees that nearly equaled the rental on the dump trucks. This gave BeeVee2 points for a LEED building through the USGBC program. They could at least get a Gold rating on this new building.

"Call it a day, John," Zach announced. Then, as if changing his mind, he turned and said, "No, call it a week. We got 'er done. Great work, man.

"Now the only thing I need to do is to remove the footing. I'll do that tomorrow myself. You guys can take the day off as a bonus. Heck, you worked a hundred hours not including the soft strip the week before. Great work! Thanks again, John."

"Mr. Martin," Cox said. "I don't mind coming back and helping you with a single dump tomorrow for the footings." The two men were out of their equipment now, surveying the demo site. Fresh dirt was evident where the floor had been. Now, there were only sixteen footing pads with connected columns left to remove. Zach had a plan.

"Okay, if you don't mind. Maybe we could use your help for about fourteen of the column footing pads. But I want to pick two for testing as I mentioned last week," Zach reminded Cox.

"And John, I expect to pay you for this." He could see a hint of relief in the contractor's face. Now, walking over to the brim of the shallow chasm, Zach feigned consideration of the pads.

"Let's see, I'll take that one over there and this one on this side. The others, you can recycle. I want to save these two for testing. They'll make fine specimens, one large and one small one."

The reality was that the large one concealed the three bodies and choosing the smallest was a subterfuge to make his selection appear random.

John Cox had one of his crew bring him a can of red spray paint. He was now busily marking the columns of the two footing pads. Zach overheard him tell his foreman to "leave these two column footing pads in place."

That was enough for Zach. He would trust that the man, wanting repeat business from BeeVee2, would follow his direction. Zach had started making some preparation of his own. He used a hand shovel to scoop up dirt under the corner of Tomb One, a term he coined and used only in his mind. He wanted to see what condition the bottom corners were in before he used the high reach machine underneath to topple the column.

Zach would make it look like he had erred and knocked it over, but there would be no one onsite to see the error. He and Bart would manage the extraction and load the columns on a single fourteen-cubic-yard Mack dump truck then conceal the decayed corpses in the back.

***

The next morning at 6:00, Cox arrived to arrange two dump trucks to receive the column footings. Zach and Bartolome had beaten him to the jobsite by an hour and already loosened the first two column footings. Bart was ready with the large front-end loader to scoop and hoist them into the waiting trucks. With the first loads hauled away, Zach focused on his work for when the pair returned in forty minutes. At 2:00 pm the last trucks had left to unload and return to the rental company. John Cox came up to Zach at the cab of the high reach machine and offered to help with loading the remaining two columns.

Zach hoped his facial expression did not betray his angst at Cox's offer.

"My guys want to hit the bars, but I'm available if you need a helping hand," Cox said.

"Naw, John. We've got it from here. I have a license for the fourteen-yard dump, and I want to be careful loading, so I don't break it prematurely. It'll be slow work. You've done enough. He wiped his sweaty brow and continued, determined to convince Cox. "You go home. Call it a weekend. I'll get with accounts payable Monday to get you paid. Two per cent, net ten all right?"

"You betcha. Ten-day payment goes a lot farther than a two per cent discount, especially on this job. It's been one of the smoothest we've had as a decon' company in years ... maybe ever. You guys are the best. I'll work for you anytime."

With work gloves off, the two shook hands at the cab of the high lift.

When John Cox departed, Bartolome carrying a large roll of burlap, headed toward the larger footing. The winter sun would set in a couple hours and there was no time to waste. Zach would use the high lift to topple the column footing and then Bartolome would do the dirty work.

"After all, it's my mess to clean up," Bart told Zach earlier.

The column footing lifted easily and toppled over just right with no appreciable damage. Zach had pulled the column over on its side pointing toward the cab of the high lift. The exposed soil and corpses were concealed from anyone at the entrance and the only exit to the jobsite.

Zach had been focusing on the job at hand and did not notice John Cox waving. He froze. "Pinche cabron," he said, letting loose a Spanish expletive.

"Sorry, Mr. Martin, but did you see my gloves there in the cab? My wife bought them for me in my rodeo days. I'd really miss them."

Fortunately, Cox approached the high lift from the left side near the project entrance where his view of the bodies was obstructed. Zach looked down and saw a pair of leather roping gloves marked M.L. Leddy's. Zach knew the brand, having grown up wearing boots from that leather company in Texas. He grabbed the gloves and tossed them from the cab.

"Thanks. Looks like you had a little accident there." Cox's statement was more like a question.

Zach answered with some bogus engineer-speak, "No, I did that on purpose. We want to get some samples underneath the footing to measure the concrete-soil cohesion after fifty years under 500 kips pressure."

"Uh huh ... uh huh," was all Cox could say, having no idea what this engineer just said.

"Well, thanks for the gloves. I wouldn't be welcome at home without them. They were pretty expensive for a working man," Cox added. "You guys take care of yourselves and don't work too late. It's Saturday, remember."

"Thanks, John. See you next project." Zach tipped his hardhat at the contractor giving him another reason to smile. He exhaled as the man turned to go.

"Thanks, my friend. Next time then." Cox walked through the gate to his truck and left.

That's when Bartolome peered around the ten-inch-thick, twelve-foot-square footing lying on its side and called to his son-in-law, "Does an old man have to do this all by himself?"

"Be right there, Dad," he yelled, realizing Bart had no idea how close they had come to being exposed.

***

Zach and Bart loaded the two column footings and three corpses wrapped in burlap into the older dump truck. Zach started to drive away from the job site when his father-in-law waved to him to stop at the gate.

Zach looked in the right rearview mirror and saw Bartolome trotting up to the passenger side of the cab, resembling a younger version of himself.

Bart opened the door and swung into the seat. He was holding a red jeweler's pouch which he had taken from his front pants pocket. They left the project at 7:30 pm after closing the chain-link fence gate and latching it with a padlock. Bart and Zach had the only two keys to the lock.

Zach was looking at the jeweler's pouch when his father-in-law said, "Zach, I've decided on a slight change of plans."

"Is this another secret?" Zach asked.

"You're my son. You should know everything. There's more to the story," Bart answered with anxiety written on his face.

Bart continued, "Sometime later, after the incident, I confessed to the priest at St. Anne's. You know him. He's the one who married you and Jordan. Padre Juan."

"After my confession and the penance that he assigned me, I carried a secret hope with me for almost two years. I wanted to talk to his mother." Bartolome motioned with his left thumb toward the rear cargo container.

"To explain to her why I did what I did."

Zach was engrossed in the story, listening and asking questions, sometimes looking at his father-in-law.

On West Picacho Street, he was headed toward I-10 and almost ran a red light, stopping abruptly just inches before the pedestrian crosswalk where a small boy with a baseball bat was walking across. Fortunately, the truck had air brakes and squealed to a stop just in time.

Zachary and Bartolome looked at each other and sighed in unison. The dump truck continued when the light turned green but much slower than normal.

"And?" Zach did not make eye contact with his father-in-law this time.

"Padre Juan is more than just a priest, son. Sometimes I think he's a *brujo* ... instead of a Catolico priest." Bartolome didn't have to explain that brujo was a Spanish term for witchdoctor. "Sometimes I think he knows more than he lets on about life, our life, and how to fix relationships and people.

"Anyway, he arranged a surreptitious meeting with me and Conchita Gonzalez, his mother," he said motioning behind them again.

"We met and talked about the incident and more. She told me that Kouris told her son to kill me, and they nearly killed my whole family. Jordan was just a baby." Bartolome looked downward as he recalled the conversation.

"He and his compadres had been drinking when they came in with their weapons drawn and even broke down the door. I didn't know they were drunk until after I incapacitated Rayaldo." Zach noticed this was the first time his father-in-law had used the man's name. Over the last few weeks, when discussing the incident, Bartolome had referred to the dead man as cabron, pendejo, mojado, goon, thug and gangster and most recently, son of Conchita Gonzalez. Everything but his name... until now.

Zach had heard Jordan discuss the psychological principle of humanization and understood that Rayaldo was now a real person to Bart.

"I killed Rayaldo first. Then when the ax was coming down, I could tell his partner was too inebriated to react fast enough."

Zach felt Bartolome staring at him, but he didn't dare take his eyes off the road. He was at a loss for words, anyway. Then he heard Bart sniffling and realized tears were streaming down his father-in-law's cheek.

"I think I did commit murder, Zach," Bartolome confessed. "It was self-defense with Rayaldo, but I think I murdered the second gunman." Except for engine noise and Bart's sniffing, silence flooded the cab.

Then smiling, Zach broke the stillness.

"Just like that Eric Clapton song, 'I shot the sheriff, but I did not shoot the deputy.'" It was a stupid, insensitive thing to say, but Zach needed to fill the pregnant silence. He couldn't bear the discomfort of his father-in-law's grief.

Fortunately, it caused the briefest smile to cross Bartolome's face before he turned to look out the passenger window at the New Mexico horizon now adorned with the yellows and reds of a desert sunset.

"It was rage, miho. I was filled with rage. I took a life because I was enraged."

At Bart's confession, a haunting memory descended upon a raw nerve for Zachary. He wanted desperately to open up to his father-in-law, but it wasn't the right time.

"So, I want to do something for Conchita," Bart continued. "... something that might make things better for her ... and give her closure.

"I want to give Rayaldo a funeral."

At that, Zach broke the private oath he made at the intersection, to keep his eyes on the road. He took his right foot off the accelerator and slowed to a stop along the shoulder of the highway.

Now Zach turned to look directly into his father-in-law's eyes.

"A funeral?" he gasped, incredulous. "You want to give the man who almost murdered you and your family a funeral? You can't be serious. The man tried to kill you, and if you hadn't reacted, he would've. And how can you give a funeral to the man who, in the eyes of the law, ran away from home in 1957 and disappeared. And now everything we're doing will be exposed. It's admitting that you killed three men. There's no statute of limitations on … killing." Zach avoided the word, murder.

"Son, you are not involved. This is on me. I must do this thing. The truck is in my name. You're not here. We'll dispose of the other two as we planned. We'll just wrap Rayaldo's body in a special way, and I'll speak privately to Conchita tomorrow morning."

***

That evening was filled with activity. The barnyard at Zach's family farm had limited lighting, and the distance from any neighbors would prevent a clue to the action even at this time of night.

The power-take-off (PTO) drive on the John Deere tractor was connected to the grain mill grinder that pulverized grain into powder and chaff then propelled the substance into an enclosed bin to store the crushed livestock meal. It would stay there until it was sacked and stored for feeding livestock on the farm. It had not been used for many years, but Zach was confident it would work properly since there weren't many moving parts to break.

The grinder was a rusted John Deere green color. It had a chute through which corn, hegari (colloquially pronounced hi-gear), alfalfa and other feedstuff was funneled into a mill.

A hopper delivered the pulverized contents of the mill to the sealed room where it would later be sacked for storage. Zach brought up a few bales of alfalfa hay, some dried corn on the cob, and a few sheaths of hegari. With the PTO connected to the tractor and the feedstuff and two decayed corpses at the ready, Bart engaged the tractor.

The grinder came to life slowly after faltering a time or two. With the speed increased enough for grinding work, Zach and Bart started the process with a few blocks of the alfalfa hay – then some corn – then some hegari – and finally Zach placed a piece of the decomposed corpse on the feed track.

Bart's scream was louder than the grinder, "Stop, miho! We can't do this!" Bartolome disengaged the grinder gear, stopping the conveyor immediately with the decomposed limb in the middle of the track. The sudden stillness was jolting.

"What's wrong, Dad? Why did you stop?" asked Zach.

"We can't do this, miho. I can't further desecrate these bodies. It's wrong. It's wrong." Zach noticed his father-in-law's tear-stained face and red eyes.

"Son, I must give these men the burial that every man deserves, no matter how evil his actions." Bartolome disconnected the PTO drive from the John Deere, then drove and parked the tractor in the semi-circular barn originally used as a Quonset hut. He returned, driving a backhoe. From the perch of the tractor he instructed Zach, "Son, bring the bodies to the scoop and lay them in. Be careful. Don't let them slip off."

It was dark, but they could see enough to dig two holes, each eight-feet deep. That done, Bartolome used the fabric to lower each body to the bottom then gently tossed the Catolico medallion into one of the graves where it landed on top of the fabric.

Bart filled the graves with care. When the soil was sufficiently compacted, he knelt beside the packed dirt and uttered a quiet prayer for each man. He stood, turned, climbed into the backhoe, leaving the pasture where Hereford cattle were still grazing. "Now the men have a quiet resting place in the shadow of the Florida Mountains, miho. May their souls be at peace. Tomorrow, I'll bring sod to cover the exposed dirt."

In the morning, they would deliver the concrete footings still on the dump truck to the recycling plant. If anyone asked, they would answer that they had completed the testing work and were responsibly disposing of the remains. It was partly true.

As they pulled out of the farm, the third corpse, wrapped in burlap, rested alone in the truck bed. Bartolome sat in the passenger seat. They were about to turn onto Highway 11 from Columbus to Deming when he spoke.

"Son let me drive. You can sleep on the trip back. You have a long day in front of you, and I have some business to attend to early."

***

Bartolome got no sleep that night. At 4:30 am, he and Zach drank coffee and ate a large breakfast at the Flying J Truck Stop on West Picacho in Las Cruces. Then Bartolome dropped Zach at the warehouse so he could grab a quick shower and proceed with final directions to the labor cleanup crew that was sure to arrive at 6:00 am.

Bartolome drove the dump truck to the recycling center with the remains of his would-be killer now in the cab with him under a green wool blanket purchased from an Army surplus store. After dumping the two column footings, he traveled to the house on Maple Street. He wasn't sure if his idea would work, but he had to try.

It was a recurring dream that haunted him. He was riding a tiger like it was a horse. The tiger turned around and asked, "Why did you bury me under a building? I have a mother, you know." This same dream had haunted him intermittently for years.

He rang the doorbell at the house on Maple Street just after 7:00 am. Conchita had arisen at 6:00 and was settling into her third cup of decaf, a routine she had adopted almost half a century before when she moved into Simon's home. It had been her property since 1958.

A year after Simon died, she moved into his master bedroom and had just installed a video monitor at the front and rear doors. She saw on the black and white video monitor, the figure of a man standing on the front porch and a dump truck parked at the street. The image stirred her curiosity.

"Yes?" she asked opening the door. Then she stopped and stared at the man she had not seen in over forty years except in passing at St. Anne's Masses.

"Madre de Dios!" she exclaimed as she instantly recognized the face of the man she had not spoken with since that day at the rectory in 1960.

"Señor Valles. Buenos dias."

"Buenos dias, Señora Gonzalez. Como esta usted?" He took care to use formal Spanish in greeting her.

"Quieres café?" she asked with the smallest hint of cordiality. Conchita invited him inside for coffee, something she knew a man in his profession would appreciate. Bartolome accepted the invitation. Dusting his gloves, Bart stuffed them in his rear pocket. He had not done a lot of manual labor since BeeVee2 had grown from the fledgling business he started in the 50's. Digging the grave with a shovel was enough to remind him of his age.

He stayed at the house on Maple Street all morning, visiting with Conchita for the first two hours. Together they shed tears as Conchita accepted his offer graciously. With one caveat. Conchita would not attend the burial. She picked out the site for the memorial, and Bartolome would be the one to dig, but she could not bear to see the body of her son lowered into the grave.

Bart dug a traditional six-foot-deep grave and, lowering the body gently, oriented it facing east as was the custom. Rayaldo would lie beneath a cottonwood tree in the backyard of the house on Maple Street. With the body encased in a large burlap wrapping, Bartolome covered it with soil for the second time.

Bartolome knew Conchita had been watching his progress from the rear window. At around 11:30 am he heard an engine start up, and a car pulled away from the circular driveway in front.

With the body now buried, Bartolome had another task.

***

"Padre Juan, buenos tardes." Bartolome greeted the priest who had been a large part of his spiritual life for almost sixty years.

After listening to Bart's request, the priest turned to collect his black vestment from the armoire in his rectory. He prepared for the Rite of Interment.

Padre Juan joined Conchita and Bartolome in the rear yard beneath the cottonwood tree while Padre Juan conducted the formal Catholic Mass including Introductory Rites, the Gospel Reading, the Homily, and the Liturgy of the Eucharist followed by the Closing Rites.

After the introductory rites, Conchita asked for a reading from the New Testament regarding forgiveness. Both Conchita and Bartolome then shared the Liturgy of the Eucharist. Finally, Padre Juan conducted The Closing Rites, asking God to accept Rayaldo's soul.

Finally, Padre Juan asked the attendees to speak to the circumstances of today's service. Conchita was first.

"Miho, I am sorry for your death. I am sorry if I misled you during your young life. I am sorry if I was not the best mother. I miss you, and I still love you. I have said prayers for you every night since …" She couldn't finish the sentence.

It was Bart's turn. "Rayaldo, I am sorry for the events that brought us together that night. I am sorry for the circumstances that led to your death. I killed you, Rayaldo. I did. I am responsible for the deaths of your friends as well. I could have tried to control things better, but I failed. I failed you and you suffered the results."

Tears flooded Bartolome's cheeks as he continued. "We had so much in common. Rayaldo, you could have been a friend. We came from the same blood. We had the same problems facing us, mixing into this white society. We were born into the same religion. We spoke the same language. We both struggled to find our way. I wish we had known each other under better circumstances.

"I am sorry, Rayaldo."

When he finished, Padre Juan nodded and invited them to join him in reciting the "Our Father."

When they finished, he added, "Rayaldo, your early departure from this earthly plane has achieved some good." Both Conchita and Bartolome looked up at this pronouncement. The priest continued.

"My son, you have brought two people closer to our Father. Your mother and Bartolome have grown closer to God and stronger in their faith. Your actions, albeit ill-advised, have knit two souls closer to their destiny and in doing so, they will bring more meaning and love to others throughout their lives.

"Your life ... and death ... were not in vain. You contributed to life's fabric. You made others around you stronger and more filled with love." He paused for a moment to reach down and grab a handful of freshly ground soil. Then, tossing bits on top of the grave, he ended the ceremony.

"Ashes to ashes ... dust to dust. Let us go in peace to live out the Word of God."

Padre Juan, facing the two, then made the sign of the cross and departed, leaving Conchita and Bartolome alone together.

Bartolome spoke first. "Señora Gonzalez—" he started, but she interrupted him.

"Please. Call me Conchita."

Hesitantly, he said, "Conchita." He paused again. "Conchita, I have something for you. I believe it was your son's." He handed her the jeweler's bag. She took it, untied the drawstrings and shook out the contents into her left hand. She held it, analyzing it for a moment and then a single tear fell from her eye into her left palm as she clutched the ring against her chest. She closed her eyes and tightened her face to prevent more tears.

"I wanted you to have it."

Silently, they stood there together for more than a minute. Bartolome noticed that she occasionally opened her eyes to gaze at the ring as if paying homage to her son's life ... and death. Then she spoke.

"You have given me something very valuable. You have given me back my son." She started walking toward the house then stopped, turned, and addressed him with stoic conviction.

"I know that all the anger I felt for you before was wrong. I now know that Padre Juan was right. Bartolome, I forgive you in my heart. You were truly acting in self-defense. Your own life and that of your family. My son had to pay for that. He was wrong. I was wrong not to try and stop him. My son's death is my responsibility. You did not kill him. I did." She walked three paces back toward him.

"Bartolome do not hold the sorrow in your heart anymore. Your act may have ended Rayaldo's life, but it was my inaction that put him there." The faintest smile crossed her face as if it were the final release she needed.

She continued, "You have carried this pain longer than you ever should've. You did nothing wrong, Bartolome. You had the right – no – the obligation to defend your family. Please let it go. You have done more than enough to make things right. It is time that you be at peace." She paused and glanced up, smiling when a bird started singing in the cottonwood tree above the memorial.

"The bird sings what I am feeling now: joy and peace. You must feel that, Bartolome. Feel peace and be with me in joy."

Bartolome exhibited a discernable sense of relief as his tense muscles relaxed. The burden of guilt was at least loosening if not eliminated. He knew that his act of returning the ring, and of course, the body was about the best thing he had ever done.

He saw the genuine relief in Conchita's eyes. But he could also detect that the heaviness of her heart was not entirely gone. Something else was there. A different pain.

-45-

NEW MEXICO, 2001

"Ray, is it? Just call me Bubba. I own the joint," Bubba announced proudly, extending his hand as if holding a treasure. "Try this baby out for size. It's my personal favorite for a handgun. Great for personal protection."

Ray Kouris had not held a weapon since 1970 and then it was a rifle. He wasn't supposed to be holding one now. Felons were not allowed to have firearms. And once a felon, always a felon. He had never held a pistol before, and it felt strangely well balanced in his hand, different than he expected. The Colt .45, designated as M-1911, was designed for a .45 ACP cartridge. It felt heavier than he thought it would. Heavy, but comfortable in his right-hand grip.

The owner at the Guns-R-Us store smugly declared to Ray, "It has plenty of stopping power with minimal recoil and relatively low muzzle blast. It's used but in perfect condition. I sold this to a judge thirty-some years ago. He never used it. And the price I'm giving you is less than I sold it for back then."

"Who was the judge, ese?" Ray probed.

"Well, he's not a judge anymore. He retired some time back. Galvan was his name. Know of him?" Bubba asked while Ray was absorbed, looking downward, caressing the .45.

"I've heard of him," was all Ray divulged, studying the pistol.

"I've got a soft spot in my heart for Vietnam veterans. I was in Korea, you know. We both had the same sort of war ... killin' the slant-eyes," Bubba said with a knowing glance at Ray.

Ray yanked on his sleeve when he thought Bubba spotted the cobweb prison tat on his elbow. He hoped the man didn't know this one represented a lengthy term. It was on the elbow to signify spending so much time with arms on a table that a spider could make a web on your elbow. If he did notice, Bubba didn't share his impression with his customer. But when he didn't request a background check, Ray figured the sale would be off the books.

"You're getting a great buy, Ray! And I'll throw in some ammo for your target practice."

Ray had told Bubba that he carried one in The Nam and just wanted to have one of his own, that he would be using it for target practice in the desert on weekends.

By the way Bubba looked at him, he could tell that his reference to carrying one in The Nam was met with skepticism. Bubba told him he was a former Marine, too, and he knew that Marine Corps infantry were rarely issued side arms.

"So, you must have been an officer," he said. "Sidearms were standard issue for officers."

That's right," Ray lied. "An officer."

Ray thought about the firepower of the .45. He only needed it for intimidation ... not to kill anyone. But he decided to be prepared.

"I'll take it," he announced. "Thanks for the ammo, ese." Bubba, who evidently was not raised in the Southwest did not seem to get the implied aspersion.

Ray had trouble fieldstripping on the counter. That gave Bubba more cause to question his claim to have had one in The Nam. Bubba fieldstripped and put it back together in less than two minutes right in front of him, then explained to Ray, "I don't need to do the safety lecture if you're a veteran. You had enough of that in boot camp and ITR. Just make sure to clean it after every target practice.

"Heck, I'll even throw in a pistol cleaning kit for you since you're a vet." Did Ray detect sarcasm in Bubba's voice? "And maybe I can scrounge up some targets as long as you promise to not leave them out in the desert.

They've got our name printed on the bottom.

"If you police your brass and bring it back in," Bubba added, "I'll give you a twenty percent discount on ammo."

"Thanks again, ese." Ray declined the box, took the pistol and stuffed it in the large inner pocket of his vest.

Bubba smiled, took his cash and shook Ray's right hand that had another recognizable five-dot prison tat.

Ray couldn't know that the pistol had been in the shop for over a year or that Bubba made a decent profit on the sale.

At just over fifty years old, Ray Kouris was tired, beaten down by life, and exhausted by all the bad luck that came his way. His efforts to achieve the American dream were thwarted in one way or another by some unknown force beyond his control.

First, his life began as a lie from his mother. He was not her grandson like she told everyone in the early part of his life, but her son … and with a man for whom she had worked as a cleaner. He started life as a bastard. He was expelled from school before heading off to Nam. Then there was the girlfriend who blamed a pregnancy on him. The final insult was his mother stealing his inheritance. Every job after the Marine Corps lasted only a few months. Then the car wreck, a trial, and prison time. Now he was an ex-con and a parolee. He was tired of failing.

He had learned some schemes in prison that would help him. Even after the purchase he just made, he still had almost $1000 from the robbery of two Circle K stores last week. The camera would not reveal his face hidden by the woven ski mask he wore. He was in and out in less than a minute each time, not enough time for the cops to respond to the silent alarm triggered by the clerk's boot. He used a short section of pipe held inside a vest he wore to simulate the barrel of a handgun. Ray learned from prison mates that he shouldn't keep up that practice. Police would increase their patrols to these convenience stores in the coming weeks. He would have to find another way to raise money. He might even find work at a construction site to satisfy his parole officer.

Ray Kouris was determined to succeed in some way. Others had taken what was his for a long time now. It was time he took some of that back.

The Colt was still in his vest pocket. He had not loaded it yet. He wanted to get the feel for using it before he carried it loaded. At least now he could throw away that short pipe section he had carried around in his vest. Now he needed a car. Walking and this bus crap was not hacking it.

At least he had a place to stay for now. As a parolee, he was given temporary quarters in a halfway house with other parolees. It wasn't the Ritz, but it was free.

He got off the bus at Picacho and Valley Drive. It was the closest he could get to a series of car dealerships where he might find some cheap wheels.

Walking toward the first dealership located on Valley Drive, he noticed two men in a truck pulling out from across the street. They headed in the direction from where he got off the bus. He kept looking as they traversed the street and went the opposite direction. The driver looked familiar and the passenger, too. Maybe. He couldn't quite remember.

"Madre de Dios," he said when he spotted the sign on the warehouse they had driven from. The sign said BeeVee2 Construction. "Hot damn! I can't believe it. My luck is about to change."

Ray reconsidered his first plan and shifted to a newly hatched Plan B. Now he had two means of extortion. "Double your pleasure ... Double your fun..." he sang.

***

Back at his halfway house for the night, Ray was happy with his newly purchased car, a hooptie, parked on the street. He found a car he could afford and paid the $900 in cash. It was a 1981 Ford Escort sporting one donut tire and no spare. One headlight was out. There was no radio, only a hole from where it had been extracted by a thief who broke the driver's window to gain entry.

He still felt good about the purchase. He had bargained the price down more than half. Part of the red $1895 grease mark was still on the windshield. He thought the salesman relented simply to get rid of him. That's okay, he thought. I'll take it however I can get it. At least I'm not walking.

***

"Kouris, your room was a mess this morning. And remember, you're not supposed to smoke in here. Do you want me to report this to your PO?" The middle-aged woman had poked her nose into Ray's room unannounced.

"That's not me, ese. I don't smoke. I can't afford it," he said, smirking at the housemother who earned her living by overseeing a bunch of ex-cons.

"I'll clean my room," he said, hoping that would be enough to keep her from reporting him to the PO.

"It'd better be tomorrow. You have a job yet? 'Cause if you don't by Friday, you'll have to go to the unemployment office to look for work or you'll lose your place here."

"It's only Monday, ese," he responded implying that he had all week. "I got a car. It'll be easier to get a job … and keep it now." She closed the door but failed to engage the latch. He knew she was non-verbally reminding him that there was only a certain amount of privacy available in this housing arrangement. "Just one more way she gets on my nerves," he whispered.

-46-

NEW MEXICO, 2001

Conchita was at the sink, looking out the kitchen window at the grave in her backyard when the doorbell sounded. She glanced at the remote video monitor mounted over the refrigerator to see who it was. She dried her hands on her apron and untied it, flinging it toward the kitchen table. She was both charmed and angered by the unexpected visit from her son who had grown up here.

He had come to his childhood home for several reasons. First, she was his mother. Second, she was old. She was over eighty now although she carried it well. She still walked around the town, even to get her mail from the post office. And she was the only one who came to visit him over the past thirty years at La Tuna. Except for his cellmates, she had been his only contact with the outside.

But the real reason he came, he admitted, was that she might be willing to help him. After all this was partly about her first son, Ray's half-brother.

"Mama, I never thanked you for coming to see me all those years." Conchita looked up from her work, cutting off the tips of green beans and preparing them for cooking. Like all mothers, she wanted to be appreciated by her children but now she had a bad feeling about the comment. What was to come?

She stifled a shiver down her back and responded, "I'm your mother, Ray. I don't like to see you hurting. It tore me up inside when you ..." She couldn't finish the sentence. She lowered her eyes, turned to face him and braced herself for the answer to her next question.

"Why did you come here, Ray? Why today of all days?"

"Que paso hoy? he asked.

"You may not remember, but I can never forget. Today is the day your older brother died." She refrained from saying the day your brother was killed.

"Oh ese, I'm sorry Ma. I didn't know that. Remember, I was just eight years old. But I'm glad you mentioned it. There's something I wanted to tell you."

Now she was glad she had braced herself. She knew there had to be something. He never would've paid a social visit ... just to see her. He wanted something. "Would you please stop saying ese to me. I'm your mother. Don't speak in that gutter language to me. What is it you want? Do you have a job yet?"

"Mama, do you know who's in town?" he asked ignoring her questions.

"Who, Ray?"

"That man who killed Rayaldo ... and his son-in-law. I saw them this week. They're here," he announced as if he expected to be rewarded for his discovery.

The fact that he knew this stunned Conchita. She tried to hide her feelings by turning away from him.

"What does that have to do with you?" she asked in trepidation of the answer.

"Well, you told me a long time ago that he killed Rayaldo. You didn't do anything about it, so I am. You always told me to fight like a man, so ... I'm going to." He said it with pride in his voice.

Conchita turned swiftly to face him down. "Oigame! You leave that man alone. What's done is done. You'll wind up back in prison ... or worse."

"What's worse than prison, ese? ... Oh, sorry."

"You could wind up like your brother, ese. She threw the term back at him as a way of deriding his lack of maturity. "You could be killed yourself."

Stunned by her reaction, he failed to form a witty response. "Besides, it is none of your business. What was done is between that man and God." She hoped that would end it, but it didn't.

"Mama, I can at least confront him about it and see what he does. I might have a payoff offered to me for my silence." He pulled up his sweatshirt to reveal the Colt .45.

Conchita became furious. Her reaction did not seem like it came from an eighty-two-year-old woman. She put down her knife and walked toward him, pointing her finger at him.

"You listen, Ray. You don't know what you're doing. You are playing with fire here. You will get yourself killed." Her shouting was out of character and shocked him. "So, you have a gun! Did it ever occur to you that he might have one too? Or that both might?"

"No, it didn't," Ray said, looking sheepish but not for long. He straightened up and, with renewed bravado, said, "Hmm. Thanks, Ma. I'll have to prepare for that."

That's when Conchita uttered words that Ray never expected from his mother. With a bright red face and clenched fists, she spewed profanity in Spanish. She followed the expletives with an order.

"Get out of this house, and don't ever come back. I reject you as my son! Get out!"

***

Ray left the halfway house the next morning at daybreak, missing group breakfast, ostensibly to look for construction jobs. He had no intention of working a regular job on a construction site but knew he might line his pockets with some cash. His puta mother's words didn't bother him. He had a weapon and intended to get what was rightfully his.

He reached for the Colt .45 hidden under the dash of his hooptie. He kept it there since his room in the halfway house was subject to surprise inspection. After jamming the pistol into his belt, out of sight, he took two full clips of ACP ammo and stuffed them in his pocket.

Ray needed to make an appearance at the jobsite for an employment application. He would look for the Ford crew cab and make sure his targets were not on site since they might recognize him.

He knew, from scouting the warehouse, that Bartolome and Zachary were staying there, arriving back from work well past quitting time and leaving before sun-up. He would break in and hide out in the warehouse until they came back.

At 4:00 pm, Ray parked his car three blocks away and walked toward the warehouse. The matron expected him at the halfway house by 6:00 pm, but lights-out was not until 10:00. He would be done by then.

***

It was 5:00 pm, and after a week of excruciating stress, Bartolome approached his son-in-law and suggested knocking off early. "We both need some quiet time away from the construction site and the stress," he told Zach.

Their drive to the office that had been their home for the last two weeks was quick since it was close to the demo site. The crew cab pulled into the site after Zach unlocked the chained gate. Bartolome parked and the two walked into the warehouse, throwing their work attire in the bin at the entrance.

Their makeshift living quarters consisted of two cots at the rear corner, near the toilet and shower. The plan was for each to take a shower then hit the nearby oasis for a Mexican meal and a *cerveza* (beer). Zach would clean up first while Bartolome used the desktop computer to Skype Catarina.

"Como esta pendejos?" The voice came from the shadows cast by artificial light in the interior, windowless office. The two men froze when a dark figure emerged, each looking first at the man with the pistol in his hand and then at each other.

Zach was the first to speak. "Look, we don't have any money, man. Would we be living here if we had money? We've been working and just wanted to clean up and have some dinner."

When the gunman stepped into the light, Zach saw the sly grin. "Sure, you do, ese. You're rich, both of you. I know better. You don't remember me … ese?" Ray spoke directly to Zach. At that point, Zach recognized him. He was sick at the thought of what could happen. Bartolome seemed clueless as to the man's identity but not for long.

"Both of you owe me, and you're going to pay up," Ray said, waving his pistol toward the two men.

He addressed Zach. "You, pendejo … you killed innocent people in The Nam. I was there. I saw it. That village looked like World War III, ese." With a swagger, Ray moved slightly closer to Zach. "You're going to owe me for the rest of your life, ese."

Bartolome looked at his son-in-law in confusion, "What's this all about, miho?"

Then motioning toward Valles, Ray said, "And you, old man … you killed my brother, ese … and two others. I know. My mother told me all about you. You're going to owe me as long as you live."

"Muchacho, there's a lot you don't know about that night," said Bart. Your mother and I have become acquainted and we—"

Ray cut him off. "Don't call me boy and don't talk about my mother, pendejo. Leave her out of this. This is between you and me.

"The only thing we have to talk about is how much you will pay me to keep my mouth shut, until you die, cabron (asshole)."

Zach could tell Bart was trying to keep Ray talking. He used the opportunity to consider their options for escape.

"Hey Ray, how's this gonna work?" Zach asked, trying to keep his voice steady. "Are you opening an account at the bank and we give you money each month or what? And what if we're late one month? Are you going to the police and tell your story?"

With that, Ray became enraged. "You think you're so smart, white boy! I'll fuckin' kill your white ass, pendejo." He was just a couple feet from Zach when he swung his right hand and backhanded Zach with the pistol.

The act of hitting Zachary with the pistol caused an unexpected consequence. The Colt .45 discharged echoing inside the metal frame building. Both Zach and Bart landed on the floor, unsure of what had happened.

Then, backing off a bit, Ray looked around, confused and shaken. He steadied the gun with two hands and pointed it toward the floor where Zach and Bart lay.

"Put the gun down, Ray."

Conchita had found the warehouse after calling the Las Cruces City Building Department. She didn't know what she would do, but she had to do something. She parked her car at a dealership using the ruse of waiting for service work the next day.

The car was easy to drive, and at her age, ease was important. It was 5:30 pm and she guessed that Valles would be returning soon to the warehouse. She walked the two blocks on Valley Drive and saw the crew cab already parked out front.

During the walk, Conchita decided to tell Bartolome and Zachary what her son was planning instead of going to the police first. The rectangular warehouse was a metal frame building with two large overhead doors on either end with a man door on one of the longer sides.

As she approached, she noticed that the door was ajar, and she could hear voices inside. One of them sounded like her son. Then she heard the discharge of the gun. She let herself in, but quietly.

Conchita noticed Valles and Martin both on the floor. She saw bloodstains on the concrete around Valles. She spoke, this time with the authority of a parent.

"Put the gun down, Ray."

Conchita was aiming Simon's cocked revolver straight at her only remaining son. She had hesitated to carry it in her pocketbook for protection, but now she was glad she had it.

"What are you doin' here, Ma?"

"Put the gun down now!" she demanded again.

"Ma, I got this. Leave me alone, ese. This is for me to do, not you." Bartolome was bleeding from the .45 ACP round that had entered his left scapula, passing through his shoulder. He needed medical attention.

Zachary crawled slowly toward his father-in-law.

"Dad, how're you doin?" A pause. "... I mean ... besides the gunshot and all." Bart gave his son-in-law a weak smile. Zach opened the clothing around Bartolome's wound.

Now Ray moved toward the two on the floor, still aiming the pistol at them.

Do you want to join your brother?" Conchita asked. "No, Ma. I just want what's mine."

Unexpectedly, the man door opened. It was Enrique Garcia.

Surprised by the noise, Ray turned his attention to the door, now aiming his gun at Enrique who stood half the length of the warehouse away. A second gunshot erupted inside the metal building ... then a third ... and then silence.

Enrique had escaped the trajectory of the slug as it bounced off the red iron column near the door, making a hideous racket.

Conchita's aim, on the other hand, was precise and the impact deadly. She had shot Ray, piercing his heart. He fell to the floor, dead before she walked up to him with Simon's pistol still firmly within her grasp.

Enrique called 911 after checking on his old boss and best friend. He saw that Zachary and the woman were unscathed. He reported that a gunman had been killed and there was one man wounded. Police were on their way.

"I'm sorry, miho. I am so sorry," Conchita said as she knelt, tears flowing down her cheeks. She reached over, closed his eyes gently and caressed his cheek. She noticed the La Santa Muerte Catolico medal she had given him when he was young.

"Thank you ... for ... saving ... our lives, Conchita," Bartolome said between gasps.

"Is that her?" Zachary whispered to Bartolome.

"Conchita, es mi hijo, Zacharia. Zach, this is Conchita. She saved our lives, son."

"I know, Dad. I was there."

Conchita nodded and returned her attention to her son.

Sirens filled the fragile stillness. Then two uniformed policemen entered with pistols drawn and pointed them at the group. They secured the scene and removed the two pistols that were already on the floor. One made a call on the microphone attached to his uniform announcing to the team outside that it was safe to enter.

More uniformed police entered, followed by a stretcher carried by two EMTs, a woman and a man. It sounded like half the Las Cruces Police force was outside the warehouse. Two plain-clothes detectives entered as well.

The two men huddled at the entrance after surveying the incident, then pulled Zach and Enrique to different corners of the warehouse and questioned them briefly.

Soon, a photographer was inside taking pictures of the crime scene. Enrique had taken one detective to where he heard the impact of a slug. They were looking for it on the ground now. Police were interviewing Conchita who would not remove her gaze from her lifeless son while answering questions.

The EMTs placed Bartolome on a gurney. A transparent medical bag attached a small plastic hose to a needle in his left arm. They were rolling him out to an ambulance when Zach stopped the procession.

"Dad, how're you doin?" he asked his father-in-law again.

"A little light-headed, son. I'll be okay." Now looking at the EMT. "Right?" he asked her.

"He'll be fine. Just a flesh wound. Looks like it went through."

"I'll be right behind you, Dad," Zach said. Then after looking at the detective's notepad, he added, "I hope."

After fifteen minutes, the detectives had completed their initial interviews and regrouped to discuss the case. "The old woman already confessed she did it," one detective said to his partner. "The guy she killed was her son. Can you believe it? Apparently, he was here to rob these two guys, and she caught onto it and followed him. There seems to be some history here."

"The dead guy's an ex-con," he continued. Thirty years in La Tuna according to the NCIC. He had a gun he wasn't supposed to have. His P.O. said he missed two of his last three meetings. He's obviously dirty."

"Same story I got from the two contractors," said the second detective. "It seems there was a fracas and the gun discharged hitting the old guy. Then Mom here came in and created a 'Mexican standoff'. This other guy entered and surprised the gunman who shot at him. That's when Mom dropped her son.

"We'll get ballistics to run the weapons and forensics to look for GSR residue on the dead guy, but we can do that at the morgue. Let's see if we can wrap this one up. I do need to interview the old guy. But maybe I can do that on the ride to Memorial General with the ambulance."

"Right. We've got pictures now. We can secure the place and handle the rest from the office."

"I see no reason to keep the old lady, do you? It looks like she kept it from being a murder investigation. She's a well-known rich widow. Lives over on Maple Street. She's not going anywhere."

"No, of course not. Let her go. Heck. Let everyone go. The stories match. The evidence is consistent. No one is hurt all that bad. If we need her, we know where she lives."

-47-

NEW MEXICO, 2001

With Ray dead, Zach's worries should have been over. After all, there was no one left to tell any tales about his unspoken secret. He hadn't told Jordan about Ray's death yet, mainly because he wasn't sure it would register with her correctly until he could explain everything.

He didn't rehearse speeches like his father-in-law did. Telling his wife something like this was hard enough without trying to follow a script. He was finally ready to express his deepest fears to the one he had loved for over thirty years.

They were together at home on Williamsburg Street in Arlington. Zach had returned last night with Bart after his father-in-law's release from the hospital. Bartolome asked Zachary to withhold the events from his wife and daughter until after they both returned.

Zach complied with the request. In fact, he hadn't explained much about the last three weeks when he and Jordan talked each night on Skype, the cheapest way to communicate. Bartolome had told Zachary to take a week off to rest up, and Zach took advantage of the invitation. "Jordan, I need to tell you something …" He lowered his head in sorrow. Time seemed to stop.

He was not aware of how long he hesitated.

"Zachary, I am listening. I am here ... listening to my husband. Honey, what is it? You're shaking."

"Jordan, I did something ... when I was a kid ... really when I was in The Nam." As soon as he used that term, he cursed himself. It was a term Ray used, one he despised.

"I'm going to tell you the truth about that night, the one that earned me the Bronze Star. But it's hard, you know? I did some things...." He paused to consider his next sentence. Jordan remained silent but laid her hand on Zach's arm.

"There was a lot going on, of course. It was war after all. I was young, but I should've had better judgment." Now he shook his head in disgust.

"Please don't ever think you need to withhold anything from me, Zach. I love you and I am here for you whenever you need me ... times like this, Zach. I'm here for you." Grasping his strong arms, Jordan turned him toward her.

For the next hour Zach told his wife the truth ... at least as he remembered it. It was the hardest thing he had ever done, acknowledging a wrongdoing to the closest person in his life and not until they'd been married for almost three decades.

With Jordan's coaxing, Zach acknowledged that many events during combat were never clearly known. Back and forth the dialogue went regarding the incident as Zach remembered it. Jordan applied her psychology training to get to the heart of what happened. Zach drew on memory clouded by thirty years of anxiety. Jordan knew how to help Zach uncover the truth.

Jordan could tell this confession was tough for her husband. After all, he always carried a commanding presence. He was accustomed to telling people what to do on a construction site in no uncertain terms. He had told her once that he must use profanity with subcontractors to be taken seriously.

Now, he was faced with trying to comprehend his own deeply buried psychosis. He had never had to follow professional advice like this. It was new territory for Zachary Martin. Jordan treaded cautiously, using professional techniques for memory restoration.

"Zach, start from the end and work in reverse the details of what happened that night." She knew the classic technique for determining deception also worked for judgment clouded by guilt. She took notes as a clinical psychologist would do with a patient. Over the next few minutes, Zach's recollection improved with several 'ah-ha' moments. After that, Jordan tried another technique.

"Here, show me what the scene looked like." She pulled a sheet of paper from her notebook. "Draw it out for me like a map. Or do you still have your grid map?" She recalled seeing a picture of the laminated map he had folded and kept in the leg pocket of his jungle fatigues.

"No, I think the map is long gone. Here's what I remember the scene looked like. The company was here on a small hill. The LP (Listening Post) was out here a klick or so. There was a road between Liberty Bridge and An Hoa. We ran down that road at top speed for almost twenty minutes until we were within earshot of the LP." He related the story again and again. Each time, there was a noticeable improvement in the clarity of his memory. After each retelling, Jordan added a new dimension to the memory-enhancement technique.

"Zach tell me about the smell of war. Do you recall what you told me one time? What was that like?"

"Oh God! It was awful and invigorating at the same time. Between my own sweat and the smell of helicopters, the napalm, the rifles, the white phosphorus candles, the blood of the wounded, it all mixed together and..." He didn't finish the thought but looked into Jordan's eyes with a thousand-mile-away stare.

That did it. Suddenly, he had a recollection that stopped him in his tracks.

"Oh my God! I remember now about my conversation with Clevis May before he went out on LP. We were both watching a line of men walking in formation toward a village. I thought they were farmers who lived in the village. I told him they were not VC (Viet Cong). He said these guys were NVA (North Vietnamese Army)." As Zach looked in the distance, pausing, Jordan was careful not to interrupt the flow of his memory.

"The NVA were notorious for screwing with villagers. We found numerous villages where they conscripted the men and killed the women and children, destroying their village. Was that what happened that night? Were we seeing villagers besieged by an NVA unit?

"I need to piece this together. Keep asking questions, Jordan. You triggered something that could be important. When I called air strikes and mortars, I might not have even touched a civilian. They may have been gone by that time. I was only killing the NVA. How can I know that?"

"Zach, who might have seen this besides you two? Clevis died that night, right?" She already knew the answer. She mentioned Clevis to trigger emotional memories, which were always more precise.

"No, not that I remember. We were talking with Billy Braun ... then Greek walked up to us. We thought he was just trying to get out of perimeter watch by walking around the ....

"Oh my God! He was going back to the perimeter ... on the same side as the village. He would have had a perfect view." Zachary strained to recall who else might have been there. Then the epiphany occurred to him.

"I remember now. Jenkins was on the LP we rescued, but Greek ... or Ray had told us he was going back to ... to Jenkins who was on perimeter watch. Ray must have been paired up with him on perimeter before Jenkins was deployed to the LP.

"If that's so, the two of them might have seen it together. How 'bout that? Ray might have seen the NVA chase the villagers off but didn't report it to the company CP. Then he tries to reverse what really happened and use that against me for his own gain." Jordan didn't understand the last reference but was interrupted by her husband's praise before she could ask.

"My wife, you're a damn good psychologist. Is this what you do for a living?" His question was not just frivolous banter. He had always wondered what her day-to-day routine involved.

But now he needed to add the postscript about Ray's threats. "His name was Ray Gonzalez Kouris. We called him Greek." Jordan drew a faint recollection of a name from the past.

"Was that the same Ray Kouris from Las Cruces?" she inquired.

"There can't be too many people with that name in Southern New Mexico," answered Zach. "Why? Have you heard of him?"

"It was a psychology class event, once, before you and I met."

Zach's brain went into overdrive. "He was in your psych class? I thought he was a high school dropout."

"He was, Zach. Our professor had us attend a court sentencing for a drunk driver who killed someone. She served as an expert witness. She wanted a few of us to see the psychology profession in action. I was in the back of the courtroom taking notes. Yes. That was the name. Ray Gonzalez Kouris. I remember the mixture of Greek and Spanish. The judge threw the book at him. As I recall, the judge added every charge possible to extend the sentence."

"Yeah, he did. Thirty years in prison," Zach informed her. "I saw that in the newspaper a few days after he went to prison. It was the harshest penalty for a traffic infraction in New Mexico history.

"He killed a guy while driving drunk, but apparently it was his manner in court that offended the judge the most. He was indignant, baiting the dead man's family with sneering expressions, all while witnesses testified that he despised white people. He was racist himself, blaming all his woes on someone else.

"Heck, I even gave him work," Zach continued. "That ended badly too. He probably stole a tool and then accused me of being racist for blaming him. And I never blamed him. I just asked if he'd seen it. He stormed off and quit then threatened to expose what I did in Vietnam. "But Jordan, there's more about Ray. He's dead. His own mother killed him just last week in Las Cruces." Jordan, now left without the composure she always relied upon, leaned forward, giving the remark her full attention.

"You're kidding. What happened?"

"It's a long story, but he tried to extort money from your father and me. The most important thing to tell you is that your father is okay. Ray shot him, but your dad didn't want me to tell you on the phone.

"What? Dad has been shot! And you didn't tell me?" She stood and began pacing, all composure lost now.

"He didn't want to alarm you. He was okay, so I agreed. Ray had a pistol but didn't know how to use it very well. He pistol-whipped me and the gun went off, hitting your dad in the shoulder."

Jordan was on her cell phone calling her mother, who had just learned the news the night before. Catarina assured her daughter that Bartolome was fine except he was complaining about her pampering. He didn't like being the focus of attention.

With that news, Jordan sat again and re-engaged the conversation with her husband. "He tried to bribe both of you?" she asked.

"It wasn't the first time Ray tried that with me either. I gave him a job when I was in college, before I met you. He recalled the incident at the village and tried to sucker me into a payoff. He was a coward, but he was always quick to find a way to make an easy buck.

"Thank God I didn't do it, although it was mainly because he never showed up. He tried to lure me into a meeting at a restaurant in Las Cruces. I went and waited for him, but he never showed up. It was around the time of that car wreck, just before my father passed away. "Son of a bi...." he caught the obscenity before it left his tongue.

"I'll bet he was in jail!"

"So, what happened with his mother?"

"Well, that's why we had to alter our return schedule. The police had to interrogate us. Your dad had a day or two recovery in the hospital too. You see, we were involved, as well."

Jordan, aghast that both men she loved had been in jeopardy of losing their lives, fell into Zach's arms, needing comfort of her own.

But there was still the haunting anxiety in Zach's mind. Even though Ray's extortion attempts would never bother him again, he needed to know the truth.

-48-

WASHINGTON, DC, 2002

Jenkins didn't even have a first name that Zach knew. So, he followed the only thread of information he had. He started at the Marine Corps Historical Center near Eighth and I Streets in Washington, near the Navy Yard, right across the Potomac from his home in Arlington.

The center had kept exhaustive records of all personnel and unit activity since the Marine Corps was founded on November 10, 1775. Both current and former Marines celebrated that date every year. Zach recalled the celebration the year he was in Vietnam. He was in the bush when a CH46 helicopter brought hot chow, one cold beer for each soldier, and a huge birthday cake. He smiled at this memory as he departed the Metro train at the Navy Yard exit on the green line.

The short walk to the historical center was not easy for him, as he struggled to plough through eight inches of freshly fallen snow. An armed Marine Corps security guard assigned to provide safety since the recent events of 9/11 greeted him at the entrance.

Zach found the records he was searching for in an electronic bin, identified as 127.3.2 Personnel Records. He searched within the time frame

268 - Lynn Underwood

of December 10, 1969, a date emblazoned on Zach's memory, the date of the event. He also cross-referenced unit assignments, in this case, Third Battalion, Fifth Marine Regiment, First Marine Division during the same time period.

After three hours, he found what he wanted, a name. Until then, his only clue about the Marine in question was a last name. He learned that Jenkins was Marcus Jenkins from Kitty Hawk, North Carolina. Zach smiled at that reference. He and Jordan had spent many summer vacations at the Outer Banks, lapping up the sun and enjoying the sand. Kitty Hawk was a great little beach town. And the best place to eat there was John's Drive Inn near mile post four and a half, he recalled.

Now for the next step. Where was Marcus Jenkins now? With his service number, Zach could access other pertinent records.

"Gunny, do you have any idea how I could find a former Marine I knew in Vietnam?" he asked the gunnery sergeant who doubled as security and librarian. Gunny was in un-dressed blues. This was a legitimate uniform that included dress blue trousers with a khaki dress shirt and tie with the Marine Corps tie clasp.

"Sir, the Marine Corps does not keep those kinds of records, sir." Zach was happy to see some traditions hadn't changed. The sergeant was detached from the commandant's headquarters and residence at Eighth and I Streets.

"They still make you say, 'sir' as the first and last words out of your mouth, huh?" Zach inquired.

"Sir, yes sir," the sergeant replied with a grin.

"But there is a possibility … a slim one," the sergeant suggested, "that if the Marine in question immigrated to the nation where he was posted, we will have that record. But as I said, it is only a remote possibility. Right over here, sir."

On a green screen, Zach noticed the gunny inputting the service number and last name and cross-referencing in the current location section in the database he was now using. A single result popped up.

"Son of a bi …" Zach jerked with a start. "Look at that! He moved to Da Nang. Hot damn!" Now all he needed was a printout of Jenkins' last known address in Da Nang.

Offering profuse appreciation to the gunny, Zach started to leave when the gunny asked him if he wanted to look up his own record.

"I'm afraid you might not let me out'a here if I do. I may be in the brig by dinner, Gunny," he said grinning.

Zach left the museum in high spirits and with a name and an address. As he was trudging through the snow toward the Navy Yard Metro stop, he made a cell call to the BeeVee2 office manager who doubled as the company travel agent.

"BeeVee Squared. Helen speaking. May I transfer your call?"

"Hey Helen, it's Zach. Can you get me on a round trip to Da Nang in the next day or two?"

"Hey Zachary. Are we branching out to the Eastern Hemisphere, now?"

"No, Helen, it's not business, but it's still something I've gotta do. Don't expense it. Charge it to my personal account."

Next, Zach called Bartolome and asked for a few more days off.

-49-

VIETNAM, 2002

The country bore some resemblance to his faded memory. He remembered the shape of the top of the hillocks around the area. Liberty Bridge was still there although upgraded to a four-lane bridge now. There were settlements on either side of the river at the crossing of the Song Thu Bohn. The outpost that had been overrun while he was there, was long gone. The road to An Hoa was paved with modern traffic signs and a rudimentary median. He passed by the Phu Nahms where they had conducted lots of search-and-destroy missions.

The driver passed An Hoa Village, the area where the Fifth Marine Regiment had its headquarters in 1969. The runway was still intact. His jeep escort said it was a regional airport now, with a prop carrier that shuttled passengers to and from Da Nang, Chu Lai, and other cities within what had been called "I" Corps.

Vietnam had a storied political geography. The country was divided into pieces for tactical reasons. Right now, Zach was in the northern most section. It was called I Corps but really it was Roman numeral I for 1st Corps. The breakaway republic was divided into four corps from north to south, hence I Corps was the northern-most sector of South Vietnam. I, II, III and IV Corps was how the Army of the Republic of Vietnam military referred to the various areas of responsibility.

And there it was, just across the Song Thu Bohn River. Zach had waded across this stretch of the Song Thu Bohn many times into the Arizona Territory. If he didn't have the river's bend to establish his bearings, he never would have guessed though.

Houses and other buildings now dotted the region. He saw what looked like subdivisions with paved avenues, streetlights and electric poles providing utilities to modern-looking homes. He wondered what kind of building codes the local contractors had to contend with.

As they continued along the modern four-lane road, he turned to his travel partner and asked, "So, Jenkins, how long have you lived here now?"

"Going on twenty years, Marty. I moved here after visiting three times. I had to tame the same ghosts that are still plaguing you. So, I came back here ten years after I was medevac'd. Did you know they put me on a hospital ship for three months before I went back to Pendleton?"

"No, I didn't. We never heard from you and assumed you rotated back to civilian life," Zachary responded to his old combat pal, albeit one he hadn't known well back then.

"The U.S.S. Sanctuary. I came back to the real world from the Philippines after getting flown there on a helicopter from the hospital ship. That was when I could finally walk around the ship three laps without crutches."

"Marty, you know my injuries were pretty severe. I was hit with shrapnel in several places including my posterior. I also took two rounds, one in the arm and the other in my groin. They said if I hadn't gotten medical attention when I did, I would have bled out.

"You saved my life, Marty ... you and Second Squad."

Jenkins looked at Zach and added, "You know the guys from Second Squad told me about you that night ... that you really weren't part of the squad, yet you volunteered to come out there after us. I remember you were a forward observer. Why'd you come out there? Why'd you risk your life to come after us? You didn't need to put yourself in that kind of danger."

"It just seemed the right thing to do, I guess. I mean, we're brothers, right? There was no one else who could run FAC and medevac," Zach said. "You woulda' done the same for me, right?"

"I doubt it." Jenkins held a sly grin as he answered the man who was responsible for saving his life. "I'm not John Wayne, ya know."

***

They were back in Da Nang after a reunion tour of the land where both had been plunged into adulthood, albeit still as teenagers.

"Hey Marty, you never told me how you found me," Jenkins said. "You'd be surprised what kind of records the Marine Corps keeps on us. I'm wondering now if they know about those LURPs (Long Range Patrol Rations) I helped liberate from the Recon Marines in An Hoa?" Zach grinned at Jenkins.

"You know, between Billy Braun, my radio operator and me, we crammed three dozen LURPs in our foot lockers. We ate on those for weeks. They were tasty and a lot lighter to hump in the field than C-Rations." Again, Zach let a grin spread across his face.

"Yeah, they were pretty good, Marty. Did you ever notice coming up short on supply one time?" Jenkins was now the one with the sly grin. "No shit! You did that?" Now, laughter erupted between the two.

Then Zach answered the question.

"Yeah, Billy accused me, and I accused him. We finally just put it to our failing memory or miscounting."

"Why did you come here, Marty?" Jenkins asked with a face betraying his concern for the unexpected encounter.

"Well, I need your help, Jenkins. It's about our time in the country."

With a sigh of relief, Jenkins said he was only too happy to help the man who saved his life.

When they arrived at the local watering hole, only one ordered a beer. Zach noticed that Jenkins ordered seltzer water. Maybe it was early for Jenkins, but Zach knew he needed a beer.

After an hour at the bar, Zach was happy that the price of beer was cheaper than it was in Arlington. Jenkins wasn't sure how he could help his visitor. They had only served a short time together. It was a serious time, but both were now older men with lots of miles.

"So, what's this help you need, Marty?" Jenkins asked.

"Do you remember the night you were medevac'd very well?" Zach started.

"Of course, just like I remember the time I lost my cherry," Jenkins joked.

After two hours in the bar and only a ten-dollar bill from the waitress, Zach smiled. He would have been dancing if he could have maintained his balance.

Jenkins remembered the night well. He also remembered an exchange with Greek and the line of NVA. Finally, he told Zach what he so desperately needed to hear.

"The fuckin' NVA that marched into that village killed two that I saw, a woman and a child who threw himself over ... what must have been his dead mother."

"No shit. Really? What happened then?" Zach asked.

"I suggested to Greek that we tell Farnsworth. He told me not to. He thought we had some sort of 'night act' or something. I think he was just a lazy asshole, but he was senior to me. Hell, everyone was senior to me. I may have been a fire team leader, but I'd only been in the country for a few months.

"Well, about that time Farnsworth came around and assigned me to the LP so I had to leave. I took one final looksee through the field glasses and saw them marching what was left of the villagers away from the area," Jenkins added.

The look on Zach's face must have conveyed relief.

"Marty, if you're feeling guilty about bombing that vill', don't. There were twenty NVA regulars there, man, and not one civilian."

After emptying the seltzer water, he added, "Well, maybe two, the two killed in front of the other villagers by the NVA."

Jenkins went on. "They did that to make them get the fuck out of Dodge, if you know what I mean. You had righteous kills man! And you saved my life."

A tear wound its way down Zach's face. Jenkins had returned the favor to the man who saved his life in 1969. Zach's self-recrimination could come to an end.

"Thanks man." It was all Zach could utter at that point. "Thanks."

"Something ... else ... Marty," Jenkins announced hesitantly. Zach could tell Jenkins wasn't sure how the man he knew thirty years ago would take this news.

Jenkins pulled something out of his pocket. "Here's a photo album of my family, still back home of course," he started cautiously. Zach took the small album.

"I got married and had kids, you know. Then I got divorced." He sounded if he were attending an Alcoholics Anonymous meeting. "She couldn't understand what I was going through." He looked straight at Zach.

"Did you know that the Arizona was in an area with a lot of Agent Orange? I went to the VA after I was separated from the Marine Corps to register for disability. They told me I was in an area with the poison. They put me on the

Agent Orange registry." Still looking at Zach as if for a sign that it was safe to keep going, he continued.

"Well, I got sick one time and I had no health insurance. So, I went to the VA. They more-or-less ignored me. They said the symptoms for whatever illness I had was not on the Agent Orange list." He mocked a sarcastic chuckle.

"Then I hit the bottle. I drank most all the time. I was in pain. In retrospect, I know I was drinking to numb the pain, but it got to be a habit, you know, look at my watch and see it was 9:00 am then grab a beer. I drank all day and night. I think it musta' been pretty bad for my wife … calling her names and all. Then, I hit bottom and found myself in an alley waking up and hearing garbage men loading trash containers. Well, I went back to the VA and let them check me into rehab, and I slowly crawled out of the gutter. But not before my marriage ended."

Zach scrolled through the album, trying not to look at Jenkins and create further discomfort for the man.

"Thirty years sober this month," Jenkins announced proudly to Zachary, toasting with his bottle of carbonated mineral water.

"That rehab clinic also found what was wrong with me. I had malaria … for a year! They treated me for that."

"No shit? I got a case of that there, too," Zach said.

"I'm pretty sure that came from Vietnam. There wasn't an outbreak of malaria in Kitty Hawk, if ya know what I mean. And the fuckin' VA didn't even catch it. They didn't even take a blood sample," Jenkins added.

"Well, as I say, the marriage ended but not before we had a child, a boy. Here he is right here at five years old. He and I were playing catch the ball out front." Jenkins was now pointing to the picture in the album Zach still held.

Zach looked at the picture carefully, giving it his full attention. It was the picture of a war-buddy's child. He was convinced that Jenkins missed this child very much and longed for a reunion.

"He's a beautiful young boy, Marcus," Zach said, intoning Jenkins' first name and now looking at him with respect and admiration.

"That's not the reason I showed you, Marty. You're important to him, you know." Zach looked up puzzled.

"You're looking at Martin Jenkins. I still call him Marty." Jenkins stared at the table then slowly raised his head.

"I didn't know your first name, man. I named my son after the guy that saved my life."

Zachary was stunned into silence. He could only convey his emotion through facial expressions.

"I'm glad you're pleased, Marty. I've thought about you ever since that night. Every time I use my son's name, I can see your face in the light of those white phosphorous candles coming down ... right about over there." Jenkins pointed south and west.

Finally, Zach spoke. "Jenkins ... sorry ... Marcus, I don't know what to say. I've never had that happen. I'm honored. I feel humbled."

A moment of silence served as a chance for both men to recover from the emotional intensity. Zach was first to break the silence.

"Marcus, this means more to me than the Bronze Star they gave me. Thanks, man." He pulled out a handkerchief, wiped his eyes and blew his nose. "But I gotta' meet him, Marcus. Where does he live?"

"In Virginia, about an hour away from DC. It's a little place called Culpeper."

After that, the two men talked for another half hour outside the bar before saying good night. Jenkins offered Zach a lift back to Da Nang International Airport the next day. Zach accepted the offer because he wanted another opportunity to talk.

Zach returned to his hotel and Jenkins went home.

***

Marcus Jenkins would remain a lifelong friend to Zach. They exchanged contact information including Facebook and Skype names. They promised to plan a reunion for members of their unit and stay in touch for as long as possible. But they also explored the possibility of getting together in the U.S. Zach really wanted to meet Martin Jenkins.

Jenkins had granted Zach what he could never give himself: absolution.

Zachary's parents instilled in their son some rigid guidelines for life. In his youth, neither Zach nor Billy could dance, attend parties, or date girls until each was sixteen years old. Premarital sex was a sin. Divorce was also a sin. It went without saying that murder was a sin. Both their church and the Martin household were inflexible on those dogmatic rules.

In retrospect, Zachary knew objectively that combat conditions and war in general brought about circumstances outside normal social mores. But he also realized his parents could never have predicted his circumstances when they arrived at their ethics and handed them down to him.

After considering a similar effect on his father-in-law, Zach gave a silent prayer of gratitude for the end of a lifelong ordeal.

***

The first leg of the flight back was twelve hours long and passed through Hawaii like it did in 1970. Zach got off at Honolulu International Airport and waited the two hours until the second leg of the return flight direct to Reagan. He passed his time in shops and looking out the window of the Diamond Head Concourse.

He meandered to Gate 15 of the terminal and thought about where he had been in 1970. The last time I was here, I was twenty years old, he thought. He considered the changes he had experienced since that time. He had grown up in that one year in Vietnam. He had learned what camaraderie was all about. He learned to be a leader. He learned about his many strengths.

He also learned about his weaknesses. As a young man, he had his share of bouts with rage. Over the next thirty years he lived with the consequences of that uncontrolled rage. He still had a temper that was evident when a driver cut him off in Northern Virginia traffic, but it was more controlled.

And now he had a namesake whom he had to meet. Marty Jenkins from Culpeper, Virginia. Could he ever return the favor his war buddy had done for him?

-50-

New Mexico, 2004

At eighty-five years old, Conchita was mostly tired every day. Her daily task of freshening up the secret grave of her first-born was about all she could manage most days. Earlier as she stood at Rayaldo's grave, her tears fell on the memorial in her backyard. Yes, they were tears of grief and regret, but this morning, she also felt revitalized and exhilarated.

"Padre, I swear it. This is the truth. I am not lying and I'm not exaggerating. It was the most profound event of my life," Conchita proclaimed with a look of absolute honesty. "I know what I saw was real. It was more real than me talking to you right now."

Padre Juan leaned forward on the office couch in his rectory. "My child, please tell me the story again, so I can feel the warmth of God from within your heart," the priest pleaded. It was the third time he had heard the story that morning. Though each telling was identical, she added slightly more detail.

Drawing her breath as if preparing to step off a cliff, Conchita closed her eyes, straining to recall the incident from the beginning.

"The light was overwhelming." The best way she could describe it was that it was a flash of light and then she was somewhere else. The most overwhelming sensation—the one she had the most difficulty explaining to the priest—was the sensation of not being in her backyard. She found herself in another place and clearly another time.

"I had been at Rayaldo's grave praying, using my rosary. I was on the third Hail Mary when I just wasn't there anymore." She opened her eyes and looked straight into Padre Juan's eyes. "I wasn't there, Padre. I just wasn't in my backyard. I was some ... where ... else." She said it as if she were straining to believe her own words.

The rectory was completely silent, the quiet serving as the perfect backdrop for this profound revelation.

"Where were you, my child? Tell me what you saw. Who were you with?"

"I was there with Him! It was the Lord Jesus himself. I saw him. He looked right at me. I heard the words in another language, not Spanish or English. But I understood them. I understood everything!"

She was now staring out the rectory window. The sun shone from behind Padre Juan's face. It was casting rays of sunlight in an arc above his head.

The image reminded Conchita of the retablos on display in the church rectory. These paintings from over a hundred years ago, popular in Mexico at the time, were by Mexican artists of various patron saints or other religious figures unique to a family. Itinerate artists of the 1800s painted them on tin flats cut from olive oil cans. The artist would lead a burro from town to town laden with these tin flats that had been cut with a crude tin snip. He would take up shop to paint for hire.

"Padre Juan, I saw Jesus. Others called Him by a different name, Yeshua."

"Go on my child. Go on." She could tell the priest believed her. She was more honest than she had been in her entire life.

"It was at a gathering on a small mountain in front of a Jewish temple built into the mountainside almost like part of a cave. I was kneeling on a trail next to the open temple. I was near a woman who had been flung down by a crowd of men who dragged her to the temple where Yeshua was teaching. She was scantily clad, almost naked.

"A man walked out of the temple and crouched to see if she was hurt. She had bruises and scrapes on her body. The man who had been teaching from the scriptures in the temple knelt where she was and gave her his robe to cover her body. One man in front of the crowd spoke first to the man who had given his robe. He looked like an older Jewish rabbi who was clearly in charge of this crowd. He said, 'This woman was caught in the act of adultery. Moses' writing says we must stone her to death.' It seemed from their manner that they were trying to test this man and waited for his answer."

She paused to catch her breath then looked downward and continued.

"The man, Yeshua, was on his knees still comforting the woman who whimpered and moaned, expecting death from the mob. The crowd had encircled the two and I was on the inside ... kneeling ... just a few feet from the woman. The leader of the crowd chided the man, using his name, Yeshua, in a patronizing manner. He kept trying to trap him with his questions. He spoke several times about the Law of Moses. The man, Yeshua, still kneeling, started writing in the dirt with his finger some words in a language I did not recognize, but I could read it." She lifted her head to look straight into Padre Juan's eyes.

"Padre, I could read this strange language. I saw what he was writing. I know what he wrote." She delivered this with the conviction of an eyewitness.

"Tell me, Conchita. Tell me again. What was he writing?" The priest asked the question although he knew the answer.

"He was listing the sins of each man standing in the crowd. In the sand, he wrote several sins, one at a time, making sure that each man was able to read the name of the sin: thievery, enslavement, drunkenness, fornication outside marriage, murder and others.

"Father, this man, Yeshua, kept writing the sins of those around him who had demanded his answer. Each time he would look up at a man for a few seconds and then write another sin in the dirt, using his bare finger. Then he would move to the next man."

She paused to recall another detail of the story.

"He stood up, looked at a man, then wrote a sin with his finger in the sand. He looked into the man's eyes before moving to the next. When he had finished, he stood, holding a rock he had picked up from the footpath, and addressed them, saying, 'Which of you is pure of heart and without sin? That man may have this stone to condemn her. You, who are without sin may cast at her.' He offered the same stone to each of the dozen men. One by one they dropped their heads, turned and departed. At last, he offered the stone to the leader. With no one else to follow him, he left, looking back every now and then, until he was out of sight down the trail."

She told the Padre who had closed his eyes to listen and was now beaming with delight at hearing the story unfold. Seeing his gladness was enough for Conchita to continue.

"Seeing no one left, Yeshua turned to help the woman stand. She arose, still wearing his robe that hid her naked body. He then spoke to her and asked, 'Woman, is there no one here to accuse or condemn you?'

"She looked around, her eyes following the trail beside the temple and replied, 'No one, sir.'

"He bade her to leave, saying, 'Neither do I condemn thee. Go and leave your life of sin.' She left, thanking him and vowing to live a faithful life."

"Please be strong my child. Tell me what else happened."

"Padre, that's the miracle. I know it seems that all of this is miraculous, but what happened next has been a true blessing from God.

"I had been kneeling the whole time in my backyard. Then the Man, Yeshua, knelt close to me. He looked in my eyes and saw right through me. He wrote on the ground with his index finger. Again, the writing was not in a language I recognized, but I could read it!

"He quoted Moses, naming the sins of which I am most ashamed:'Thou shalt obey your parents and honor them; Thou shalt not kill; Thou shalt not commit adultery.'"She was alive with excitement. "Father, then ... then he did something else.

"He turned to me with eyes that pierced my soul. I noticed his left hand moving back and forth on the ground. I changed my vision to the source of the movement. He was erasing the words of sin as if he were a teacher at the blackboard. I turned back to see his face.

"His expression was of love, pure love and forgiveness," she said. "He uttered the most tender words to me while his hand wiped away my sins. 'Your sins are forgiven.'

"With a rush of blood to my head, I glanced back at his left hand, now soiled with dust. He was rubbing his thumb against the tips of his other fingers. He then raised his left hand to show me, as if to convey that my sins were now like the dust falling to the ground. Then he uttered one last sentence. 'Tell my son that I am proud of him.'

"Then another blinding flash of light surrounded me. Or was it within me?

"Suddenly, I had been returned to my backyard, still kneeling at Rayaldo's grave with my thumb and forefinger rubbing the twenty-third bead of the five-decade rosary.

"Father, I felt forgiven, completely forgiven, for all my sins." She expressed overwhelming joy. "I understand forgiveness, Father. For the first time, I understand. What I forgive in others is forgiveness for me."

Raising her gaze from the rosary she was holding, she looked at Padre Juan with puzzlement. "But Father, what did he mean, 'Tell my son that I am proud of him?' Who do I tell?"

"That is a mystery, my child. For all of us are His sons and daughters." The Padre smiled knowingly and bowed to utter a silent prayer of gratitude to his Father.

***

Zachary and Bartolome attended the funeral Mass. They were among the few who attended. Conchita had only a few friends. Those she did have, however, were close, very close.

According to Padre Juan, "She departed this world as she entered, with purity of heart and no regrets."

That was true. She said so in her will that was read shortly afterward to the only beneficiary named: Bartolome Valles.

Her estate was larger than the one she inherited from Simon. She invested wisely, and although she had no regular income from a job, she was able to multiply Simon's already sizable estate by a factor of forty. For tax purposes, an accountant validated the seven-figure sum estimated in the will.

The Last Will and Testament of Conchita Gonzalez was in her own handwriting:

"November 25, 2004

To my dear friend, Bartolome Valles,

After paying off personal expenses, debts and taxes, I leave to you my entire estate of real property, bank accounts, investments, assets and other tangible property, including my home and its contents on Maple Street.

In return, I ask that you do one thing for me. In the rear yard is the grave of my son, Rayaldo Gonzalez. I ask that you relocate his body to a proper gravesite near my other son, his half-brother and me, in the Las Cruces Masonic Cemetery. I acknowledge to the authorities that his death was accidental and fully my responsibility.

My heart is pure, and I have no regrets. My life has been a joy. Concepcion 'Conchita' Gonzalez"

After the Last Will and Testament was entered into record, the police were contacted who excavated the grave, confirming identification of the body. The Medical Examiner's Office determined through DNA analysis, that the body, although extremely decomposed, was directly related to Conchita and was probably that of the missing Rayaldo Gonzalez Kouris. Rayaldo's circumstances of death were impossible to determine, according to the ME's office, so the police chief, after reviewing the missing persons record, listed 'accidental' as the cause of death.

With the case closed, they exhumed and buried his body in the Masonic Cemetery beside his mother. It was the second funeral Mass held for Rayaldo. Padre Juan conducted the Mass as his last official act as a priest for St. Anne's Iglesia Catolico. Zachary and Bartolome both attended. They had flown back to Las Cruces twice in the last month to monitor progress on the new high-rise.

As heir, Bartolome sold the estate of Conchita Gonzalez, and donated all her assets to several charities including St. Anne's Iglesia Catolico and a host of orphanages in Northern Mexico and Dona Ana County.

Bartolome, now seventy-three years old, would officially retire next year, return to Las Cruces, and leave the business to Zachary and Jordan Martin, who were already grooming their son, Billy Martin, to take over in a few years.

Zachary Martin and Billy Woods remained as close as the brothers they were.

Zachary and Jordan traveled to Culpeper, Virginia to meet Marty Jenkins and his family. But first, they picked up Marcus Jenkins from Reagan International Airport. He stayed in Culpeper long enough to forge relationships with the grandchildren he had never met.

Padre Juan bar Yeshua was last seen on foot, walking toward Mexico. He had told the newly appointed St. Anne's priest that he was going on a pilgrimage. The only thing he took from St. Anne's was a single white yucca bloom from his beloved garden.

ABOUT THE AUTHOR

Raised on a farm in Southern New Mexico near the Mexican border, and learning Spanish from an early age, Lynn Underwood was immersed in Hispanic culture. Joining the Marine Corps at 18 and serving in Vietnam, Lynn saw the underbelly of war and cultural upheaval. With degrees in engineering and journalism, Underwood has written nine non-fiction books on construction. He served as a building official since 1984 after a short time as a home builder.

He and his wife live in Williamsburg, Virginia.

This is his first novel.

ACKNOWLEDGMENTS

Six people need special acknowledgment in the creation and execution of this book:

- Glenda White for her love and patience,
- Carroll Bailey for his vision
- Cindy Murati for her regular, thoughtful advice
- Larry Underwood for his daily calls
- Cindy Freeman for being more of a teacher than the excellent editor she is
- Jeanne Johansen for her faith and trust in a new author.

1 27

Made in the USA
Middletown, DE
03 August 2021